Dearest Mother Superior,

I know you worried over my loss of position in St Louis but I assure you, I have found myself in a much better situation. I am cooking for the ranch hands at the Harrison ranch outside the small town of Sweetwater, Kansas. I had fears that I wouldn't settle in this quiet western town but now find I love the silence of the nights, the genuine people who live here and the welcome I received without reservation.

There are successful business women here who I would like to get to know and become friends with. The men I work with remind me of the boys I helped raise. All are away from home and without loved ones so we are one another's siblings of the mind. I have found the teasing and friendship I thought I had left at St Michaels' Foundling Home again.

Sweetwater, which I believed was just one more stop on my travels may be where I belonged all along. The town has been growing ever since it was chosen as one of the stops along this track of railway. I see prosperity everywhere I look and happy, content families. If there are others who need a place to feel welcomed and safe, they would find honest work here.

I keep you and the others always in my heart and prayers.

Your Faithful Servant, Callie

Harrison Ranch
&
Macgregor's Mail Order Bride

by

Susan Payne

Sweetwater

This is a work of fiction. Names, characters, places, and incidents are either the product of the author's imagination or are used fictitiously, and any resemblance to actual persons living or dead, business establishments, events, or locales, is entirely coincidental.

Harrison Ranch & Macgregor's Mail Order Bride

COPYRIGHT © 2019 by Susan Kay Payne

All rights reserved. No part of this book may be used or reproduced in any manner whatsoever without written permission of the author or The Wild Rose Press, Inc. except in the case of brief quotations embodied in critical articles or reviews.
Contact Information: info@thewildrosepress.com

The Wild Rose Press, Inc.
PO Box 708
Adams Basin, NY 14410-0708
Visit us at www.thewildrosepress.com

Publishing History
First TWA Edition, 2019
Print ISBN 978-1-5092-3029-7
Digital ISBN 978-1-5092-3028-0

Sweetwater, Book 1
Published in the United States of America

Dedication

The Sweetwater stories are dedicated to my husband whose sense of romance still takes my breath away.

Harrison Ranch

CHAPTER 1

With the help of the conductor, Callie stepped down from the train to the well-worn platform of the neat brick station. She gazed around taking in the first sight of her new home. Somehow, she knew this was to be it. The end to her journey of finding where she belonged. A place where she could make friends and a life, she could be proud of living. To repay all those who helped her make it this far. To reward their belief in her and her abilities.

Not that being a cook for a couple dozen ranch hands was that much of an accomplishment but it was for an orphan from New York. It was for a girl the nuns who raised her feared would never make her first birthday. She showed them all, though. And she wasn't about to stop doing so now. She may be little but she could do this man's job as well as anyone. She wouldn't lose this position merely because she was a woman.

Brushing her hands down the plaid dress of muted greens and rust with shiny onyx beads buttoned right up to her chin, she dislodged much of the soot that had blown in the open train windows coating everything. Wishing she had taken time to find a mirror on the train to make sure she looked presentable, she spent the time familiarizing herself with what she could see.

Searching the platform for anyone meeting her, she straightened the small box-style hat perched atop her untamable orange hair. The naturalness of which was

1

proven by the sprinkling of freckles across her otherwise porcelain cheeks and nose. Her green eyes were her best feature. She knew she appeared young and untried but she was wiser than many her age. Living in an orphanage her whole life might not have prepared her for much but she knew what she knew well and that was what would get her far in this world. She fingered the gold watch pinned on the front of her dress as if unconsciously. Touching it to make sure it was still there. Her talisman on her travels into the west.

The conductor, a grandfatherly type man, smiled saying, "The porter will be right out with your trunk, Miss. It was a pleasure to have you on board. I hope you enjoy your new position out there on the ranch. I think those cowhands are in for a real treat." With that, he stepped back onto the stairs, waved his hand to the engineer and disappeared into the train that had been Callie's home for the last couple of days - all the way from St Louis.

As promised, the porter brought Callie's trunk, which contained her most treasured possessions and Callie gave him a small reward along with her thanks.

The thin young man with a bright open face, tipped his hat. "My privilege, Miss."

As steam built up in the engine, the call for all aboard rang out over her head and the train pulled noisily away. Callie could see the town off to the left behind the station. A clean, wide main street with several well maintained two-storied wood structures on either side made Callie sigh with contentment. She just knew she was going to like living in Sweetwater.

Since it was Sunday, there wasn't activity on the street but Callie thought she could see some buggies and a buckboard down near the far end in front of what must be the church. She didn't see any building that appeared to be a hotel and was starting to worry her transport to the Harrison ranch had been detained or wasn't coming at all. If she were a man, they might think she would make her own way to the ranch. She didn't want to start out being a burden to someone or showing up late. She had been eager for this job and knew she had been lucky to get it.

Sunday would be a difficult day to hire a rig and then she would still need good directions, although she had no experience with handling a horse and buggy. Something she may need to rectify now she was no longer living in a city where public transportation was readily available.

Just as she was turning to let the stationmaster know she may need to leave her trunk with him, she bumped into a short man standing directly behind her. Callie's first thought was that Chris Cringle had appeared early since the man was much the same height as Callie at five feet. He had a long white beard, a pipe hanging out of his mouth, and was wearing a bright red plaid shirt and black boots.

Callie gave a start and exclaimed, "Oh, I'm sorry, I wasn't looking where I was going."

The man grabbed his scruffy ten-gallon hat off his head and asked, "Are you, St Michaels?" His light blue eyes crinkled at the corners as he looked at her with interest.

Callie answered, since this must be her escort to the ranch, "It's Miss, but please call me, Callie. It's less of a mouthful."

The man gave a nod of his head and a smile that showed through the thick white mustache and beard.

"Well, don't that beat all? We're gonna have to write Mr Herbert, that attorney in Kansas City, a great big thank-you note for hiring you. My name's Sully, short for Sullivan since it's less of a mouthful."

Holding out his hand, Callie put her much smaller gloved hand into it. The man shook it energetically and continued, "Yup, we're gonna thank Herbert greatly."

Callie retrieved her hand, laughing at his enthusiasm. "You haven't even tasted my cooking, yet. What if I burn the biscuits? Or feed you beans every day?"

"Miss, you can feed them boys anything you want and they'll come back for seconds just to see your smile." Sully moved over to the trunk and tipped it up on its wheels asking, "This yor only luggage besides the bag you got ahold of?"

At her nod, Sully started toward the other end of the platform where a buckboard was waiting for them but not before he took notice of Callie's limp. The tap of her boot heel followed by a much lighter one was a rhythm Callie was used to. Well, Callie thought straightening her back, it doesn't hold me back from cooking or doing any of the duties Mr Herbert mentioned. She was strong and healthy and could do anything a male cook could do in regards to the job. Her boss, Mr Harrison, and the ranch hands would have nothing to complain about. She would make sure of that.

Sully went to the rear to heft the trunk onto the wagon bed before securing the back gate. Callie, after swinging the carpetbag of personal items into the wagon, stepped up to the buckboard's seat without waiting for help. Callie liked to show she could do anything any other woman could do - any other perfect woman could do.

As Sully climbed up and untied the reins from the break, Callie explained, "The trunk's a little heavy because I packed some cooking utensils and spices. Things I thought might be difficult to find here. St Louis has such a wide variety of foods and stores and I wasn't sure they would be available this far west."

"You might be right with that. We tend to furnish everything we need from the farm garden and raise all our own meat. Sometimes we trade with our neighbors. The Harrison beef is much sought after," Sully said proudly.

As they drove down the center of town, Sully gave a vocal guide of the various businesses, especially those he thought Callie should know. "Now the butcher here in town slaughters all the meat for us and makes some of the pork into sausage and such. He makes up the headcheese and pickles the beef tongue, too. Smokes the best bacon and hams I've ever had. We get all our cheeses from him and he says it comes all the way from Wisconsin by train. Anything else you want he can get it for you."

The trip through town continued along that vein with Callie absorbing all the interesting tidbits and swinging her head from one side of the street to the other trying to memorize which buildings were which from dry goods to the milliner. They drove past the church with its white steeple and the waiting buggies and wagons out front. Would she get time off to attend? She wouldn't ask until she knew more about her job and the ranch hands' needs.

Sully became quiet once they left the town behind so Callie took the opportunity to ask some questions about the ranch and the men she had been hired to feed.

"Sully, you said the men would eat anything I fed them but, really, I would like some guidelines as to what they expect. I mean, Mr Herbert wasn't very forth coming as to how many men there actually were or what kind of a food budget I would have. I don't wish to disappoint them in any way. Can you help me?" Callie was taking in the scenery which she found so much more fascinating than city streets and other conveyances as they bounced down the dirt road that was wide enough for two buckboards to pass each other.

Sully thought a minute before answering, "There's twenty cattle-hands including myself right now and one that tends to the chickens and hogs but he usually don't eat with us. The boss has his own housekeeper that cooks for him before she goes home every day. The number eatin' in the cookhouse have dwindled down to where most of us are heaten' beans on the bunkhouse stove. And we sometimes can buy somethin' ready-made in town but most of us don't get time off during the day to make it in. As to budget, I think you just order anything you're runnin' low on. We make a trip into town weekly and I know Ol' Joe, he was cook before you, would tell us what to get for him. He didn't know how to read or write so we didn't have a list so to speak."

Callie absorbed this information, then asked worriedly, "Did Old Joe pass on? Am I replacing a long-standing favorite cook for the ranch hands?" This might be a touchy situation if she came in and changed how things were done before. Changed what the men might think as being sacred.

"Well, Ol' Joe just got too frail to continue cooking so he retired like and moved out to his daughter's place in Texas." Sully smiled and added, "I don't think anyone is gonna miss his cooking. He was what you might call a basics man. Mostly beans, some stew, and fry pan biscuits. He started as a trail cook, you know, goin' with the cattle drive but we stopped havin' those when the train rails got closer. Boss moved Ol' Joe into the cook house a few years back and he was there till about a month ago."

Callie was relieved to hear that the man hadn't died but glad, also, that his retirement gave her the opportunity to get a job. Female cooks weren't very popular and single female cooks had nearly an impossible time finding a job. Mr Herbert was somewhat dubious once he saw her size and youth but she had very good written recommendations from the Mother Superior and her last boss. And she thought she might have been the only applicant willing to travel that far for a cooking position on a cattle ranch. The pay seemed fine to her but then women always made less than a man no matter what the job.

"I've been planning menus in my head for days but if you have any ideas on what to cook to please the men, I'm very versatile." Callie was hoping to get some guidance. She knew what people ate in big cities but not what they ate on a cattle ranch in Kansas.

"Lord, child, these men are gonna be putty in your hands. Just feed them a hunk of meat and a pan of beans and they'll be happy as ticks on a hound. Most of them are about ready to eat the leather off their saddles it's been so long since they had a cooked meal. Oh, but don't try to feed 'em lamb! These are cattlemen, you know," Sully told her with a laugh.

"Well, I think I can do better than that." Callie

relaxed and enjoyed the scenery again, which was quite lovely. Trees and prairie brush with green grasses along the roadside. The road itself was dusty which meant it had not rained in a while but the rest showed the area was not going through a drought. Yellow and blue and white wild flowers dotted the fields and along the ditch. She wanted to get a closer look at them but knew she would need to wait for some free time. The flowers would probably be there throughout the fall and she smiled thinking of gathering them for the men's dining table.

"That's the beginning of the Harrison ranch just over this hill along that there fence. We'll be home soon. I'll show you round the cookhouse and you can relax the rest of the day. We'd like breakfast on the table by six each morning and supper by six at night. We don't come back in for a midday meal. Sometimes the boys take an extra biscuit from breakfast to keep their stomachs from growlin'. Sunday you'll have off right after breakfast," explained Sully.

"Oh, but the men are still at the ranch on Sunday, aren't they? They're still going to need meals. I'll think of something once I see the store of provisions. I am very resourceful. I'm used to cooking at a foundling home and feeding over seventy-five hungry growing children, many of whom were boys. That gave me lots of practice to economize on the budget," Callie replied with emphasis thinking she should be able to have three meals a day and not increase the costs by much. She had been told she could make an excellent soup out of a stone if she wanted.

The ranch they rode toward was neat and well laid out. Callie took it all in avidly. A large two-story house with a wraparound porch and plantings all along the stone foundation indicated the ranch was profitable and well managed. There were some late blooming flowers along the side and more in urns on the porch by the wide front door. Not too far to the north was a much smaller building with a front porch and white painted rocking chairs inviting any visitor to come and rest in the shade. Across the compound from that was a large barn, doors open on this sunny day with several out buildings scattered nearby. The last building, a long low wooden structure with several windows, with its porch covered by a slant roof was probably the bunkhouse.

Sully pulled the wagon close to a side door of the smaller building with the rocking chairs, tied off the reins and climbed down. "I'll just show you round and maybe get Jamie to help with the trunk a little later."

Callie's excitement had been building ever since the ranch had come into view. She hastily got down, brushed at her skirt and straightened the little green hat which was less protection from the sun than a boost for her self-confidence. After the buggy ride and predictable jostling, she checked that the short veil and brown speckled bird made from real feathers with shiny black eyes nestled right in the center, was still there. It was pure nonsense but it made her feel pretty and matched the colors of the plaid in her dress.

Sully put out his hand to help her up the steps and into the kitchen portion of the cookhouse. She wanted to tell him she didn't need the aid but then thought perhaps he was merely being gentlemanly and that it wasn't a comment on her ability to navigate stairs.

"Oh, this is wonderful and so bright." Callie looked around, taking in the two long tables with twelve chairs each and another two tables that sat eight. There were jars of eating utensils dotted along the tables and salt dishes. Both long tables were located at the front of the building and the large windows behind them overlooked the compound between the bunkhouse and the cookhouse and the barns.

Then Callie took in the kitchen. Her domain for as long as she made the men happy with their meals and, so far, she didn't see that as a problem. There was a counter with open shelves below holding large pots and some boards nailed above which held stacks of metal enameled dishes and cups. A sink with its own pump stood at the end of the counter next to the door they had entered. Another wood counter ran parallel to the first and offered Callie ample space for bread and rolls to rise.

Then Callie's eyes got wider as she inspected the large cooking stove she would get to use. Shiny nickel and black ten-plate top with two ovens plus two warming ovens and a water reservoir. There were also two fire boxes with swing style doors to control the heat. And it would be all hers to use. Wiping her hand over the cool exterior she felt in awe. If she had dreamt of the perfect stove this would be it.

Callie let out a long-held breath. "Oh, this is laid out just lovely. I don't think I could ask for more. It's so clean and well stocked with every type of pan I should need. Where are the stores? Is there a cold room? A root cellar?" she asked excitedly.

Sully, who had been looking at Callie's enraptured face, turned to a door behind him. "Right here." Lighting an oil lantern, he opened the door to show Callie shelves of canned fruit and vegetables all neatly lined up in Mason jars of all sizes and colors. Barrels holding everything from soda crackers to pickles to salted fish were standing along the base of the shelves like sentries.

Callie, still enthralled, whispered almost as if in a prayer, "Oh, here's pickled beets and eggs, hot peppers, sweet peppers, jellies, and oh, look, dried fruit and flours and sugars." She turned a smiling, glowing face to Sully. "There's wine, too. Do you suppose I could use that?"

"Sure, everything here is for the cookhouse. The Boss has his own stores and, matter of fact, it's his housekeeper, Maria, and her sister that preserve most of this stuff. They come down during harvest and put up as much as they can every year."

Sully went down a few steps and pushed open the door at the bottom saying, "This here's your cold room and the root vegetables and such are under the saw dust and straw. Most of it has just been put down here in the last few weeks. There's still ice left from last winter but that'll get renewed as soon as the pond freezes over."

Callie entered the chilled room and took in the hanging hams, the beef carcass, and what looked like sausages. There were three round wooden boxes with 'cheddar' or 'stilton' written on the sides. "My mind is just whirling with ideas for meals."

Callie noted the sanded square meat-block table with a clean cleaver and saw hanging on the side ready to be used.

She looked a little doubtfully at Sully. "Are you sure I can use all this food? Is it supposed to last a certain amount of time?"

Shrugging, Sully said, "Nope, the Boss wants the hands to be happy and this makes them happy. At least it will with you doing the cookin'."

He led her back up the steps. "Let me show you to

your room and you can rest up. I'll see you tomorrow morning."

"Now that I've seen the stores and pantry, I can have a substantial meal tonight for the men. I'll just get some of this dust off me and I'm on my way to making supper."

Callie followed Sully through the kitchen and down a short hall to a room at the back of the building with a neatly made bed, washstand and dresser. "This will be fine. I see my trunk and bag have been brought in. Please thank whoever did that for me, will you?"

Sully nodded in agreement and left Callie. She was so excited to begin. Removing her hat, she then used the water in the pitcher to wash up before hurrying out to her new kitchen.

Callie was pleased with the faith Sully had in her abilities. Not that she was afraid of failing the ranch hands' expectations but it was nice to be accepted so readily without any proof she was qualified. The fact that she was more than qualified would have Sully rethinking Callie's agreement to be a ranch cook.

Having been a sous chef at one of the finest hotels in St Louis, learning to prepare foods from around the world, being apprenticed to one of the premier French chefs would more than qualify her for this job. It would also cause people to question her soliciting such a low-paying job as ranch cook.

In fact, so much experience and skill almost made Mr Herbert pass her application by. Callie was honest and maybe, at times, blunt in her interview. She had only used her first initial and last name on the letter applying for the position of ranch cook. At the time, Callie wasn't even sure what the job entailed. But she had cooked for the foundling home since she was twelve. By the time she was sixteen, she was running the kitchen and making what had always been too little stretch to feed all the hungry mouths three times a day. She felt if she could do that, then cooking for hungry men would be an easy transition. She knew she needed a change from what she had been doing. Getting another sous chef position in St Louis was out of the question.

The hams were in the oven and the bucket of potatoes Callie had brought from the root cellar was waiting next to the sink. She saw a very round older woman with black hair braided and pinned like a crown on the top of her head enter the cookhouse. Wearing a brightly patterned skirt and embroidered blousy shirt, the woman carried a striped clay pot with lid and ceramic pitcher. Her dark gaze moved around the cookhouse before stopping on Callie.

In broken English she said, "Mi es, Maria. I work up for Mister Seth in big house. I bring you mantequilla, um, butter and the crema. I have mucha eggs, mucha eggs. Jamie bring me all the eggs and leche. Too mas, I don' need these things. You use them, you need them." And she set the full containers on the counter.

"Thank you so much, Maria. My name is Callie and I appreciate the butter immensely. I didn't see any milk here so I was trying to make a meal without it."

"El neno, Jamie, he will bring milk to you from now. I no use cow milk, I have goats," the housekeeper stated firmly. "If you need bath, there one in big house to use anytime." And with that she waved and turned back to the door.

A bath, the chance to wash the soot and dust

completely out of her hair was too much of a temptation for Callie. She knew she would have time before anything more needed to be done to supper so went to her room to gather some clean clothes.

Callie called out to Maria from the front door which was left open to enjoy the late fall sunshine. She could see the wide stairs to the upper floor and a big living space with one wall a huge stone fireplace and mantle. There was a leather couch and several comfortable chairs as well as a smattering of highly carved wood tables and chests. Colorful Indian blankets and rugs were strewn around the room adding to the welcoming warmth.

Maria came quickly and showed Callie to the rear of the house through the kitchen and down a short hall. Maria pointed proudly to the large copper tub easily six feet long, enclosed by a wooden box with a small area of space all around it to sit on before getting into the water.

"See," Maria said explaining how the stove had a water reservoir on the back where water could be heated and the handpump at the end of the tub. "Mucha important put this plug." And she drew out the word as if it were two. "If you no do, big bug or spider come in tub. Take out plug, water go out, put back plug so bug no come in. Si?"

"I understand. I don't want to see any bugs, either." Callie assured Maria that she had everything needed for her bath. Filling the tub part way up, Callie stepped into it sliding down under the water and allowing her now freed hair to be rinsed out completely. She used the special hair soap made with rosemary and thyme to wash her hair through twice, rinsing it with the water she held back for just that purpose. It felt heavenly to be clean again.

Pulling her bright hair forward over her shoulder, Callie made one long center braid while curling strands pulled themselves free on both sides of her face. She would pin it up after it dried more. Dressing in the uniform she always wore to work, consisting of a neat gray shirtwaist with white collar and cuffs, matching gray skirt, and buttoned shoes made her feel her new job had really begun. Shaking out the ironed apron, she slid her head through the top and tied the strings behind her back easily after years of practice. A white mop cap would be added once her hair dried. She finished by pinning the ever-present gold watch to her shirtwaist and gathered the rest of her items to take back.

The watch had been a gift from the nuns when she left St Michaels. Sister Mary Margaret, now Mother Superior, told Callie to pawn it if she were ever in need. It was a sort of savings account she could always depend on. Luckily, she had never gotten that desperate so she still had the lovely gift.

Maria stopped Callie on the way out and took her traveling dress and jacket saying she would clean them on laundry day. Callie tried to object but Maria was persistent so Callie finally gave in gracefully. She was finding the people at the Harrison ranch were very nice indeed.

CHAPTER 2

At six o'clock Callie was ready with her first meal at Harrison ranch. She heard the shuffling of boots outside the side door opposite the kitchen and called out, "Come on in. It's all ready."

Hearing a clang of a bell, a tall, thin man dressed in the typical gear of a ranch hand walked in hesitantly. Holding his hat in front of his chest, his head kept bobbing up and down as he spoke, "Evening ma'am. Er, Miss."

The other ranch hands trying to fit through the door were actually pushing and sliding the first man along the shiny wood floor towards her. Callie realized she was going to need to take things into her own hands.

Waving them towards her with the food resting on the work counter, she said, "Just call me, Callie. I don't stand on ceremony." Waving her arm over the table like a magic wand, she continued, "Gentlemen, tonight we have beef with barley soup, baked ham, escalloped potatoes, green beans with bacon and onion, and chopped slaw with a vinaigrette dressing followed by glazed spice cake."

Callie didn't know if it was the invitation to come in or her rendition of the menu but the group of men at the rear of the line pushed forward and the first thin man was suddenly in front of her.

Still bobbing his head, he needlessly said, 'I'm Slim, Miss Callie, glad to meet ya." And he plopped his unrecognizably shaped hat on his head and took the plate Callie handed him. Holding it out to her, she cut a nice sized slice of ham and placed it onto the plate.

"Just take what you want from the other pans and the corn bread, butter and coffee are already on the tables. I'll come around with refills as soon as everyone is served."

The mumbles continued as everything she said was passed down along the line of men. Each man held his hat and introduced himself. Each of them placed their hats back unto their heads after the introduction was made. And each of them called her Miss Callie.

Callie watched as each man sat down in a chair at one of the tables. A quiet came over the group, broken only by an occasional sound of enjoyment and the clink of utensils against metal plates. Callie took pride in the sighs of contentment as she took messy, emptied plates in exchange for a plated piece of her favorite glazed spice cake.

Then the men began with the compliments. Some shyly, saying it was the best they had eaten since leaving home to loudly stating that Miss Callie would make any man a great wife. Each man snatched off his hat as he left and thanked Callie personally for a 'fine' meal.

Finding herself with a smile on her face, she started the clean-up, humming. She was glad her first meal had been enjoyed so heartedly but she was already planning for the next one. She wanted to get some buttermilk biscuits started and boil some eggs, maybe some bread dough set to rise. Planning was the most important part of a good meal. And she felt the pressure of being behind before she even began.

The men had filed in this morning, practically pushing and shoving but removed their hats to wish her a good morning before replacing them and filling their plates. After a couple of short naps during the night, Callie was pleased that the biscuits and red eye gravy, beans with ham, and scrambled eggs went over so well. Plenty of coffee and all were quiet for the next few minutes.

Callie was pouring coffee and circling the tables with her uneven tap, tap as she told the men, "I have some biscuits with ham packed up for those who would like some to take with them. Just take one of the packages tied with string and a hardboiled egg. I'll have something ready each day to take with you. On Sunday, I'll have supper at noon and a lighter meal at six. Oh, and I'm sorry to have fed you beans but I won't do it too often."

The ranch hand named Will, a big rather handsome blond who Callie could tell thought of himself as a Romeo bantered, "Miss Callie, eating these beans for every meal wouldn't be a hardship. Simply looking upon your beautiful face and glowing hair would be enough to live on."

Callie laughed as Will probably meant for her to do. Shaking her head, she told him, "Well, I don't think that will keep you going for very long so you had just better grab one of those packets and I'll see you all tonight."

The men took the dismissal in stride and thanked Callie for the meal and lunch as they hurried out the door heading toward their respective jobs.

Cleaning up the kitchen, she kept thinking of the next meal's schedule since she always preplanned each meal. Worked out the timeframe it would need including the time it would take to get the ovens up to temperature, which pans to use for each item, and ways she could prepare food ahead of time.

She always thought of cooking being like a conductor creating beautiful music out of many individual instruments. At least that's how she thought of Chef Pasqual running his kitchen. Of course, a hotel kitchen with all the myriads of foods being served all day and into the evening had to be constantly monitored. Timing was of the essence. A sauce could break down, a fish become too well done, a salad wilt…it was all in the timing.

Both cooks and waiters needed to be prepared and trained to know the exact minute the meal had reached perfection. That was the moment it was to be placed in front of the patron. She had enjoyed the restaurant life but she thought she might like being a ranch cook even more. Here she would get to see her creations being enjoyed, really enjoyed by men who deserved to eat well. They did a hard job under harsh conditions and she found it personally rewarding to make sure they were well fed as they did so.

Callie took time during the day to study what was in the pantry and cold room. The hotel held fewer foodstuffs but, of course, the hotel had deliveries of fresh food daily. Being in a hub city brought all the food possibilities directly to their doorstep. Shell fish, shrimp, exotic fruits and vegetables. The hotel she had worked at offered six different types of mushrooms alone on the menu. The menu boasted fifty-five sauces and gravies, creamed soups and a myriad of pastries, all which had been under Callie's domain. Her creations appeared on every portion of the menu.

Cooking out west, so far from shops was going to be more of a challenge. And the train deliveries were probably a lot less dependable. Having their own meat was convenient and money hadn't seemed to have been spared in bringing in the provisions. Callie would, of course, be conservative since she didn't know whether this was to last all year and she still had to gauge how much the men consumed in a day. Their appetites would be substantial she would surmise as they were mostly young and did manual labor. She remembered from the years at the orphanage how much food a growing boy needed to be content.

Curious about a barrel that had the word 'China' written on it with charcoal, Callie decided to investigate. Taking a cleaver, she pried the top off to discover it filled with sawdust. Putting her fingers into the wood shavings, she felt a hard object so she rooted around until a pretty China cup emerged. Intrigued, she continued to dig carefully and soon realized there was a sizable set of hand-painted dishes.

Chef Pasqual had trained Callie that presentation was ninety per cent of a meal and remembering Sully had told her everything there was for her use, she began carrying the dishes into the kitchen to be washed.

At six o'clock Callie heard the shuffling of boots on the side steps and at her calling out to them, someone rang the bell. Slim led the way and Callie didn't know if he was the hungriest or the bravest. Probably, both.

He smiled whipping his worn, sweat-stained hat off his head. His hair was plastered down with pomade and he wore a bright new kerchief around his neck.

"Evenin', Miss Callie. Things shore smell good," he said shyly as his eyes widened taking in the roasted pork, mashed potatoes and gravy, buttered rutabaga, pickled beets and oxtail soup. Piles of warm rolls with honey and butter were on trays already on the tables.

Quickly replacing his hat, he took one of the pretty China plates she handed him. Nonplussed, Slim looked down at the plate but didn't miss a beat in holding it out flat in front of him, ready to be served.

The next man in line said his good evening, plunked his hat back onto his head and picked up one of the pretty plates and awaited Callie's placement of a slice of pork roast, as well.

Callie noticed something different about the men and it took her a few moments while greeting each one and slicing the roast what the difference was. Not only did the men appear less scruffy with neatly trimmed beards or clean-shaven faces, most had new neckerchiefs and even clean shirts. Callie was also aware there was a distinct smell of soap, a little less odor of cow and a little more of cowboy. Not a bad change in only twenty-four hours she thought to herself.

Spending the next half hour pouring coffee, she then passed out warm apple pie with sweet cream poured over it. All the men became quiet when given their dessert. Callie would keep a mental note that these men favored apple pie. She spent the clean-up time with a smile on her face and humming a tune she had heard in St Louis.

The men all sat around the tables after helping her clear and spent the time socializing, almost as if they were a family. Sully would tease one of the younger men about something he swore a greenhorn wouldn't do and then the others would add in their two-bits worth of advice.

Callie listened as she washed up and then went to leave but Sully called her over to sit with the men before they headed off toward the bunkhouse.

He told her the men were interested in anything outside their small world, would be interested in anything Callie had to offer in way of news from the east. They began inundating Callie with questions about St Louis and New York and everything in between.

Callie laughed, the men all seemingly mesmerized by the sound as she finished her story about a museum she had visited. "No, truly, there is this big old skeleton and I swear the teeth are as long as I am tall."

"That's not all that tall, Miss Callie," Ned teased.

She looked at him with a smile, saying, "I know that, Ned. But if that tooth was as tall as me then it must have been eating some pretty big things. The other skeleton was as long as here to the bunkhouse and had a tiny little head. It almost looked to me like they got the wrong skull on the animal."

"I bet that thing ate pakaderms," Rusty stated.

Sully asked, "What?"

Rusty repeated, "Pakaderms. They's huge animals, as tall as this porch roof and have legs like tree trunks only they's called legs. Their long nose is called a trunk, instead. It can pick up a pole or buckit or anything, even a man. And they drink through it." He finished with a flourish as if daring anyone to beat his story.

A chorus of disbelief went up among the men, some calling Rusty a storyteller only in not so polite terms.

Callie came to his aid. "I've seen what he's speaking about, too. They also called them elephants and they use them to put up the circus tents and for all sorts of work. I have to agree that something that large would feed the animal I saw in the museum. For a day or two, at least."

"Now you're both Joshin' us. Don't get dragged into his foolishness, Miss Callie," Ned told her.

Will came to her rescue and admitted, "No, I seen them myself in a circus. They walked them around the ring like they was pets holding one another's tails. And they are as big as a cabin, I swear. Must take a lot of rope to bring them down for branding."

"Well, I hope to never run into one out here in the wild, although, I might pay to see one in a circus," Ned told the group.

Sully said, as he stood to lead the men over to the bunkhouse, "Well, maybe with the train coming right through here now, a circus will take a day and stop to set up a show. I always liked them trapeze artists flying through the air."

"You mean you liked to watch the women trapeze artists flying through the air, old man." Will teased. Then realized Callie was still there and added, "Pardon my language, ma'am."

"I understand completely, Will. Remember I was raised with dozens of brothers at the foundling home. If that is the worst I hear said, I will count myself lucky."

The men filed out of the front door saying their farewells and goodnights.

The next morning, after another big breakfast, Callie finished cleaning up and thought about the last two suppers. She knew the men were excited about the menu and wanted to know what would be served at their next meal and an idea came to her. She had seen a large slate board stored behind the shelves and thought she could write the menu for the next supper or even day on the board so the men could see it ahead of time.

Callie went to retrieve the board, wiped it down and was looking around the room for the best place to hang it when she saw the perfect spot that already had a sturdy nail in place.

Setting the board up onto the counter, she leaned it against the wall, pulled a chair closer to use as a step, then climbed onto the counter. She was just bending over to lift the board to the nail when a male voice bellowed, "What the hell do you think you're doing?"

Callie, surprised by the shout, turned quickly rolling her bad foot under her. She gave a little shriek as she started to fall and felt a pair of strong arms keeping hold of her as the world righted itself.

She found herself looking into the most beautiful, sherry colored eyes with dark gold tipped lashes. A tan face with strong angles and a mouth that was wide and firmly clamped shut finished the picture.

Callie was the first to break the spell between them saying crossly, "Put me down. I'm not hurt."

As the large cowboy in white sleeved shirt, leather vest and tan trousers set Callie unto her feet, she limped a few steps away from him. He practically growled, "You are too, hurt. You're limping!"

Callie straightened to her full height, which seemed very small compared to the cowboy's six foot plus and stated, "I always limp."

The cowboy, with a hard glare repeated, "You always limp? I, oh…." As understanding seeped in he said, "Oh, well, you could have been badly hurt if you had hit the floor from that height. What did you need up there for?"

Callie didn't like being treated like a child even when she was a child so she wasn't going to allow this over-sized cowboy to yell at her about something he had no business with.

"It doesn't matter what I was doing up there. I would

have been fine if you hadn't shouted and startled me. Now you can leave and come back with the rest of the ranch hands when supper is served."

The man was good-looking and the anger only intensified the color of his eyes. "I have every right to be here and to be worried about one of my employees breaking their damn neck. Name's Seth Harrison and I expect you're my new cook."

Callie was nonplussed for a moment but then drew herself up to her full height, again, crossed her arms and introduced herself as if she hadn't just been hugged against that wide firm chest.

"How do you do? I am Callie St Michaels." She didn't put out her hand in case her boss refused to take it.

"How old are you, for God's sake? Did you lie in your letter? I don't recall it saying you were a girl," continued the man in a little less angry tone.

Callie said in a chilly voice, "A lady doesn't tell her age and a gentleman never asks."

"I never claimed to be a gentleman and I damn well expect some answers. Now."

Callie noticed that the man's big hands were clenched into fists. She felt she was boxed into a corner so admitted, "I am almost twenty-one. And everything in my application letter is true. I do not lie. I am more than qualified to do this job. Just ask Sully or any of the men."

"Hell, they'd lie through their teeth just to keep a pretty little thing like you around. Probably starve before they said a bad word about you or the grub. I came over to meet you because they were raving about what a fine cook you were and what great meals they've had so far. I never expected that they may have been over doing the praise to make sure I didn't fire you when I found out you were so pr.., er, young."

"I can assure you I have experience in cooking for large groups. After five years at St Michael's Foundling Home, I worked and trained under Chef Pierre Pasqual at the Wainwright Hotel's dining room. Working my way up to sous chef. I have excellent credentials and have won awards as a dessert and pastry chef as well as for soups and sauces." Callie was proud of her accomplishments. Accomplishments men working in the profession longer than her hadn't earned.

"Well, what the hell is this board about? This is the menu for tonight? Cream of mushroom soup? Boeuf Borg, borgug... sounds expensive."

"Boeuf Bourguignon. It's a way of cooking that makes even tough cuts of meat tender. The French peasants cooked this way," Callie said defensively.

"Hell, we even got that in the pantry?"

"You have all the ingredients. It was very popular at the Wainwright and it sounds fancier than it is. It's really just a simple way to cook beef," explained Callie hoping to placate the man as she realized he had the power, and evidently the inclination, to fire her.

"Well, these men are just simple ranch hands. They're certainly not expecting or used to this kind of a meal. I don't want them to go hungry. I need them to be able to concentrate on work."

"I totally agree. If I ever find that they are leaving their plates with food on them, I'll change my menus. I will make sure that they are well fed. I take pride in doing my job, any job, well."

"I'm still not happy about you being so, so, ah, young. It could cause problems with the hands." As if thinking about those problems he snarled, "Herbert will pay for this. Hell, they'll all pay for this." And with that, her boss turned and stomped out the front door. Callie could hear him bellowing for Sully as he took long strides toward the bunkhouse.

Taking a couple of deep breaths, Callie relaxed her taught muscles. It had been a fight or flight situation and she almost hadn't stayed to fight so she was still trembling. Her new boss was rather large and foreboding but she didn't feel that he would hurt her. In fact, he had been very gentle with her when he had caught and held her. She felt as if she had been drowning in his eyes. That is, until he started yelling at her again.

What's with that man? She's simply a cook and everyone said she wouldn't ever have contact with him. He ate at his own house. Mutinously she thought he should have stayed there.

Callie decided she would think about it later. She had a supper to prepare and a meat cleaver downstairs she could take out some of this pent-up energy on. The men deserved a good meal when they got in from working the herd and she was going to make sure they had one.

'What the hell' was Seth's thought as he headed back to the ranch house. He was still trembling inside with repressed what? Anger? Fear? Yeah, fear. When he first entered the cookhouse, he thought there was a kid standing on that counter. When she started to fall it took a heck of a lot of fast thinking on his part to catch her before she hit the floor.

And then he had her in his arms and gazed into those eyes. My God, time stood still and he wanted to stare into those green eyes forever. She smelled so good, he had to stop himself from nuzzling her neck and inhaling her scent so that he could remember it later. That scared him, too. He had held a strange female as if she were the most precious person in the entire world to him. It didn't make sense. She's just a little thing, pretty of course, and those eyes….

Even now, he could see the startled expression that turned into a smile. That is, until he set her down. Seth didn't know why he felt the need to yell at her rather than be the calm rational rancher everyone else knew him to be. Well, it was a surprise his new cook was hardly more than a child and damn pretty. But not a child. Once she was in his arms, he knew he held a woman - all woman. The right curves in the right places, the way she fit to his body as he set her down. And his body's response was swift.

Seth had to ball his hands into fists to keep from grabbing her and pulling her back to him. Then she went and folded her arms across her chest raising her very womanly breasts and bringing his attention to things best left un-noticed. Seth wasn't a skirt chaser, so why would this one little woman drive him to become a totally different man?

Herbert knew this would be like putting the fox in the hen house with all these randy ranch hands. Herbert knew Seth would never have accepted a single female cook, no matter what her age. And Sully knew it, too, yet had not bothered to warn him. Were they trying to make him look a fool? Herbert was going to receive a piece of Seth's mind as soon as he could get the letter out to him.

CHAPTER 3

Callie was browning bacon when a tall, lanky boy with straight blond hair hanging over his eyes came shyly into the kitchen. His shirt was too short at the worn cuffs and had buttons missing. His denim trousers were tied tightly around his slim hips with a cotton rope but were clearly hand-me-downs from a much larger man.

Keeping his head down, talking into his chest he mumbled, "S-Sully s-sent me o-o-over. The B-b-boss w-wants m-me to h-help you. N-n-name's J-J-Jamie."

Callie recognized the manner right away. So many times, lost kids, abandoned and treated like stray dogs ended up with stammers and such low self-esteem they had trouble fitting in anywhere they went. Callie was good at helping them. No one left St Michael's thinking themselves as a cast-off and Callie would help this boy, whatever his story. 'We are all God's creatures' was one of the nun's mottos.

"Glad to meet you, Jamie. I'm Callie and I appreciate your offer to help. You're the one who emptied the bucket of potato peelings, right?"

"Y-yes, m-m-ma'am. I f-f-feed the p-p-pigs. And the ch-ch-chickens."

"So, we have our own hogs? And the chickens give us our eggs?"

"Y-yes. M-m-ma'am. W-we e-eat the ch-ch-chickens, t-too." Jamie added.

Callie felt she was making progress. The lad was answering her and didn't seem too self-conscious of his stammer. She felt this could work out well. "I haven't seen you for meals. Where have you been eating?"

"M-M-Maria g-g-gives m-me a p-plate. Sh-she c-c-cooks g-good b-but m-m-mostly Me-Mexican."

"Have you ever done any cooking?" she asked and he shook his head. "That's all right because I have taught hundreds of children how to cook."

The boy lifted his head and looked wide-eyed at Callie. She laughed, saying, "No, really. I ran the kitchen at a foundling home I was in and every child there had to learn to cook, sew and clean their own clothes. Every week we were given a work chart and we took turns doing everything. Both boys and girls. The nuns said we had to be self-sufficient, to take care of ourselves and others. I know I'm grateful for the lessons. I wouldn't be here today if they hadn't taught me to do all those things." She watched to make sure the boy was still interested. "I was trained to be a teacher but I loved cooking so much I acquired jobs in that field. But all that other education came in handy. Like you taking care of the animals. It's a skill you have now and could probably train someone else to do."

All the time Callie was talking, she had been taking the cleaned carrots out of the water and placing them near the cutting board. "Now watch me. Keep your fingers rolled under and well back from the knife blade. Make angled cuts about this width all the way down the carrot and then push it off and start another. Got that?"

At the boy's nod and slow smile, Callie handed the knife over and watched the boy begin slowly cutting the carrot. "That's perfect," she said. "Now you only have about forty more to do." The boy's eyes got a little larger but then he picked up another carrot and studiously cut it into slices.

Callie had seared off the pieces of beef in the bacon grease and brought out the bottle of wine. Jamie's eyes became round as saucers again as Callie took a bottle screw and pushed it into the dried cork. "Never push the screw all the way through the cork or there will be little pieces of cork in the wine. I'm just hoping it didn't turn to vinegar," Callie told him as she expertly opened the bottle. Sniffing, she smiled and nodded. "Still good."

"I-isn't i-it w-wine? W-why w-w-would it b-be v-v-vinegar?"

"Well, some things turn to vinegar if the air gets to them. Cider and wine are good examples but they can still be used. Merely have to be used differently, like when you want a tarter taste." Callie smiled as she began the training of Jamie.

"It's fine. Smell this." Callie held the bottle to Jamie's nose. "See, smells like wine, no sour smell." She poured half a bottle into the still hot pan and stirred it around scraping the bottom to get all the little pieces off.

"Here, I'll give you a break. I'll peel and cut the onions while you stir the pan. Just keep moving the spoon around." As the boy took the wooden spoon and began mimicking the same movements, she encouraged him. "That's it. You're going to be a natural at this."

Jamie's chest seemed to expand as he stood straighter continuing to move the spoon in a figure eight motion.

"Now we add all this stuff together and, in a few hours, voila', we will have tender beef in a vegetable infused au jus."

"W-what i-is th-th-that?" Jamie asked, peering into the other pot on the stove. Callie noted it was his first self-initiated question regarding food preparation and smiled to herself.

"These are sliced mushrooms, a little shriveled, but still very edible. I am simmering them in beef broth and then I'll add cream near the end of the cooking. Some I'll throw into this pan with the meat as well as the rest of the beef broth and wine before covering it. Now we have a jump on the meal. The soup, the entrée' and the glazed carrots are all ready for completion."

Jamie looked with pride at what they had accomplished in such a short time. He turned to her. "I-I th-th-think I-I'm g-gonna l-like c-c-cooking."

That night, Jamie stood beside Callie as the men entered and proudly served a piece of tender beef onto each plate. Teasing, friendly comments followed from the men saying they hoped the meal was edible considering who helped cook it. Jamie took the teasing in the manner in which it was given. Not returning the banter but not shying away from it either.

As Callie began putting the kitchen to rights with the help of Jamie, one of the younger ranch hands approached her. He had his hat in his hand and nervously asked, "Miss Callie, I got some letters from my girl and I was wonderin' if you might read 'em for me? I read some but Sally's are different and I can't tell what is what."

"Well, let's see what you have. Some of the nun's penmanship was more than challenging. Go and get them while I finish up here," Callie told the young man named Ken.

"I got 'em right here, ma'am." He reached into his breast pocket pulling out several sheets of severely folded paper.

"Well, let's get over to the lamp and I'll finish the

dishes later." Callie opened the well-worn paper and began reading the neat perfect cursive penmanship taught to every young lady of means.

Embarrassed, Ken quietly confided, "I print, ma'am. I can read and write but not this fancy stuff. I don't want Sally to know so I've been sending letters to her. I print them myself but I don't know what she's writin', you see? She may be asking me things that I'm not writin' back about. I'm afraid she's gonna think I don't care but I do. Can you help?"

"Sally is writing in cursive. Would you like me to read these to you so you can write back to her?" At his nod Callie read the brief letters.

Ken was very relieved after hearing the last of the words and smiled. "Thanks so much, Miss Callie. I didn't miss very much and I can add those things to the letter I started this morning."

"Ben," said Callie, "I think you need to be honest with Sally. The girl writing those letters won't think less of you but I think she would want to know. It is always better to be up front with things. You are evidently planning to be married and I am encouraging you to tell her. Meantime, I will write down the cursive version of each letter next to the printed one and that will help you decipher letters. If you want help learning cursive, I may be able to do that in the evenings. That was just one of many things the nun's drilled into us."

Seth watched the two people, the young ranch hand and the smaller, pretty woman sitting at the end of the table with their heads close together. Man, that Ken Taylor really works fast. She's been here just over forty-eight hours and men are already trying to cut her from the herd, he thought.

Seth's voice boomed across the dining room making the couple jump guiltily apart. "I hear tonight's dinner was quite a success. I guess I should have cancelled my plans and eaten with the hands."

Ken glanced awkwardly at Callie then at his boss mumbling, "I was just goin', Boss. I'll let you know about, eh, things tomorrow, if that's all right, Miss Callie."

"I look forward to it," she answered.

Ken quickly left by the closest door and Callie turned her face up to look her boss in the eye. "Is there something I can get you, Mr Harrison?"

"No, I just heard that dinner was good, excellent by many opinions, and I just wanted to come and apologize for my poor behavior yesterday. I was caught off guard. I wasn't expecting a girl, I mean young lady, and I guess really…. I was mad at Herbert for pulling this bullshit. Pardon me, I just meant to say you were not the target of my displeasure."

"Well you could have fooled me, Mr Harrison," said Callie in her best nun voice.

"Call me, Seth, please. We don't stand on ceremony here." And he flashed a smile filled with strong white teeth.

"Or boss?" asked Callie. At Seth's look of puzzlement, explained, "Everyone else calls you, 'Boss'."

"Don't call me, boss. It's bad enough the hands do," he said as he slid his thumbs into his front pockets.

The movement brought attention to his long legs incased in worn cotton twill and the large silver buckle at his lean waist. Callie tried to tear her gaze away from the pleasurable sight and felt Seth looking at her reaction.

Quickly turning toward the sink, she realized Jamie had finished the washing-up and then left while she had been busy with Ben. Callie, taking a towel, started to wipe down the already clean counter.

"Well, if there isn't anything else, I'll just finish up here," she said without looking up from her work.

"Sure smells good in here," he said sniffing the air.

Cassie stopped working and with her hand on her hip asked, "Would you like a plate? I can fix one up for you."

Seth snatched the Stetson off his head and sat at the end of the ranch hands' table, looking expectantly at her, saying, "May as well find out what I'm paying for."

Callie smiled giving a little shrug. Typical male, his mind never far from the dinner table.

After Seth had gone through a substantial piece of beef and all the sides, he sat back in the chair and complimented Callie on the superb meal. "I haven't had a meal like this since visiting the City of Kansas. Hell, I think this beats Kansas all to H, er, heck." Then standing, he leaned over and gave Callie a buss on the cheek. "I always kiss the cook, Darlin'." Then said huskily, "And I'll be lookin' in on you from time to time."

When Callie looked up at him with alarm, he finished, "Just to make sure you're settling in. You need anything, ask Sully. And by the way, lose the cap. It makes you look like my maiden aunt." He tipped his big Stetson and left Callie standing there.

Callie knew her mouth had dropped open somewhere along the line. Was that last bit a threat or a promise or merely a simple boss to employee welcome?

Seth was whistling on his way up to the ranch house.

He hadn't been lying when he said that meal was the best he had since the Kansas beef auction. He probably shouldn't have kissed her, although she just looked so tempting standing there, smiling over his complimenting her cooking. She should know she was attractive, as well.

Besides why should the ranch hands get all her time? He would hate to lose a good cook like she was to some cowboy who gets it into his head to marry her. Herbert would have to hunt some to find anyone who could make beef taste that good. And the man wouldn't be able to come up with a better-looking cook, no matter how hard he tried.

He knew he was still smiling. The expression on her face after that little kiss had made his heart jump to his throat. If she did that to him, how were the rest of the ranch hands feeling around her? The problem of having a young single woman on the ranch was greater now that he had tasted her cooking. If he wanted more, then there would be others who did as well. Damn, that was why he never had a female on the ranch. Well, other than Maria but she was married and often came along with her husband. He knew the men wouldn't make a pass at the married woman but Callie, she was different. She appeared to be free for the asking – and that is what had him breaking out in a sweat. He could lose not only a great cook but a good hand as well. Would any man want to keep a wife like her out here in the backwoods? Seth knew he would take her anywhere she wanted to live. Give up anything he had to make her happy.

Hell, he felt like punching Herbert for putting him in this position.

CHAPTER 4

Wednesday found Callie in the kitchen before sun up again. She had been planning menus and figuring out the cost per meal. Something she had always done at the hotel and she liked to keep track of expenses, stretching the budget by using left overs for soup and planning for by-products. If you have bones, you have broth. Stale bread becomes stuffing, bread pudding or breading for fish. Nothing much left for the pigs but it keeps costs down and she wanted to show Mr Harrison, Seth, that she took her responsibilities seriously. That she knew cooking was more than an art of flavors.

Seth found her with her head down on her arms asleep at the table. Papers scribbled with notes and lists spread out in front of her. He shook his head glancing around for Jamie. Not seeing any help, he picked the small woman up in his arms, shrugged to get her to lean against his chest before carrying her into the room she slept in.

The room was neat as a pin as he knew it would be and the bed made. Seth lowered his bundle onto the top comforter and picked up the quilt folded at the end of the bed opening it over her. He looked at her shoes and bending, undid the buttons and slipped first one then the other off.

He noticed her disfigured foot, turned in at the ankle, and laid a light kiss on it. Then pulling the quilt down to cover both feet, walked quietly out of the room.

Callie woke with a start, looking around, trying to get her bearings. She didn't remember lying down for a nap, in fact, she rarely did so. She looked at the watch pinned on her apron to verify she hadn't over-slept making her late with supper.

She was entering the kitchen when Jamie brought in the dead and dressed chickens and laid them in the sink. She said, "Oh, those are big ones. You were right. They should have been used earlier this fall."

Jamie smiled. "I-I-I knew the ex-exact ones to g-g-get. They w-w-were mean and they p-p-pecked me. But I g-got em'."

"That you did, now it's Coq au vin for all. Let me show you how to cook them," she instructed her most willing pupil.

That night, after the washing up was completed, Will sat out on the porch with his guitar and kept Callie company while she sat rocking and knitting. Will asked, "You can knit in this poor light?"

"Just as I suppose you can play in this poor light," she teased back. "Once I get something started, I can knit without paying too much attention."

"And I play by ear so we're two peas in a pod." Then he began a song Callie had heard him playing on the porch of the bunkhouse Monday evening. Callie tapped her good foot to the music and clapped her hands in appreciation when he was finished.

"I wrote a song just for you because your beauty touched my heart," he said and started into a rendition of a ballad that Callie thought sounded fairly familiar.

"If I'm not mistaken, that song originally had a different lady's name in it," she laughingly accused.

"But if I had known you first, it would have had your

name," he said unabashedly.

"Just how many versions have you sang of that song? Someday those ladies are going to get together and compare notes and then you'll be up the creek. I can't believe you haven't been caught out before now."

"It's my roguish manner that makes them forgive me any minor indiscretions," he said strumming and humming a new tune.

Callie knew Will, or at least the type. He would flirt but never be serious with a woman and he would never flirt with a woman who he thought would ever take him seriously. She was familiar with the sort and felt safe enough teasing him in return.

About to excuse herself, she looked up and saw a large shadow fill the doorway into the dining room.

A stern voice out of the dark said, "You got nothing better to do then stir up the coyotes, Will?"

Will slowly stood up still holding his guitar. "I guess I can find something else to do somewhere, Boss," he said with a smile in his voice.

"Do that," replied Seth.

Seth waited for Will to step down off the porch before stating, "The men were saying you made them cocoa something. Said it was good and not what it sounded like at all."

Callie hid a smile. "I suppose you would like a plate?"

"Well, if it ain't too much trouble. I like to try new things."

Callie entered the dining room as Seth backed up to let her pass. "I could fix you a plate every night if you want. Jamie could run it up to the house."

"No, that won't be necessary. I might just start

coming down here and save Maria the work of fixin' and cleaning up from my dinner now that Jamie is eating down here, too." He watched her moving around the kitchen, heating up the Coq au vin and continued, "If that's all right with you."

She turned and looked at him, "Of course. You're the boss." And smiled as she turned back to the stove. She knew eating with the hands and saving Maria work was an excuse - but for what? Was he worried she was spending too much on food? Should she show him her ledgers with each meal's costs broken down? Or was he afraid she was keeping the hands from their chores? Of course, some of them had work after supper but most seemed to have time to sit and talk or like tonight, play the guitar.

Unsure, she finished putting the meal together and then left him to eat alone. She would figure out the right way to treat him later. When there were others around to dispel his concentration on her.

Callie was surprised on Thursday morning when a couple of the men brought in three wild turkeys they had shot before breakfast. "They've been making a racket every morning, waking us up but this morning we decided to do something about it."

Jamie grabbed them by their feet saying, "I'll c-clean them. C-c-can I have the f-f-feathers?"

"Of course. I can roast the birds for tonight's supper. A good cook is always flexible." She smoothed Jamie's hair as he passed by her holding up his prize.

Callie had time before she needed to get the turkeys into the oven and everything else was done. She had seen some of the men over at a paddock, working with the horses and wanted a closer look at the beautiful animals.

Sully nodded her way as he continued to twirl the rope over his head, talking softly to the horse he was working into the corner of the paddock. He threw the rope hitting the mark and sliding harmlessly over the horse's head. The horse reared up slightly but Sully gentled her into submission then led her into the stable.

A few moments later Seth emerged leading a large black horse with a white star on its forehead. He appeared surprised to see her leaning against the fence but then flashed that full smile at her. Taking the halter off, he patted the horse to let it run free but it stayed by Seth's side walking beside him as he approached the fence where she was leaning.

When he reached her, the horse leaned toward Callie and Seth put out his hand to protect her but without need. The horse hung its head over the top rail and nibbled Callie's hair and then lipped her neck just above her starched collar. Seth pushed him back and away from Callie.

"This is, Lothario." When Callie looked at him with wide eyes, Seth laughed and said, "Yeah, I know, not very original. He sired most of this year's foals so he lives up to his name, I guess."

"What do you do with all the foals?"

"We train some of the best cow ponies in the west. They have to be smart, strong and brave. Able to face a charging bull if that's what the rider signals. They have to keep a rope taught when needed and keep true to their training even when the rider is out of the saddle. I think we have some of the best recruits this year as I've seen yet. It takes a lot of time to train them but we have a waiting list of buyers. I like to know where they'll be going so I don't put them to auction. I sell them at horse shows and word of mouth mostly," he informed her.

Lothario had worked his way back to Callie and was again lipping at her throat while Callie laughed at the tickling of his surprisingly soft lips. She rubbed his velvety nose and told him what a beauty he was and what a flirt with those long black lashes, to which the horse listened, enthralled, as completely smitten as a horse can be with a human.

Callie looked at Seth and thought he looked a little flushed, a bright-rose color intensifying from his shirt collar to the top of his cheeks. Too much sun, thought Callie and then said, "I better get back. The bread has probably risen by now." Turning she gave one last pat on Lothario's muzzle and went back to the cookhouse.

Seth waited until he thought Callie would be well out of hearing range. He slapped the horse on the hindquarters. "Damn horse. I don't know if you were intending to embarrass the hell out of me or just bragging. Now put that thing away and behave yourself. I won't bring another lady to visit if you can't be trusted to act like a gentleman." Then Seth walked back into the stable leaving a well-endowed Lothario rubbing his chin on the top fence rail.

Callie started the clean-up of the bread making thinking about tonight's altered menu and looked up to see Seth ride over to the cookhouse. She stopped wiping the table and went out to see if Seth wanted anything. Lothario kept pulling on the bit and stepping toward the porch while Seth held back on the reins.

Finally, Callie stepped down off the porch to speak to Seth lifting her hand to rub the velvety black nose.

Lothario quieted as soon as Callie stepped toward him. He nuzzled Callie's neck and snorted quietly at her, blowing warm breath into her face.

Seth was a little frustrated for losing control of his mount although he couldn't fault the horse for having good taste. He explained, "I came over to see if you needed anything from town. I have to go in to pick up the payroll and I can put in an order at the mercantile for you."

"I don't need anything for the pantry but I would like some plaid material, enough to make a couple of men's shirts," she answered still rubbing Lothario's nose.

Seth immediately lost his good humor. He didn't like the thought of Callie sewing shirts for another man. "Doesn't sound like something I would be good at. It might have to wait till you get into town. I'm sure you would get just what you want then."

He pulled back on the reins and Lothario backed up, spun and headed toward the ranch gates at a cantor. Seth didn't come down for supper with the hands that evening.

CHAPTER 5

Seth had seen Gregg, the owner of the adjoining ranch closer to town, ride in and waited to hear the knock on the door that never came. Curious, he looked out his front window just as Gregg stepped up to the cookhouse porch and began talking to Callie.

Grabbing his Stetson, Seth slapped it on his head. What business did Gregg have with Callie? They didn't even know each other, did they? If Gregg was only saying a friendly 'howdy' he should be done by now and heading toward Seth or Sully.

Neither Gregg nor Callie noticed his approach, they were so engrossed in their conversation. Seth was almost close enough to hear what Gregg was saying now. Seeing Callie's apparently worried expression and repeatedly shaking her head negatively had Seth on the alert.

Gregg was saying, "I heard the other men say you were really good, had a lot of experience from working at that big hotel in St Louis. I have to have someone do it and I thought, since you are so close, you would be the best choice." Gregg was almost pleading and then continued at Callie's shake of her head. "I really need this. I'll pay more than your going rate."

And when Seth heard that and saw Callie's face pinched in worry, he couldn't stand any more. Taking one big step up onto the porch, he spun Gregg around by the shoulder and punched him in the jaw. Gregg, unprepared for an attack, flew from the porch and landed in the dust on his buttocks.

"Get outta here, Gregg. Go back to your own ranch."

Without watching whether Gregg did just that, Seth turned back to Callie, the shocked expression still on her face. She had stood up and would have gone to Gregg's assistance but Seth stood between them and he wasn't planning on moving no matter what she said.

Seth was almost pleading. "Look, Callie, I know it was hard for you, hard for any woman to make it alone, without family. You may have done things that you weren't proud of but you don't have to do those things anymore. There's no need to make money on your back for some man just to feed yourself. Any us here would give you whatever you need without asking for anything in return. You're not some whore without friends."

The sound of the slap echoed across the compound and back to the stunned couple on the porch. The two ranch hands next to the paddock stood stock still, one man holding the other's arm, their heads close together. Jamie was halfway from the barn, both hands balled tightly into fists at his side.

Callie's green gaze locked onto Seth's as his cheek started to show the red imprint of her small hand. Everything stopped. Even the birds seemed to have dropped from the sky.

Breaking the silence, Callie raised her hand to her mouth, and said, "Don't you dare follow me!"

She ran as fast as her limp would allow her into the cookhouse and the sanctuary of her room locking the door behind her. She stared in dread at the door handle expecting Seth to kick it in at any moment. She had never hit another person in her life. Never. What a hateful, hurtful man to attack her for no reason. To say those awful things. What had she done to make him so angry? What had just happened?

Seth watched as Callie ran into the cookhouse. He looked towards the men by the paddock and they were still there, glaring at him. Jamie had turned away but not until the hurt and pain showed plainly on his young face. Gregg was riding out through the ranch gate and Seth felt the heat and sting of his cheek but thought it best to ignore it. He stomped off the porch and went toward the ranch house. What had just happened?

Callie was starting to shake now. What had she done wrong? Why had Seth yelled like that and say all those hurtful things? Why would he be so mean to her? She would need to leave. She could not stay here and have the men look at her, like some whore? Is that what they thought? Callie had gone through something similar while working with Pierre.

The men in the hotel kitchen would sneer and say rude comments behind her back about her and Pierre, her mentor. He was old enough to be her father and he treated her as a daughter. Callie lived with Pierre, his wife, Lizette, and their two daughters, both of whom were about the same age as Callie. They had made up a happy household and still thought of each other as family. The talk eventually caused Callie to be dismissed from her sous chef post. She had not wanted Pierre to lose his position by defending her against the slander. But the talk spread and she wasn't able to get another job in any of the city's hotel kitchens.

Pierre told her to ignore the other cook's comments. That they had been said out of jealousy for her talent. That the men saying these things were ignorant pigs that were not fit to clean the floors after her.

Well, Seth Harrison wasn't fit to clean up after pigs!

Tears began filling her eyes and running down her cheeks. Taking up the carpetbag, she sat it on the bed. She opened a drawer and took out her neatly ironed aprons and placed them on the bed beside it. It wouldn't take long to pack her clothes.

A soft tapping at her door drew her attention as Sully said softly, "Callie, are you all right? Can I talk with you?"

Callie answered, "I'm fine. Don't bother yourself, I'll be all right." And sniffed.

"Callie, child, the boys, they said you and the Boss got into some tiff. I'm havin' a tough time understanding what happened. What did he say to you that got you to hittin' him?"

Callie went to the door to better hear Sully. "I was simply talking to Mr Gregg about baking and decorating his wedding cake. He's getting married in two weeks' time. He had heard I had been a pastry chef and had decorated cakes for famous people. I told him that I worked most of the day for Se…Mr Harrison, and all the ingredients here belonged to the ranch. I couldn't see how I could bake a cake without taking time and money from Mr Harrison. Mr Gregg didn't see it that way. He said Seth wouldn't mind and he would pay anything it cost. But I still couldn't figure out how to get it there and set it up. Men don't seem to realize there is more to a large cake then simply baking it."

"I don't understand how that could make the boss mad enough to punch Gregg and then tear into you."

Hiccupping, she said, "I don't think it had to do with M-Mr Gregg. I-it had t-t-o do with me-e-e." At this sad admission, Callie's tears broke through and she began sobbing into her apron.

"Oh, Honey child." Sully tried to sooth her. "I don't believe the boss would ever think badly of you. This must be some mistake."

"He said awful, hurtful things. He said I did things I wasn't proud of. And he said I made money on my back a-and I don't even know what that means but he said it like it wasn't nice." And with that admission, hiccups interspersed with the small sobs that nearly broke Sully's heart.

"I don't know what that boy could have been thinkin'. I'm sure you must have misunderstood what he said," a confused Sully explained.

Callie stood closer to the door, bowing her head in shame and whispered, "He called me a whore."

Then Sully heard wrenching sobs on the other side of the door. All he could think to say was, 'Child, I don't know what devil got into that boy but I'm gonna find out. How he got the wrong end of the stick, I don't have the vaguest idea but I'm gonna have a serious talk with him."

Callie said quietly, "Thank you, Fath, I mean, thank you, Sully." Callie felt the relief and calm as if she had attended confessional and cleansed her soul of all bad thoughts. She could continue with her packing.

But now anger was replacing heartbreak and Callie was going to show everyone that a St Michaels isn't beaten down that easily. They were only words. Words that should not have been said and that they tarnish the speaker more than their target.

Sully was still outside the door. "Why don't you just rest, Callie child, and me and the boys will make do tonight."

Callie's voice was raw from crying but said, "No, they'll be coming in expecting a good meal. I have it mostly started and I'll serve it. I am the cook here and no one is going to say I didn't do the job I am being paid for right up till the end."

"All right, but if you need help, just give me a call," the old man told her.

She didn't understand everything but she was unwavering in her sense of rightness. No one should be treated as she had been and she was strong enough to leave. Perhaps there was work in town until she earned enough for a train ticket further west. This couldn't be the only ranch in Kansas needing a good cook.

Sully walked into the ranch office without knocking and sat down. "Well, she's stayin', for now. What the hell did you think you were doin'? You actually called that little girl a whore?"

Seth's feet hit the floor nosily as his boots dropped off the desk. He sat straight up then asked, "She said that? She thinks I called her a whore?"

"Well, did you or didn't you. It's not a word used in everyday conversation."

Seth tried to explain. Tried to remember exactly what he had said. "The word did come up. I don't remember how, right now."

"Let's start from the beginning. Why in the world did you sucker punch, Gregg? He's been our neighbor for over ten years now," Sully asked exasperated at his boss's behavior.

"He was propositioning Callie. I heard her tell him 'no' and he just kept at her," explained Seth crossly.

"I don't know what you heard, or thought you heard, but Gregg was asking Callie to bake one of them fancy wedding cakes for him and his bride next weekend. She said she couldn't cuz she didn't have time and the ingredients she used would have been yours."

Seth sat quietly, replaying the conversation between Gregg and Callie in his mind. A thoughtful look came into his eyes as he said to Sully, "I might have got that part wrong."

Sully let out a sigh. "Yeah, you got that part wrong. But what about all that other stuff? I know when I hear someone with a broken heart and that poor girl is heart-sick that you said such awful things about her."

"They weren't about her. I was trying to tell her it didn't matter to me, to us, what she had to do in the past. That she had people that cared for her now and that she should never feel she should turn to a stranger for help or money when she had us. I don't know how she got it turned around." Seth tried to explain himself again. "I was trying to say I didn't judge her for her past."

Sully gazed at him sadly shaking his head sorrowfully. "You don't see how that may have sounded to Callie or anyone else within ear shot? I've got a bunkhouse full of men ready to draw straws as to who's gonna knock your block off. That little girl wasn't ever in the kind of situation you're talkin' about. Anyone talking to her more than five minutes can tell she's an innocent. You let jealousy control your hands and your mouth. We may lose the best cook we've ever seen just because you can't admit you want to rope and brand her, so to speak."

"What are you saying? I've no interest in Callie in that way. I just don't want her hurt by some fella wanting to put another notch in his belt," he answered angrily.

"Let me put it like this. You're a stallion." At that comment, Sully was interrupted by Seth blowing air through his lips but he continued, "No, you're a stallion and you've gelded all the rest of us."

Seth sputtered denial but Sully continued, "Me and the hands, in your own mind so to speak," explained Sully. "Anytime any o' the hands got too friendly or were alone with Callie, you found some reason to go over and break them apart. You saw another stallion, Gregg that is, come into your territory and start sniffin' around your mare. Boy, you got the scent of that mare in your nostrils and you've been fighting the attraction somethin' fierce. No one is gonna be safe until you cut her out of the herd and put your mark on her. And by that, I mean marrying her. I won't let you break her heart again. She's not that kind of girl. Practically raised as a nun, you know."

Seth thought about what Sully said. Some of the feelings he had felt over the last week started to form a pattern. Disgusted by his lack of understanding himself, he asked, "So what do I do now? Go over and blow my breath up her nostrils? I don't have the slightest clue how to make this right. I certainly didn't mean to hurt her feelings or make her leave." Panic set in. "Got any ideas?"

Sully got up and hit his hat against his leg. "None. I've never seen a man make more of a mess in courtin' a woman than you have." With that he turned and walked out the door.

Seth watched his oldest and best friend leave, thinking 'thanks a hell of a lot'.

Seth did have to face the truth that he was attracted to his ranch hands' cook. She was pretty and friendly and he liked the way she smelled. Hell, even his horse liked her and Lothario knew good horseflesh.

How was he supposed to get close enough to her while all his other employees watched him - them? He had never been in this position. Had never been this close to being attracted to a woman. He needed to explore how strong the interest and attraction between them was because he thought she might feel the same.

At lease he thought she did. Of course, that was before the fiasco today. How did what he say come out sounding like an accusation? He had thought, from what he knew of her job experience, she had worked some hard jobs. Dishwashing and low-end kitchen positions. He knew those jobs didn't pay very well. He just wanted her to know if she had to resort to less than savory ways to make her way in life, she no longer had to do so. He would gladly help her out with any expenses or debts she may have.

He had thought she might consider Gregg's offer. That was the whole problem. He was angry that his neighbor was propositioning his cook before he could. What did that say about him? Sully was right. Seth wanted her but wasn't ready to be a man about it.

He regretted making Callie cry and for saying anything that would drive her away. He will have to find a way to apologize and let her know he would never think badly of her again. She was an important part of the ranch already and her leaving would cause half his hands to leave, as well.

Not that he cared about that right now. Right now, he had to figure out how to apologize without offending her all over again. How to explain he was wrong without saying exactly what he was wrong about. And then, how to get her to see him as anything but the ass that embarrassed himself and her in front of everyone.

CHAPTER 6

Callie stood in front of the steaming standing rib roast. It had been slow cooking all day and she had paired it with garlic-roasted potatoes, green beans with pecans, sautéed cabbage with bacon, and her special French bread rolls. Jamie was serving the French onion soup topped with a toasted piece of bread and melted goat cheese.

She knew her eyes were still red from the afternoon of crying but hoped no one would remark on them. Pasting a smile on her face, she called out, "Come on in. It's ready. Ring the bell for the others, please."

As usual they began their shuffle in. The first man in, Slim, snatched his hat off his head and pushed a handful of late fall wild-flowers towards her. The very same kinds she thought of picking for herself at one time.

"Thank you, Slim. They're lovely. I will place them in this jar for all of us to enjoy." She took up the fork and carving knife and placed a slab of rare roasted beef onto his outstretched plate and added a small ladle of au jus. The next plate was put forward and she greeted that recipient with the same easy friendly manner. Another bouquet of flowers showed up, this time already in a pitcher of water and Callie accepted them graciously then served Rusty a portion of meat.

Callie was touched the men were trying to sympathize with her but weren't sure how to go about doing that. It made her sad that she may be leaving them just as she was forming these friendships.

A sudden shift in the atmosphere and a rise in

mumbling brought Callie's head up from the slice of meat she was carving. Someone had replaced the ranch hand who had been waiting in front of her. She looked straight into the sherry colored eyes trimmed with golden lashes.

Callie's smile disappeared and she bit down hard on her inside cheek to keep from showing any emotion.

Seth wasn't wearing his hat and held the plate out in front of him, a hesitant smile on his lips as he said, rather too robustly, "Miss Callie, this sure smells great. Thought I'd come down and have a meal with the rest of the men."

Callie looked down at the roast and fought her instincts to yell, throw something, cry or run - anything to get away from this man. Instead, she pulled on some inner strength and searched around in the bottom of the pan for the piece of roast end she hadn't planned on serving. Picking it up between the fork and knife blade, she slapped it onto the empty plate. The au jus splashed on to Seth's shirt and vest but only a slight flutter of his left eyelid indicated he was aware of it.

Callie raised the full ladle and inquired, "Au jus?"

The entire row of men stepped back toward the door as one cohesive unit and stared with wide eyes at the hypnotizing drama playing out before them.

Seth politely replied, "Thank you, no." He continued down the counter covered with food and then sat at one of the smaller tables. Sully picked-up his plate from the ranch hands' table and went and sat next to Seth, speaking quietly.

Callie looked expectantly at the next man in line, then realized she was still glaring daggers and relaxed her features. "A nice rare piece for you, Jake?"

Seth finished his meal and left the dining room quietly. Sully moved back over to the hands' table and soon the meal was finished and Callie and Jamie did the washing up.

Callie had turned out all the oil lamps in the dining room and stood looking through the front windows toward the bunkhouse. The men didn't stay and talk as they had become used to doing. Including her in their day's work and asking about things they had a curiosity about.

These men were very dear to her already. They had become the big noisy family she had missed since leaving St Michaels. How was she to start over again? Pierre would take her back into his home and family. However, the hotel had made it clear she was too much of a distraction in the kitchen and she could not regain her old position.

That was why she had applied for this ranch cook position in the first place. She would let Sully know her decision tomorrow and ask if he could let Jamie drive her into town to catch the train. She wasn't sure when it came through but it couldn't be more than a day. She knew there was a Sunday stop.

She would say goodbye to the men at breakfast. It would be difficult and she was hoping she wouldn't find herself crying. They had been welcoming and kind to her right from the beginning and she was touched by the sympathy they showed her this evening. But she was a St Michaels' graduate and she would survive. Merely in another place along the path God made for her.

Large warm hands came to rest on both her upper arms. Callie startled. She hadn't heard Seth enter the dining room.

Seth held Callie lightly but firmly. He felt he could get through this but only if she didn't look at him with those sad, accusing, green eyes.

"I apologize for everything I said. It all came out wrong and I didn't mean any of it the way it sounded. I didn't mean to hurt your feelings," he told her earnestly.

"Then why did you say them? I don't understand. I didn't do anything and then you were yelling and scaring me. You said I made money on my back and I still don't know what that means...and neither does Sully," she finished with a 'so there' moment.

Seth had to quash a smile but said, "It means I'm an idiot. I'll explain it sometime when we know each other a little better. But just believe I was the one in the wrong. I made all the poor decisions. Not you, Callie." Taking a deep sigh, said, "God, you're next to perfect."

He closed his eyes and bent his head to inhale the perfume of Callie's shampoo, the perfume of her.

"But the men heard, and Mr Gregg...what will he think of me?" whispered Callie still worried about the aftermath from the altercation of that afternoon.

"I sent Sully over to Gregg's ranch to apologize and explain that I thought he was here to rustle my new cook. Sully told him that you'd bake him that cake as my gift to him and his wife, so I'm hoping you'll stay. Don't make more of a liar out of me then I've already been. And the men didn't really hear any of the words. They just saw me yelling and were ready to come to your defense but then you slapped me and that pretty much put a stop to it." He smiled in self-deprecation.

"I'm sorry I slapped you. I have never slapped anyone in my life. I feel so, so, I don't know. There are better ways to stop an argument than with physical violence," she said in a whisper.

"Why do I think that is a quote from some nun?" he asked the back of her head.

"Sister Mary Margaret. She was in charge of discipline and never raised a hand to any of us. Not an easy thing when taking care of children who sometimes grew up on the street."

Seth was tired of not seeing Callie's pretty green eyes so he turned her to face him.

She noticed he was still wearing the shirt and vest he had on at dinner and said quietly, "I'm sorry I splashed your shirt."

"I'm sorry I didn't ask for the au jus. It was really good," he answered smiling.

He pulled Callie in for a hug and nuzzled the top of her head. "Am I forgiven or can you give me some penance or something to earn a way back into your good graces? No one wants to see you leave. I don't want to see you leave. Please stay, Callie." He seemed to pray into her hair. "Don't leave, don't leave me."

"I still don't understand what happened but I think you don't want it to happen again and that's all I need to hear."

Seth leaned down saying into her ear, "I never want it to happen again. Ever." And he pulled her toward the table as he shuffled backwards.

Spreading his legs to balance himself, he sat on the edge of the table. He reached out to pull Callie against his chest. Wrapping his long arms around her, he held her to his warmth. Callie stiffened, unsure as to what he was planning.

"Come here, Darlin', I don't want to have to yell

across the room to talk with you. Now relax, I'm not gonna do anything that would have them nuns worrying," he said in that slightly husky voice he used only with her.

It was a comfortable position, at least for Callie. She had never had a big man basically surround her. She felt protected and consoled and, something else she had no words for and no one to ask. Callie felt herself lean in and enjoy feeling fragile and feminine and wanted. It was kind of a heady experience.

Seth inhaled deeply. Callie's unique scent, vanilla and spice and warm clean woman filled his nostrils. He nuzzled her neck just beneath her ear and the urge to nibble overcame good sense. Seth sucked the creamy ear lobe into his mouth, just lipping it, and when that wasn't satisfactory enough, he sucked the soft skin along her neck.

It must have tickled because Callie hunched her shoulders but didn't pull away. Seth laughed to himself and continued with little kisses down to the edge of her collar. When Callie bent her neck and hunched her should on the one side, that left the other side unprotected and the same little kisses and skin sucking was administered there.

Seth became hungrier for more and took possession of Callie's lips, covering them completely and sucking her bottom lip between his as he pulled away. Callie's eyes were closed and Seth took that as an invitation to continue. He tipped his head at an angle and again feasted on her lips that were beginning to swell with need. Slipping his tongue between her moistened lips, he entered her warmth, rubbing her tongue and receding and thrusting again, mimicking the age-old advance and retreat motions of mating couples through the ages.

"Have you ever stepped-out with a fella before? Had a special beau?" he asked into Callie's ear as he began the trail of exploration again.

At Callie's confusion, he explained, "I'm asking if you would allow me to court you. I'm giving you a choice. Nothing would change here - your job, your life would remain unchanged if you tell me to get lost. I would honor your wishes in this matter. If one of the other men has caught your attentions, I'll accept that. If not, I would like to have the opportunity." Seth leaned back putting some space between them whether for her benefit or his, so that each could think with a clear head.

"I've never had a beau and I have a feeling you would make a grand one," she said shyly then smiled up at him.

"I'll try to make a great one." He finished with a quick kiss on her lips that were still shinny and pouting for more.

"I'll see you tomorrow after breakfast. I'll be heading into town and I thought you could come with me if you want to," he offered hoping she would agree.

"What time will we be back?" she asked thinking about the meal.

"It should only take three to four hours total. Will that work?"

"That will be fine."

"Then I'll see you after breakfast. Sleep tight." Without another kiss or touch, Seth left Callie standing in the darkened room.

Seth headed back to the house, trying not to show his discomfort but he didn't want to adjust himself in case Callie was watching out the window, or God forbid, one of the hands was out taking a smoke.

Why couldn't he just tell Callie he wanted her and be done with this. She found him attractive, that much he could tell. If he was a stallion then why couldn't he just nudge Callie into a corner and cover her? Just that thought had him in more pain as parts of him welcomed the idea. Well, he didn't have a full-sized tub for nothing. He was going to fill it to the brim with water right from the hand-pump and sit in it until he had more control of his manhood.

Stallion or not, Callie could bolt anytime and he needed her to come to the same realization that he had. They were to be a tandem team and there was no way around it.

Callie lay on her bed, watching the moonlight move across the wall like a sundial marking off the hours. She was excited about going to town with Seth. She was excited about his asking her to step out with him. She was excited by the way his mouth on hers made her feel, inside where the nuns said women had to be careful not to mistake lust for love.

She never had to understand that before. Actually, she thought she had it all under control since she never had been tempted to 'lust' with anyone before now. Because she had not been tempted, she thought she was in control. That was before Seth Harrison had come into her life.

Now she knew she was not immune to 'lust'. Just as the nuns had warned all the girls in the home, they could get caught up in 'lust' and lose their immortal soul. Not that Sister Mary Margaret said as much but she seemed more down-to-earth than many of the nuns at St Michaels. Callie had been under that nun's authority far longer than any other. Sister Mary Margaret was whom Callie looked to for guidance right after the Virgin Mary.

Callie would pray for direction and then write a letter to Mother Superior at St Michaels. She felt the need for advice, to help her sort out feelings. Her natural female feelings. She knew she should be attracted to a man, to want to join with that man and to marry that man to form a family. But she needed help to know how to know when she met that man. How would she know if Seth is the man she is fated to marry?

After breakfast, Callie dressed to go to town. She had slept surprisingly well after all the drama of the past twenty-four hours. Putting her little green hat on, she smiled at the little brown bird peeking out of the netting with its bright eyes. Taking her reticule, she put her gloved hand through the loops. Going out to the porch, she heard the buckboard pulling up just as she arrived.

Seth jumped down and ran around to help Callie onto the wagon seat that had a cushion this time to sit on. She took the basket she was carrying and placed it on the floorboards under her seat.

"Not very fancy but it gets the job done," teased Seth as he spoke about the ranch's transportation.

"It's fine. There were many times I would have given an eyetooth to have anything besides shanks mare to get around on."

"Lothario is going to have his nose out of joint if he sees I'm leaving with you and these other horses. He seems quite taken with you." He gave her that grin that always made her smile back.

The trip to town went by quickly. Seth asking a lot

of questions about Callie's growing-up and having all those other children around all the time. Callie learning about Seth growing up an only child on a farm distant from any other families. He had a dearth of relatives on either side, leaving him now with only some second cousins back east.

Town was busy on Saturday in the fall, a day when many farmers and ranchers came in to trade and purchase items for the winter. Seth nodded to most of the other wagon drivers and riders passing them going the other direction already done with their reason for going into town.

"Once snow and cold weather gets here, travel is limited so everyone has to stock up now. I have to pick up some lumber for the new calf boxes from Thompson's dry goods store so I'll drop you off at the mercantile," Seth told her.

Callie was impressed by the quality and quantity of fabric she found at Murray's Mercantile. There were also a lot of readymade clothing. Callie commented on this to the woman, Helen, who was cutting material per customer's orders.

"Oh, that's because there are so many unmarried men working the area ranches and farms. The requests for readymade clothes are very demanding," Helen explained.

Callie was holding a pair of canvas trousers up to herself trying to judge the right size when Seth walked into the store.

"Trying to start a new fashion, Callie?" he teased.

"Just trying to gauge the right size for Jamie. He has out-grown and worn out his two shirts and I told him I would show him how to sew. I can use the buttons on his old ones but that is about all that's still usable. Cuffs and collars are too frayed and faded to turn. I think everything he has are hand-me-downs from the men and I want to change that."

Seth looked chagrined and asked, "That plaid material you wanted? That was for Jamie?"

Callie looked at him humorously and said, "What would I do with plaid shirts. I mostly wear my uniforms." She continued to look over the readymade shirts in a size that would fit Jamie.

Seth felt badly for not looking for the material for her and took up a shirt saying, "I think he would like this one. It will bring out the blue in his eyes, too. Maybe he can get a girl to walk out with him." Then he added another pair of trousers and two more shirts to the pile of union suits and socks Callie had going already.

"What about boots?" Seth asked looking at a sharp looking pair of leather boots with a metal guard on the heel.

"It's hard to say. His appear all right, but he may have them stuffed with paper to make them fit. I really think we need him or at least need to take a drawing of his foot and bring it back before we buy any."

"We'll bring him next time. That way we'll be sure of the size."

Callie liked the thought of there being more trips into town together, even if Jamie came, too. It held the promise of a future. Something Callie realized she had never planned for before. She worked hard at whatever job she was doing at the time but she never had long-term plans of staying in any one place. Being an orphan meant she had no permanent home or people to call her own. She knew a few other graduates of St Michaels whereabouts but mostly once they reached eighteen, they made their own way in the world as she was doing.

She had not planned on what she would do when she turned eighteen until the nuns practically packed her bags for her and sent her westward on the train. Then she was hired as a scrub when Pierre found her and felt sorry for her. She started by washing dishes and cleaning the pots and pans at the Wainwright hotel.

She got a break when Pierre needed her to watch the saucepans in an emergency. He was impressed with her ability when it took him longer than he thought away from his stove. Callie had saved the sauce and several other items from ruin.

But with all her pre-planning for her meals, she never made plans for when she was finished at the hotel restaurant. Just as she had no plans for after the Harrison ranch.

Callie went to take the coins out of her purse when Seth told the proprietor to put everything on his account and he would take care of it at the end of the month as usual.

Seth said, "I have one more stop unless you would like to go for a cup of tea or something."

"I brought a picnic we could eat on the way home. There are jars of grape juice and some buttered bread with ham and goat cheese. A couple of slices of spice cake if you want something sweet," Callie offered.

"That sounds great to me. Jamie sent this parcel with me to drop off at the dress shop."

"What could Jamie be sending to a dress shop?"

He shrugged. "Don't know. Gave me this back at the ranch and asked if I would deliver it. I told him I would."

"Well, I trust Jamie but I would feel better knowing

what he was up to. I also know teen boys." She smiled. "Let's see the package."

Seth took the slim bundle wrapped in the paper and string used on the packets for the hands to take with them for their midday meal.

Callie accepted it and felt gently up and down then said, "I think I know what it is. These are the turkey feathers. He is selling feathers for the dressmaker to use in boas and hats. I noticed she made hats as well as dresses when Sully drove me through town."

"Well, don't that beat all. The kid just keeps thinking and planning. He's going to own the ranch someday if I don't watch out." Seth laughed, somewhat in relief he wasn't doing anything against his better judgment.

He took the package into the shop across the street while Callie stepped up into the wagon and that is where Seth found her on his return. Pulling himself up onto the seat, he turned the team toward the ranch.

A few miles out of town, Seth pulled the wagon toward one side of the road under some shade trees. "This is a good place to stop if it's all right with you."

Callie agreed and Seth helped her down from the buckboard. He grabbed the basket and seat blanket and they walked a little way from the horses to sit in the long, dried grass.

Callie said, "I had no idea this area was so beautiful. I guess I thought everything this side of St Louis was the wild west."

Seth chuckled. "Well, we are a little short of females and a few of what might be considered refinements. We have our own forms of entertainment and a lot of us get to visit the big cities for things like museums and theatre.

Although I can't rightly say I miss 'em out here. Guess I always have better things to do like take a pretty girl on a picnic." He flashed Callie one of his drop-dead gorgeous grins.

Callie took the food and jars out of the basket trying to get her equilibrium back after that smile. "Well, that kind of flattery can't go unrewarded. Try this grape juice Maria put up. I like it better than wine."

Callie asked, "If your mother taught you to read and write before you left for school in town, who taught you all you know about ranching? The horses and training?"

"That was all Sully. He was a lot younger, of course, but had all the experience. My Dad knew cattle and getting them to market in good shape but Sully said we should be breeding and training our own ponies. We started out with a few wild mustangs and then purchased some stock for height. Now we have the best of all of them."

"From what the other hands say at meal times, they think you have some of the best animals around Kansas. That has to make you proud."

His sandwich forgotten, he nodded. "I guess. It was just one more thing to make the ranching go easier. That is where my thoughts go for about anything I do. Sully, too, I suppose."

"It is a shame your dad passed before the ranch got this big."

Seth thought for a moment then said, "I think he could see it all coming together before he died. He told me he was proud of my hard work and knew Sully would never leave me. I think he passed easier knowing the ranch would go on."

"Sometimes, when I am thinking about life, I realize

it isn't the big things that matter the most. It is the everyday things we do people remember and end up meaning the most. It is what the nuns tried to instill in us. Not to take our blessings for granted and to pass on goodness whenever we could."

After their light meal and a little small talk, the two cleared up their make-shift picnic and the rest of the trip was uneventful. To Callie it could not have been better.

Callie was excited to call Jamie to the kitchen to show him his new clothes. He ran in and stopped abruptly when he realized what was piled on the counter in front of her.

She smiled and said, "I know we were going to make you some shirts but Seth thought you should have both. Having the readymade gives us more time to work on the shirts we are sewing together. And I can't sew the heavier trousers. It takes a machine and I don't know where to borrow one."

Jamie was slowly going through the pile, treating each item like a precious jewel, even the underwear. He asked, "Th-these all f-for m-me?" At Callie's nod he said, "Wow, I n-never had s-s-so m-many th-things b-before. Th-th-thanks."

Callie smiled at his enjoyment of the clothing. "Just like a birthday."

"D-don't know." He brushed his hand over the blue plaid shirt as if to make sure it was real.

Callie asked, thinking she knew the answer already, "You never had a birthday gift?"

"N-never had a b-b-birthday. D-don't kn-know it," he replied as a matter of fact.

Callie made a decision. "A lot of the children at the foundling home came to it without any history. My birthday was set for me because they said I was a newborn when they found me on the doorstep, June 6th. The nun's let other orphans choose their own birthdays. Some chose their saints' day, others the day they entered the foundling home. We all got the same last name of St Michaels if we didn't know our own."

"D-don't h-have a last n-n-name e-e-either," Jamie said with a lost look in his eyes that Callie recognized from the expressions on so many new orphans' faces, one of desolation and despair, hopelessness at its highest level.

"Well, this is an opportunity for you then," Callie said happily. "Now you can choose a last name, too. It doesn't need to be today. You can take your time."

"I-I w-was using W-west when I-I g-got here. I-I t-traveled w-with a f-fella n-named, West. H-He s-said I-I c-could c-come w-with h-him. M-my m-mom l-left m-me w-with m-my aunts. N-nobody w-wanted m-me s-so I-I w-went w-with him b-but i-it d-doesn't s-seem r-right w-with h-him g-gone."

"Well, you choose a birthday and I'll bake a cake to celebrate. The last name can be decided any time. Then I'll file it and make it all legal for you. Do you know how old you are?"

"B-bout f-f-four t-teen."

"Okay, fourteen it is. Your next birthday whenever you say," said Callie decisively.

Smiling, Jamie folded the new clothes to take back to his bunk.

CHAPTER 7

It was after dinner and Callie hadn't seen Seth since their trip into town. She thought of their conversation and all the things they covered. Then she thought of all the things they hadn't covered. She gathered up her sponge bag, clean clothes, and walked the short distance to the house hoping to get a bath.

Maria met her at the door as she was leaving. "Meester Seth not home. You need help with el agua? Water?

Callie shook her head. "No, I'll be fine. Go home to your husband. I'll close up when I am done."

The bathroom was as clean and pristine as it had been the first time Callie used it. The tub, with the plug firmly in place, stood waiting for water. The water in the reservoir was hot and Callie took the bucket and filled the tub to a decent depth for soaking. She added cold from the handpump then climbed into its cocoon shaped warmth. Sliding down blissfully until only her face and the tips of her breasts were above water.

Callie washed her hair and tried to dry it in front of the stove but gave up and braided it for sleep. She left the bathing room as neat and clean as she found it and refilled the water in the reservoir. Walking back through the quiet house, she admired its beauty before leaving by the front door, pulling it closed behind her.

Seth arrived to the ranch, noting all seemed quiet and secure. Just the way he liked it. He put Lothario into his stall and took care of him for the night. Taking the lantern with him up to the house, he looked over to the cookhouse and saw all was dark there, too.

Not a surprise, Callie got up early to make sure the hands were fed a good meal. He smiled because he missed eating at the cookhouse tonight. He wondered what outlandish sounding meal she had prepared. He was beginning to get used to eating with the hands if it meant being near Callie. Getting time to watch her smile and tease with the others, sometimes have a word or two with her himself.

Entering the house through the office, he immediately sniffed the air. He went into the hall and turned left to the bathing room. As soon as he reached the door, he felt as if he were truly home.

Lighting the lamp, he saw a hair pin dropped by its base. He took in a deep breath of warm moist air, warm moist woman more likely. It hit him in the gut so hard he felt he had to sit on the bench next to the tub. Rubbing the side of the copper, he found it still warm, warm from her bath, warm from her body. Callie had just been in here. He had probably just missed her. His body part that was always happy to think about Callie made itself known.

Seth stood up and adjusted his trousers. God, this was torture, smelling her soap, knowing she had been naked in this room, smoothing a washrag over her skin leaving steaks of soapy bubbles. Standing and letting the water slide down her soft, fragrant skin in streams.

Oh, my God, this bouquet that was the essence of Callie was going to drive him mad and there wasn't any escape from it. He was going to smell it all night. He just knew it. He didn't even consider taking a cold bath, to dissipate the smell of Callie, to make it less potent. It would be impossible, anyway. Sully had been right all along. Seth had the scent of her in his nostrils and there was only one way this could all end.

After breakfast Seth showed up looking tired, Callie thought. "Didn't you sleep well," she asked concerned.

"Just got in a little late. I got talked into a card game and one thing led to another," he explained. "I came to ask, since this is your half-day, if you wanted to go on a real picnic. Maria said she could put together a meal for us and I could show you some of the ranch."

"That sounds like fun. I would love to see the working part of the ranch. So far, I haven't seen a live cow, err, cattle. I should be done after one o'clock and Jamie was going to handle the evening meal, so I don't need to be back at any set time either."

"I'll pick you up then," he told her as he left for the house.

Jamie was finishing the dishes when Callie heard Seth's voice from the porch. She had changed out of her uniform and was wearing a white shirtwaist with lace at the cuffs and collar and pearl buttons down the front. The skirt was a rusty brown with embroidered leaves and vines around the hem. She was going to forgo a hat since it was breezy and she didn't want to have to chase after it or keep looking up through it to see Seth.

Going out to the porch, she saw Seth up on Lothario, evidently talking to the horse since no one else was around. Callie hesitated and stared at the large animal. "We're not taking the buckboard? I don't know how to ride. I've never been outside a city before and I took public conveyances everywhere I went."

"No problem, I'm gonna take you right up here with

me," Seth said with a grin indicating a place in front of him. "Besides the buckboard can't go where we're going. No two tracks to follow, just wide-open space with rolling hills and the prettiest little lake you ever saw."

"I'm not sure…," she said hesitantly looking up at the high saddle where she would be expected to perch. The once friendly horse looked anything but that now.

"You're not going to disappoint Lothario, are you? He's been excited about the trip since I told him this morning." That made Callie laugh, as he knew it would.

"Oh, well, I wouldn't want to disappoint Lothario." Now that riding on Lothario was a reality, Callie was worried about the logistics of getting on the huge beast. "How do I get up there?"

"Just take my hand and I'll pull you up here in front of me," said Seth as he maneuvered Lothario to stand quietly beside the porch. Callie reached her hand up into Seth's and was lifted easily in front of the saddle.

Callie tried to find something on which to hold. She had never realized how tall a horse was and how high the rider sat. She felt a little heady looking down and panic began to form in her chest.

Seth said quietly in her ear, "Close your eyes and lean back against me, Darlin'. Let the horse do the work and don't worry about fallin'. I'm not letting you go."

Then Callie felt the movement of Lothario's gait slowly rock her into a relaxed mood.

After a short while, Callie opened her eyes and was able to enjoy the height she was at to see everything. Being smaller than most adults, she felt like the queen of all she surveyed sitting high-up on Lothario. Seth being so close helped make her happy, too.

He started talking about points of interest such as where the hands are stationed, how many cattle were in the pastures they were passing through, when he had purchased certain parcels. They had been riding a ridge dotted with small bushy trees and underbrush. It followed a meandering stream, which opened onto a dammed-up pond. More of a small lake that lay like a jewel in the middle of the golden pastures surrounding it.

Callie smiled and exclaimed, "Oh Seth, it is beautiful. I wouldn't have expected to find something like this out here. Has it always been here or did you form the dam?"

"It was here way before me. The stream has always had enough water. The pond freezes over in the winter and you can skate on it. I nearly broke my neck a few winters ago testing it out," he told her trying to make living at the ranch sound fun.

"That's not something I'll need to worry about," she smiled without explaining that her lame foot prohibited such activities.

"Maybe I'll carry you around like a doll."

"After telling me you took a fall? Not likely." The subject seemed to have become too personal so to change the subject, she asked, "What are these trees with the waxy greenish fruit?"

He allowed her to lessen the tension between them. "I only know them as a Prairie crab apple. They have a real pretty pinkish white flower in the spring. There are a lot of them up and down the river," he explained as he pulled Lothario to a standstill. "I'm gonna dismount and then I'll lift you down. Lothario won't move so don't worry."

As Seth reached up for Callie, she placed her hands on his shoulders and let herself be lifted then set on the ground next to him.

Holding her to be sure she had her land legs back, he reached for the bag and blanket tied to the saddle. "We'll sit over here, I think. Let me walk around in the grass for a minute to scare out any critters that may have thought they had a safe spot to sun."

Callie looked apprehensively around, prepared to jump if anything too dangerous came running her way. Nothing moved except a very confused toad that once disturbed continued in an ungainly hop, hop, hop toward the brush. Callie smiled in relief and helped spread the blanket on the now exorcised ground.

Seth asked, "Are you hungry, yet? I ate a big breakfast but that was hours ago."

"You mean, you are hungry and simply asked to be polite." At his grin, she finished saying, "I haven't eaten either. Since you told me Maria was fixing the food, I wanted to make sure I got to try true Mexican cuisine. I never pass up an opportunity for authentic food."

"Maria sent along quite a lot of food for only the two of us. Let's see, we have enchiladas, rice and beans, pickled peppers, corn tortillas and beef tips with peppers. I reminded her not to make this too hot. You're a gringa and not used to these really hot peppers yet," he explained as he set out the items.

Callie had been placing a portion on each plate as Seth handed her the jars. It all smelled so good Callie's mouth watered. "I can hardly wait."

"Well, let me get you something to drink in case Maria's idea of mild and mine differ. She doesn't hold back for me. I get exactly what she and Carlo are eating for the most part. Here it is. Sangria, which seems to change every time Maria makes it. Probably has to do with what fruit is available. Here try this, Darlin'."

He handed Callie a cup holding a wine mixture with a beautiful bouquet of citrus, cherry, and could that be peach?

"Mmmmmm. That's just downright pretty," she said closing her eyes and concentrating on all the different flavors hitting her tongue at once. "I'll need to get a recipe for this. It makes me think of long warm summer nights, barefoot in the grass…."

"Skinny dipping?" teased Seth with that gorgeous grin flashing at Callie.

"I don't have any memories of skinny dipping, sir. The nuns frowned on such undertakings, although I do remember some of the boys one summer getting caught swimming and brought back by a constable."

"Sounds like skinny dippin', to me," he said with a smile. "Try some of these beef pieces wrapped in a tortilla, one of my favorites."

Callie tried some of everything and took Seth's suggestions as to how to eat the various items, as well.

"Do you think the meat in these enchiladas is goat? It doesn't seem to taste like beef," stated Callie trying to decipher the little corn wrapped parcels.

"It wouldn't be the first time she fed me goat," replied Seth dryly. "But don't let the hands know or they'll never let me live it down." And he laughed watching her expression change to worry.

The food was good but a little hot for Callie's inexperienced pallet and she found drinking the refreshing sangria helped alleviate the intensity of heat on her tongue. Soon she found herself exceedingly happy with the food, the day, and especially Seth.

"Tell me about the man you used to live with," Seth said casually.

Confused Callie asked, "The man I used to live with? Oh, Chef Pasqual? He is the most marvelous man, generous and probably saved my life. He took me home and his wife, Lizette, opened her house and her heart to me."

Seth was surprised by her answer. Herbert had made it sound as if she had lived with a single man for the last few years. "He had a wife? Tell me how you two met."

"I had gotten too old to be kept on at St Michaels so I was 'graduated'. The nuns sent me to accompany the orphans who were to go on the train to the western states and territories. I didn't know any of them. None of the children were from St Michaels. The sisters there never let any of us be adopted if they couldn't check out the couple first. Chef Pasqual came into the train car looking for a sturdy boy to do the washing of the pots and pans at the hotel's restaurant he managed. All there was left was me - a scrawny, too small, female. He must have felt sorry for me, well, I know he did. I heard him tell Lizette that was why she found me in her kitchen."

She looked chagrined as she spoke. "Lizette never argued with Pierre so I was taken in and treated like their own daughters who are only a couple of years younger than me. I miss them terribly but we write and someday we may meet again."

"So, you did end up doing the pot scrubbing?"

"Yep, that's how I started." She began wrapping up some of the food. "A few weeks later, one of the head cooks cut his hand severely and Chef Pasqual was busy trying to stop the bleeding. With him busy, the food on the stove was going to burn. The entire staff had been preparing for a large dinner party due to begin in less than half an hour. There wouldn't be time to remake all the soup and sauces. I couldn't do anything to help the injured cook but I could keep the food from being ruined."

She shrugged. "I took over watching the cream soup and kept the sauces from breaking, which means they would separate and turn lumpy. When the kitchen got back to normal, Chef Pasqual was impressed with my ability and decided I might be of more use becoming a line cook. Later I became the only female sous chef in the hotel's history. I made history and I'm proud of it."

"Then what happened?" His brows drew down in confusion. "Why are you cooking for a bunch of ranch hands?"

She didn't want to think about that part of her life. It was still painful but less so now that she had landed at the Harrison ranch. She was feeling more and more at home here although he would need to hear it at some point and it may as well be from her. "That was due to a series of half-truths and ugly rumors. I was accused of using my womanly wiles to get Chef Pasqual to give me promotions that I wasn't qualified to receive. Passing up men in the kitchen who should have my job some people thought. They said I was living with him."

Callie fumed remembering the unfairness of the accusations. "I was young enough to be his daughter let alone that Pierre was not that kind of man. He loves his wife and he loves his daughters and my being there was making that all seem wrong. I told him to fire me and I went looking for a different job, away from the politics of a large dining room kitchen. That's the story. Not very exciting and not very pretty, I'm afraid." She finished the last bite of filled tortilla and drank another large gulp of sangria

"Well, I for one can testify that I've had your cooking and it's better than what I get in any of the fancy hotel restaurants in the cities of Kansas or Topeka," he assured her.

Callie smiled her thanks and raised her empty glass in salute.

They had packed away all the food except the second jar of sangria. That was simply too good to put away, yet. Callie watched as the tall lean man beside her stretched out on his side of the blanket tipping his Stetson down over his eyes.

"Are you planning on taking a nap and miss enjoying this gorgeous day?" she asked incredulously.

"No, Darlin', I'm going to enjoy this gorgeous day by taking a nap." And his lips quirked into a teasing grin.

"Hmmm. Maybe you're right." Callie lay down on her back then turned toward Seth and complained, "But I got a lumpy spot." Wiggling over to lie against Seth's side, she snuggled into his warmth, which was redundant considering the blistering sunshine.

Seth didn't move. He barely breathed. When he finally heard the even breathing of Callie sleeping, he exhaled a whoosh of air he had been holding. Damn, this was going to be a long day. First, he had to try to ignore Callie's cute little behind rubbing his nether regions all the way here. Of course, his nether regions had not ignored her. The rocking of Lothario's gait had added to the intriguing feeling of almost having sex without all the fun.

He had a difficult time concentrating on the scenery

and points of interest all the while wanting to tear Callie's clothes off and have his way with her. Now he has the opportunity to do just that and he pretends to be asleep.

When Seth woke up, he was wrapped around Callie's small form. She must have moved in her sleep because now she was practically flat against his stomach and, considering the degree of his arousal, had been there for quite a while.

Just then, her head tipped up and a small, welcoming smile appeared, as she said quietly, "Hi."

That's all it took. Seth slid down to be face to face and took her lips in a long sought-after kiss. He drank from her lips like his life depended on it, as if it had been too long since receiving succor.

Callie opened her mouth to accept the warm tongue seeking entrance. She snuggled against Seth, trying to get closer and Seth reveled in that closeness. This was part of his fantasy, lying close to Callie, alone without the possibility of interruptions and kissing her soft swollen lips.

This close to Seth's chest, Callie worked her hands between the buttons so she could feel the hair roughened skin, warm and inviting. Her hands traveled further and wanted Seth to mimic her movements.

He soon got the silent message and slowly opened the buttons down the front of her shirtwaist, giving her time to stop him if that was her wish. It may kill him but he would stop if she wanted. When the shirtwaist was opened, Seth cupped one blossoming breast through the camisole. It was made of some sheer material and trimmed with lace and frustrated Seth because he couldn't find a way through it and he really wanted through it to her soft skin.

Driven by sheer desire, Seth placed his mouth over the budding tip and let his moist warmth bring a moan from Callie as she arched to give him access to both breasts. Seth again took her cue and paid homage first to one than the other but his ministrations always left one breast cooling while the other sought his attention. Seth covered one nubbin with the palm of his hand and massaged it with a small circular motion. The other he devoted his tongue and mouth to.

Callie was starting to show signs of uncontrollable lust. She had placed one leg over Seth's hip and struggled to get her lower portion closer to his. Too close if this was supposed to be just some light petting session. Seth never thought it would go farther than that. He wasn't prepared to go much further than that and he wasn't sure Callie was either, no matter what her body was telling his at the moment.

Taking his hand and mouth off Callie's breasts, he tried to cover them with the sides of her shirtwaist. He remained close to her, kissing her lips and eyes and neck but he tried not to respond to her rubbing her body against his. Did not respond with anything like his body was screaming for him to do, at least.

"Callie," he said softly. "Darlin', it's getting late. We have to get going or it will be dark before we get home."

Callie looked up at him with heavy lidded eyes and soft pouty lips, trying to make sense of where she was. Sitting up, holding the front of her shirtwaist together she blinked saying, "Oh, yes, sorry. I must have fallen asleep." She looked down so he couldn't read any emotions on her face.

"I'll get Lothario." He could have whistled. The horse was trained to come on command but Seth felt Callie needed time to recover herself. Hell, he needed time to recover himself.

It wasn't going to be easy to forget how willingly she came into his arms and how generous she was in her responses to him. It boded well for their future together but it was going to be hell on his control today.

He walked Lothario over to where Callie stood with the now folded blanket and saddlebag, which Seth took from her. Lifting her onto the horse by her waist, he mounted the saddle behind her. Although Seth could tell Callie was trying to sit straighter, her hip was resting against his appendage that had already taken about as much as it could without bursting.

Seth tried counting backwards from one thousand but that was too easy and not taking up enough of his thoughts so he listed the reasons for not making love fully with Callie. The main reason was that it might make her run and he may never find her again. That possible loss was what kept his hands on the reins and his mind on anything but Callie.

CHAPTER 8

Callie left Seth taking care of Lothario in the stable and had gotten to the cookhouse in time to find Jamie serving the jambalaya and corn bread. The dessert would be a smorgasbord of left-over sweets from the week. This was a good meal to use up the little bits and pieces that didn't make it into the soups. Callie tried to concentrate on anything besides what was uppermost in her mind. Fearing Seth would come to say goodnight, she felt she couldn't face him in front of the others.

She declined a plate saying she had eaten too much of Maria's good cooking but in reality, she wanted to be alone to think more about what had occurred that afternoon. What she had let occur. The nuns had been very free with their warnings for young girls overcome by their emotions. Many of the orphans were the outcome of just such loss of control.

Laying on her bed, she had more opportunity to think about her actions. In her youth and ignorance, Callie had nodded and agreed that there would be nothing worse than to be overcome by such passion and produce a child that wasn't wanted by its parents. The nuns had not been specific as to what constituted such behavior but they seemed to think that all young girls would recognize it when it happened. But the nuns also insinuated that it was something men did to, and not with, girls. It was a non-participation event, something that was done to them not with them.

Callie had definitely been a participant. She might even be considered the instigator. After all, Seth was sleeping and she practically crawled into his trousers. It was humiliating to think how she had thrown herself at him. Should she apologize? How does one go about doing that? A formal letter saying that although she deeply enjoyed what he did to her body, she is apologizing for forcing him to pleasure her?

Callie turned into her pillow, chagrinned. How was she to face him? She let him suckle like a babe at her breast and she had enjoyed it - a lot. And worse, he knew it. He was the one who finally called a halt to the - what would it be called, her deflowering? His deflowering?

Oh, Callie, she thought to herself, you are never, never to drink sangria again.

Leaning against Lothario's neck as he finished brushing him down, Seth asked, "Is this the way it always goes if she refuses you? Doesn't present? I'm sorry I put you through this pain." He gave a last unconscious pat to the horse's rump as he locked the gate behind himself.

He walked towards the house but he was looking toward the cookhouse. If he saw Callie in the dining room he would go over and nonchalantly ask her to go for an evening walk. He wanted to explain away today. He wanted her to know he didn't expect anything more from her. He wanted her to know he didn't expect it to happen again. He wanted her to know that he didn't think this meant she had made up her mind about him.

But he didn't see a sign of Callie, only Jamie at the sink. Damn, he really wanted to talk with her before she talked herself into running. She hadn't said anything on the ride back and Seth didn't know what to say. He felt she was in a fragile condition and didn't understand fully what had happened between them. He didn't know if he would be any good at explaining it but at least he could convince her it was natural and normal and not anything to be frightened about. At least not with him.

Daylight couldn't come soon enough but Seth didn't think sleep was going to help him pass the time any faster.

Seth was awake and as soon as the lamp's light showed through the cookhouse windows, he was off his porch and eating up the space between with long strides. He stopped short when he saw Jamie standing by the counter cutting biscuits. Callie was at the stove and she looked up when she heard the door open. She gave him a pleading expression.

"Can you find time to talk with me later, Miss Callie?" He asked as Callie nodded silently and Seth left to return to the house.

He had given Callie the time she asked for but was worried she would choose to do something rash the longer he let her think. He knew she would understand his motives when he explained he was serious about a relationship between them. Although it happened faster than even he could believe, he wanted to marry her, to be her family, to take care of her the rest of his life.

Deciding it was time for them to talk, he stalked through the house in time to hear the buckboard coming through the gate. As he looked toward the cookhouse, he saw Callie standup and give a squeal. She ran toward the buckboard, which was now stopped and threw herself into the arms of a young man who had jumped down from the seat and readily picked her up spinning her around.

By the time Seth got to the wagon, it was moving

off toward the barn leaving Callie and the stranger, a rather handsome stranger if Seth were to be truthful. Black wavy hair with startlingly blue eyes and dimples, hell, what real man has dimples? And dressed like a city slicker right down to the derby. They still stood with their arms around each other's waist. There were tears running down Callie's cheeks but they were tears of joy. She was simply beaming with delight.

Seth lost his breath looking at her. She was glowing with happiness. He didn't believe he had ever seen her so contented.

"Seth, Jamie, this is Matthew St Michaels," introduced Callie. "We haven't seen one another for years. He tracked me down and decided he has a few days to catch up with me about all the others." She turned back to the smiling stranger and sighed, "Oh, Matthew, it is so good to see you. I missed you so much. How long can you stay?"

"Only a few days this time. I'm lucky I caught a ride with Sully. When I asked around town about how I could get out to the Harrison ranch, someone yelled over to the dry goods store. The next thing I know, I'm on my way here to you," said the young man with a big smile meant only for Callie.

"I'm sure there's an empty bunk in with the hands. I'll check with Sully," she said.

"No need." stated Seth. "There's plenty of room at the ranch house."

"We don't want to put you to any trouble," Callie responded somewhat shyly he thought.

"No trouble. Just drop your bag off up to the house. Maria will be glad to have someone else to mother." Starting to continue to the stables, he spoke to Matthew,

"I'll see you later this evening then."

When Seth reached the stables, he turned enough to see Callie and Matthew going into the cookhouse and Jamie heading for the barn. Damn, they'll be alone for hours. How was he going to speak with Callie if he can't get her to himself? At least he'll be able to keep his eye on Matthew. If he didn't show up tonight at a decent time, he'd go down to the cookhouse and find him. He wasn't a light sleeper for nothing. He might even set up a trap that would let him know if Matthew tried to sneak out during the night, too.

Matthew and Callie talked over each other just as they had since childhood. Finishing each other's sentences and beginning thoughts that the other had only just begun. Callie put Matthew to work peeling potatoes while she got the chicken ready for the oven. Rubbing the poultry with sage and other spices, she was full of questions.

Callie said again, "I really needed to talk with you, Matthew. You've always been so grounded and knew what you wanted out of life."

Matthew looked closely at Callie and could tell she had something important weighing her down. He said quietly, "You know you can tell me anything. I won't judge and I won't scold. What's happening?"

"I'm attracted to Seth," she almost whispered.

"I can understand that. He's a good-looking man, if you like the type. And he owns this whole big ranch and, I think, he kind of likes you, too."

"Do you really think so? That's part of the problem. I don't know if he's merely bored and I'm the only single female around or if he is getting serious or even could ever be serious."

Matthew had stopped peeling potatoes and asked intently, "Has it come to that? Or is there a problem that it will come to that?"

Callie understood what 'that' was. "I don't think so. I mean I like what we've done so far. But I don't know if that means I am falling in love with him or if I'm maybe like my mother."

Callie looked so forlorn Matthew got up from the table and walked over to her.

Holding her in his arms, Matthew felt all the old protective instincts come forward in a rush. Callie didn't deserve to be hurt and especially not by a selfish son-of-a-bitch that couldn't see what a jewel he had the possibility of possessing.

"I've been with a few women. Most I've had strong feelings for but for one reason or another it didn't work out for us. It didn't matter to me if they were virgins or not, hell, I sure wasn't one. But I know how you were brought up and I don't think you could give yourself to a man and then let him walk away. I think it would break you into a million pieces. I think it's alright to fool around a little, kiss and pet, heck even show a little skin to each other. But until you have a commitment from the man, I recommend that you remain faithful to staying chaste."

Rocking Callie back and forth, Matthew gave her a kiss on the temple. Then said as he let her go, "Anything you do would be forgiven. You've got all those good deeds stored up for just this kind of stormy day."

Trying to get back to a normal conversation since Jamie could come in any time, Matthew said, "I can't believe you're making eggs Benedict for these guys.

They really are eating high off the hog."

Callie must have thought so too and replied "Well, it became a favorite of Pierre's when he worked at the Delmonico and as sous chef, I made the Hollandaise for everything. It really isn't all that difficult and I enjoy making less common dishes. I have to keep my talents fresh. I made quiche Loraine' last week" She laughed at Matthews mock look of horror.

"How did that go over?" he asked with a grin.

"I had to tell some of them it was egg pie and then everyone was fine with it."

Seth spent the day doing unnecessary physical labor that usually was done by the lowest man on the totem pole or one who had gotten in Sully's bad books. Sweat was dripping off Seth's chin when he heard Callie cooing to Lothario. Wiping his face off with his shirtsleeves, he rolled them down as he went through the door to the paddock that held Lothario.

"Be careful, he's been known to bite strangers," Seth warned Matthew when he saw who accompanied Callie.

"Oh, not this gentle beauty," replied Callie rubbing Lothario's nose and allowing him to lip her neck with his soft mouth, contentment written all over the big horse's half-closed eyes.

Seth looked at his horse and thought, with derision, 'what a smitten beast'. Then realized he was actually jealous of Lothario. He could nuzzle and kiss Callie, right here in the open and she allowed it, even encouraged it, yet Seth couldn't get close enough to talk with her.

He was annoyed with his horse's attraction to Callie,

with Matthew's closeness to Callie and with Callie for keeping Seth at arms' length. But most of all with himself because he would allow it to happen as long as Callie was happy.

He nodded as he left the paddock heading for the ranch house. He thought it best to stay away from the newcomer or possibly end up saying something he would regret. Well, maybe not regret exactly but something that would disappoint Callie with him. He would rather not do that. Not while he was so unsure of her feelings. The last thing he wanted was to need to chase after her if she decided to leave with her 'old friend'.

Seth had planned on staying away from the cookhouse. He came in and Maria had left a dinner he didn't touch. Instead he went directly into the bathing room to wash the stink of sweat and manure off himself.

The water didn't have to be cold, thank God, since all his thoughts of Callie that day had to do with worry rather than lust. Who exactly was this Matthew St Michaels? Had they been married? Cousins? Certainly not brother and sister, she was from a foundling home. The foundling home - that has to be their connection.

Raised together? Probably, but that doesn't mean he could discount that there wasn't a sexual attraction, a bond in place over years of living together. Damn, he wished he had asked more questions about her years at the home, but there hadn't seemed to be an urgency to know everything right away. He had thought they had time to get to know each other. Maybe he had waited too late.

Seth went down for dinner at the cookhouse and smiled and talked with the men in line and then sat at the table where Matthew had taken a seat.

"Tell me a little about yourself, Matt. I can call you Matt, can't I," asked Seth sociably.

Nodding, Matt replied pleasantly, "Well, there isn't much to tell. I'm a pretty plain living guy. Not too much to know."

"I find that hard to believe. After all, you were able to find Callie way out here. That must mean something," said Seth affably.

"Oh, that. We both keep in touch with Mother Superior Mary Margaret, one-time Sister Mary Margaret, and she keeps track of everyone. I don't know how the woman does it. She must have some kind of system but she always knows where everyone is and what they're doing," he said smiling. "Now that I think of it, that isn't too different from when we were children."

"So, you wrote to this Mother Mary Margaret and she sent you here?" asked Seth nonchalantly.

"Well, she sent me to a Chef Pasqual in St Louis. I knew Callie was in the city but I was trying to give her some room to grow. Make life what she wanted for a change and not needing to worry about someone else. Pasqual was hesitant to tell me at first but then realized the relationship between Callie and me and told me about her accepting this job. I was going to be traveling up to Topeka so I took this detour to stop and see Callie."

"That's some detour. And a trip to St Louis? Must have taken you a lot of time and money just to see an old friend," Seth said conversationally pretending to enjoy what he knew was a deliciously roasted chicken and stuffing that tasted like sawdust in his mouth.

"Well, Callie's more than an old friend. I mean, you see her. She's beautiful. And such a sweet person. I've never met anyone with a more generous and open heart. She's going to make a wonderful mother. She was made to have a family. We used to dream about one day having big families and dozens of kids. Probably because we couldn't visualize anything less to make a family. I think we both have gotten a more realistic number of children in mind now," Matthew told the other man, watching Seth's reaction.

Seth didn't have a comeback for anything Matt had just said. Did the other man and Callie really have an agreement to marry and raise a large family? Does she melt in that man's arms like she had in Seth's?

Matt seemed satisfied with Seth's reaction and said, "Callie sure hasn't lost her touch with a roasted chicken and these livers and onions are so moist. Usually, they come out dry and tough when anyone else tries to cook them." He took another healthy mouthful smiling around the fork tines.

Seth took a bite of the food but it all tasted like dust. He had lost his appetite the more he spoke with the other man. Matt seemed like a nice guy and he had a history with Callie. She seemed happy with Matt and she had never committed herself to Seth in any way. Just a little heavy petting that Seth could see she regretted immediately.

Seth finished his meal and left before dessert was served. He left without thanking Callie for a good meal, which was unlike his usual habit. He did make a point of telling Matt he'd see him up to the house and emphasized how people working on a ranch went to bed early since they got up so early. Matt seemed acceptable to those rules.

CHAPTER 9

Matt was up early the next morning heading for the cookhouse and Callie. The coffee was already made and thick cut bacon sizzled in the pan. Callie brushed back a wisp of hair from her forehead with the back of her hand and gave him a little kiss on his cheek.

"Everything smells great as usual. You know you're too good of cook for these cowboys. Come back with me and I'll help you get a situation at one of the hotels or dining rooms in the City of Kansas. It's a thriving city and there must be dozens of places looking for talented chefs," urged Matt.

"Matthew, I am content here and these men are as deserving as the next hungry man whether it be here or the City of Kansas. Besides, you said you will be relocating further west with this promotion," she reminded him.

"I know, but I would take you with me. I just feel you're not as happy here as you thought you'd be. I can't stand to think of you unhappy and alone way out here."

"That's pure cupboard love talking. Besides, I am hardly alone. There are over twenty men in here at least twice a day."

"Yeah, but that's just it, men. You have no women to talk with. Who do you gossip with?" he teased.

"I've never had many women friends. They kept getting adopted or married it seems. There are a couple of younger women here I would like to meet. One is marrying the neighbor and I'm baking her wedding cake and the other owns a dress shop in town. I simply haven't gotten around to knowing my schedule yet. I'll find time to visit and I write Mother Superior and Lizette, Pierre's wife. She has always treated me well."

"The offer stands," he said as Jamie entered the kitchen's side door with more wood.

Matthew St Michaels, the sleeves rolled up on his ironed shirt and leather boots only a city slicker would wear, highly polished and devoid of a scuff on them anywhere, crossed the dusty compound. He entered the barn but saw his target in the dim light immediately. Walking over to a stall, he placed one booted foot on the lower railing. Seth was brushing a piebald and didn't stop although he knew Matt stood there.

Matt said in a friendly manner, "Callie is making pies and helping Jamie with his reading so I told her I would take a walk. I'll be leaving in the morning to catch the train and Sully offered a ride since he was going in anyway. In case I didn't see you again, I thought I would thank you for the hospitality."

Seth didn't reply but kept brushing the mare's long tail so Matt continued, "And to warn you if you hurt Callie in any way, I'll be back to knock your block off and take Callie away with me."

At that statement, Seth stopped brushing a moment but then continued as if nothing untoward had been said.

Matt had more to say though. "She's the most beautiful woman in the world and I'd marry her in an instant if I thought she would think of me in that way. I could change her mind but I'm not sure it would make her happy right now. She's unhappy. I can tell. And confused and a little afraid, of herself I think, but you're the cause of it. Callie is the sort of girl that believes in the vows to honor, obey, and love. They were brow-beat into us by the nuns. I want you to do the honorable thing and walk away from her if you're not serious. If you don't love her."

"What's love got to do with it?" asked Seth still brushing the docile horse.

"Callie spent her whole childhood in the foundling home hoping to get adopted by a loving family. I saw her hopes get crushed more than a hundred times and I swore she would never feel alone or unloved as long as I was alive."

He stopped again as if readying himself to hear it all. "Why wasn't she adopted?"

"Because people are hypocrites. Saying they simply want a child to love but really meaning they only want a perfect child to love. A red-headed runt with a limp didn't qualify. Sometimes the nuns took her with the other girls her age to parade in front of prospective parents, you know, just so she didn't feel left out but after a while Callie accepted, she wouldn't be adopted." Matt sighed heavily. "I told her I was glad since that meant we would be together always because I was never going to be adopted either. Once a boy was over three or four, they were pretty much going to live out their youth at the foundling home. But she cried. It broke my heart then, and it still does now."

"Yeah, I know. What about those orphan trains I heard about?" asked Seth glad that Callie never got sent on one.

"Mother Superior was very particular about the placement of 'her children.' She vetted every couple and made sure they had a good Catholic upbringing. She refused to even allow the kind of people that sorted through the foundling homes looking for pretty little girls and handsome, feminine looking boys. Obtaining new blood for the brothels is only one dirty little secret that the public is kept ignorant about. Mother Superior was very street wise and, now that I'm older, I think there was much more to her story than we, as orphans, ever guessed."

Seth had gotten angry listening to Matt talk about Callie's life and the possibility that some unscrupulous person would prey on helpless children, prey on a child without the protection of a family. The horse lifted its leg in protest at the agitated brushing. Seth returned to reality and patted the mare in apology. He turned to the next horse waiting for his attention.

Matt assured Seth, "Whatever lucky fella puts a ring on her finger, Callie will have to love."

"But what exactly is love?" asked Seth exasperated and surprised that he had spoken out loud. Asked this stranger who he wanted to be rid of not bond with.

"Beats me. Kind of like an orgasm, I guess." Then explained at Seth's stunned look, "You know, hard to describe but you sure as hell know when you've had one."

Matt continued, "Look, I sort of like you, Seth. I know that Callie more than sort of likes you. If you don't come up to the mark, I'll ask her to marry me and keep asking until she does." With that he turned and left Seth thinking…about a lot of things.

That evening after dinner, Callie announced it was Jamie's birthday. Sully had already spread the word and there were little gifts, some wrapped and some not, on one of the side tables. There was also a frosted cake with Jamie's name written in yellow frosting on top. Jamie was a little embarrassed by all the attention but took it all in good grace as each man gave his congratulations.

Seth was a little late but when he entered, he set a cowpony saddle on the table next to the cake. Jamie's eyes got wide as he asked, "F-for me?"

"All yours, Jamie. I know you've been saving to buy a horse so you can go out with the other hands someday but you can use your new saddle to practice with the ranch horses until you do."

Callie blinked the tears from her eyes. No need to embarrass Jamie any more than he was already. Having a weeping woman bawling all over him wouldn't make anyone think of him as a grown man. She sniffed and grabbed hold of Matthew's hand and squeezed. He returned the squeeze, knowing she was happy for Jamie and this milestone in his life.

"Callie told me to choose a last n-name so I thought about it. Her and I have b-been reading about history and I want to be Jamie Franklin. B-Benjamin Franklin started out doing all sorts of things like p-politics and writer and p-postmaster." A round of applause went up. "Th-thanks for everything. I-I really like all my g-gifts. And I'll sh-share my cake." He grinned at them all.

The ranch hands all laughed and went to get some plates while Callie said there was pie as well for anyone.

Matt helped Callie with cutting and serving the pie and sometime during the commotion of cake cutting and pie serving, Seth disappeared from the dining room.

The next morning, Seth watched from the front window as Callie hugged then kissed Matthew goodbye. Oh, not a mushy, tongue in the mouth kiss. After all, Sully and Jamie were both standing there but a kiss nonetheless. Callie stood and waved until the wagon was through the gate and out of sight.

Then he watched as she bent her head, picking up the end of her apron to wipe her eyes. Seth wanted to run to her and hold her and tell her she wasn't alone. But according to Matt that wasn't what she wanted to hear. She wanted to have someone tell her he loved her. Could Seth ever be that man?

He watched till Callie limped up the step and across the porch through the door of the cookhouse. Then he turned and headed to the office. He had some work to do and a lot of thinking. He still ached for Callie. Still dreamt of her soft small body beneath his, still smelled her hair, her scent in his room, on his pillow although she had never been there.

Seth didn't understand how he could lust after Callie but not know if he could love her? Lust wasn't love, he understood that. But what was this allusive thing that people everywhere seemed to spend their whole lives searching for and never finding? Or maybe they do.

His parents seemed to have gotten along very well. He never heard a cross word between them and his father grieved, silently and privately when Seth's mother passed away. But was that love? He wished his mother were alive so he could ask her or even his father. He supposed at this age he would be able to talk with his father about such intimate subjects - or maybe not.

Wishing he had been older before his father passed and able to talk to the man about his feelings for Seth's mother wasn't going to be of help, now. Did two people know they were in love and then marry or did love come simply by marrying someone. Out here in the west he knew of many who married simply because it was easier. A man needed a wife and family to make it out here.

Couples married for a lot of reasons and love didn't seem to come into play in most of those marriages he knew about. Having sons to help with the land, to take it over when the father became too old to keep it up alone. The same seemed to be true for daughters. They tended to be the ones who helped the aged parents when the time came. Those were the reasons he knew for getting married. Solid, un-emotional reasons to tie yourself forever with someone.

Seth understood a parents' love and a child's love but not a wife and husband kind of love. He was attracted to Callie and wanted her in a way only a husband should. But did that mean he should marry her? Tie them to one another for the rest of their lives? That was a commitment he wasn't sure he could do. Could live up to.

He could ask Sully but Sully's experience with the ladies was pretty slim to none and he'd just warn him not to hurt Callie. Hell, Seth didn't want to hurt Callie or make her go running to Matt. So, where did that leave Seth?

Stepping toward the cookhouse, Seth hoped to find Callie alone but he heard her talking with someone before he got to the doorway.

"Okay, hold it like this, firmly, then with pressure lift it up then down, up then down, that's right. It's all in the pressure. The movements change according to the petals you're making." Callie smiled as she looked up from the frosting flower she was making with Jamie when she heard footsteps on the porch.

Callie's smile disappeared quickly but Seth wasn't going to let that distract him. "I just wanted to tell you I thought your, er, Matt was a nice guy. I'm glad he could find the time to stop by for a visit."

Callie smiled at Matt's name as Seth thought she would as she said, "No matter how long it's been between seeing each other, we start up right where we left off. As if time didn't count."

Jamie called for her attention and asked, "I-is this right?"

"Very good, just keep practicing. You don't want to know how many times I scraped the frosting off and did it all over again." She laughed then turned back to Seth.

"I'm starting the flowers for the Gregg's wedding cake." Since there was no reaction from Seth, she continued slightly more relaxed, "I make them ahead so they will dry and harden a little so they are easier to work with when I place them on the cake. Of course, Jamie wanted to try his hand at them. He actually catches on very quickly."

She smiled fondly at her pupil. "We will have to store them well away from the stove or they'll melt. I can't put them in the cold storage because they can also absorb odors and we don't want onion flavored flowers."

"You can store them at the house," offered Seth.

"No, I think my bedroom will be far enough away. I need to paint them with a food dye so I'll want them close," she explained.

"Are you all set with transportation to the Gregg's ranch?" he asked solicitously.

"I am packing everything up as well as possible and Jamie is driving me over in the buckboard. Then helping me to assemble the layers and do the final trim."

"Sounds like quite the undertaking. If I can help, let me know," Seth added sounding unsure of what he could do to help.

Callie let out a sigh after Seth had left. That went much better than she had feared. Maybe things would get back to normal and she could stop worrying about how to leave the ranch.

CHAPTER 10

There was a light tap on the bathing room door. Callie had finished rinsing the soap out of her hair and was submerged in bathwater that had turned milky from the suds.

"I'm in the tub. You'll have to wait a few minutes," she called out.

Seth replied, "I know. I just want to help you wash your back." And waited expectantly for her answer.

"I don't think that's such a good idea, Seth. I don't think the nuns would approve that activity at all. In fact, I know they wouldn't," she answered breathlessly.

"Come on, no one will know and I'm certainly not gonna tell the nuns," he teased.

"The door is locked and I'm all wet," she replied reasonably.

"Then it's just as well that I have a key."

Callie heard the key turn in the lock and the door open behind her. She gave a squeak and hunched forward submerging her naked breasts.

Walking to the stove, Seth ladled more hot water into the tub, warming the cooling bath. He silently went to the end of the tub and picked up the damp sponge sitting on the wooden ledge.

Squeezing the sponge several times, he said, "I like this thing. I may have to get me one for myself." Lowering the sponge into the warm bath water, he lifted it to squeeze the water down Callie's back. He took the bar of soap and rubbed it against the sponge to build up the lather and washed Callie's back going slowly over every inch all the way to the water and lower.

She shivered but not because she was chilled. In fact, she would say the opposite was probably closer to the truth. Saying in a weak voice, "I don't think you should be in here. I can wash my own back."

Seth leaned over and whispered in her ear, "But I can do it so much better." And began a trail of kisses and nips down her neck to her still damp shoulder.

Callie instinctively raised her head to allow him access to her throat so the kisses and nibbles could continue to the other side as well, as Seth accommodated her.

Startled when Seth began sponging first one breast then the other, she tried to slip further under the water, but that didn't stop Seth from his ministrations. Instead, Seth's mouth left Callie's neck and began to feast on her lips.

Callie moaned, which was almost Seth's undoing. He was glad his trousers were taut against his raging arousal, held in check by his position and the way the material stretched tightly across his pelvis.

"Please don't moan, Darlin', it's gonna un-man me," whispered Seth into her mouth as his head descended. He again covered her lips with his own, allowing his tongue to taste the warmth within.

Seth slid the sponge from the well-cleansed breasts lower to parts that had yet to have his attention. The first, almost tentative wipes of his hands near the junction of her thighs was with the sponge as a protective shield between his skin and her most intimate part. Then the sponge was floating and Seth had renewed the movement letting his hand slide easily into her satin channel and nearly entering her body.

Callie tried to rally herself. "I am sure this is something the nuns would not approve." She added breathlessly, "Are we about to commit a sin?"

With a chuckle, Seth answered, "Not exactly, Darlin'. I'll let you know when we're about to sin." His lips brushed her skin. "In fact, you'll be the first to know." He returned to kissing her mouth and allowing his fingers to rub, back and forth, over a most interesting nub.

Seth continued thrusting his tongue into Callie's mouth, imitating what he really wanted to be doing to her and risking embarrassing himself. He couldn't prevent his hand from its mission. He had the honor of watching Callie's face, eyes closed, two front teeth over-lapping her lower lip to silence a moan that escaped anyway.

Her body stiffened with her climax and then her eyes opened in amazement, gazing directly into Seth's, before becoming slumberous.

She whispered her small question, "Are you sure that wasn't a sin?"

Seth couldn't stop himself from kissing her deeply as he calmed her with gentle rubs of his hand against her mound.

Taking his last kiss, he said, "You better get out of this water or you're going to get pruney. I'll see you tomorrow. Don't overthink what happened tonight, Darlin'. Everything will be all right. I promise." Standing with difficulty, he left.

Callie took a moment to return to reality. She tried to standup but her legs wouldn't obey so she waited a moment then tried again. As she reached for the towel on the bench, she kept reliving what had occurred. It started out so innocently. Helping her wash her back but then…then what happened? Was that what the older girls used to giggle about? What they used to tease the boys about? She had never understood them at the time.

No wonder people sinned so much. Callie wasn't stupid. Anything that felt that good between a man and a woman must be a sin. She would need to pray on this for forgiveness. She had never meant to sin with Seth. She would pray for his eternal soul, too.

Dressing quickly, Callie cleaned up the bathing room. She didn't want Maria to ask any questions in the morning.

Seth sat in the dark office going over what had just happened. It had all started with his sitting at this damn desk listening to Callie get ready for her bath. He could practically hear her unbutton each button on that damn drab uniform. The sigh as her camisole was pulled up over her head. The stockings being rolled down, one by one, until he knew she stood there naked for him to see if he only took the chance, the chance that she wouldn't turn him away.

And he had been right. She had been ready for another lesson in making love. Hell, he certainly had been. This night was going to haunt him far longer than her simple flowery scent had. The feel of his hands sliding over her water-slicked skin and then the expression on her face as she reached her pinnacle. Such awe and amazement of her first, he'd bet his life on it, orgasm.

Seth heard Callie leave and waited a few minutes to make sure she wasn't coming back for something she had forgotten. His shirtsleeves were wet past his elbows and he didn't even want to think about the wetness of his trousers. Well, a cold bath wouldn't be needed tonight although his penis hadn't given up hope all together. Seth hadn't had this problem since he had wet dreams as a raw boy. He went into the bathing room to clean himself up. Chagrined, he peeled off his trousers and started pumping cold water into the big copper tub once again.

Callie lay in her bed, a rosary clutched in her hands. What exactly had Seth done to her? It was beyond wonderful in one way and terribly embarrassing in another. To let someone, a man, touch her like that and then to let all reason and training and control go. To allow a man such intimate knowledge of her body's response. How did he know she would like it, enjoy it so much? Seth hadn't been surprised as she had. She realized he had been working toward that very outcome.

His promise that everything would be all right. What did that mean? Did he think he was going to get to do this again? That she was going to let him have such liberties again? And what if she did? What did he get out of it except to have control over her? She wished she had someone to ask but she knew even if she were back with the nuns, they wouldn't be much help. Callie fell asleep before she had completed one Hail Mary.

Callie and Jamie pulled up to the Gregg's ranch house about an hour after breakfast. Getting down from the wagon's seat, she met Mr Gregg as he came out of the house to greet her.

A pretty, blond woman with bright-blue eyes followed him out exclaiming, "I'm Julia Minor, soon to be Gregg, and you must be, Callie. May I call you,

Callie? It is so nice to talk with another woman. Well, my mother and sister are here for the wedding but they will be leaving tomorrow and we," here she blushed slightly, "Ben and I will be off on a trip to San Francisco. I am so excited. I told Sully that you didn't need to bring the cake over. I could have sent one of the men to get it. You've already done so much by agreeing to bake it." Julia finally came to a stop to take a breath.

Callie laughed at the other woman's exuberance. "Well, it is going to take a little while to assemble so if you can show me where you want it set up, Jamie and I can get started and then get out of your way."

"Oh, no," Julia pleaded. "Please stay for the wedding. I don't have many friends here and I want to count you as one of them. It's not going to be ornate but I would love for you to stay. There will be music afterwards. And, of course, cake."

Callie had worn her best plaid dress with short jacket over it, the green hat with the little brown bird that Jamie seemed intrigued with, and gloves. The same as if she had known ahead of time so agreed that she could stay. Supper had been planned and there was enough time to put in an appearance before heading for home.

Removing her hat and gloves, Callie slipped an apron over her dress as she directed Jamie with moving the largest part of the cake. After setting the other two white frosted layers in place, Callie stirred the colored frosting again to get it ready to be piped over seams between the layers. She used the green frosting to draw vines and leaves that would 'hold' the pre-made roses.

Jamie watched every movement and interspersed questions with words of awe at the design being created right in front of his eyes and seemingly without a pattern.

When the cake was adorned with the piping, frosting ribbons, and vines, Callie carefully un-wrapped the pink and yellow roses that she and Jamie had made and placed them gently in the nest of leaves made for them on the cake. A spun sugar heart was placed on the top tier and then Callie backed up to look over her work.

"Miss Callie, I've never seen anything so beautiful in my life," said Jamie breathlessly, his eyes never leaving the cake.

Callie smiled with tears in her eyes. It was the first sentence Jamie had ever said to her that he hadn't stammered.

Not wishing to make him self-conscious, she replied, "Why, thank you Jamie. But remember, you helped make this cake, too."

Callie offered to help with anything else to give the bride and her family time to dress and soon other people began arriving in buggies and buckboards. Even though Julia had said it was to be a small wedding, it seemed that people had passed the word and many had travelled quite a way to wish the popular Ben Gregg and his new bride many happy returns.

A wood platform set up to the side of the porch had been decorated with urns and flowerpots with late fall mums and black-eyed Susan's. There was an arch where the ceremony was evidently to be held and a pleasant looking minister wearing black stood nodding and smiling at the guests as they made their way to the benches and chairs set out. Mr Gregg came from the rear of the house and stood next to the minister and the crowd hushed craning their neck to get the first sight of the bride. Several men took their positions and a fiddle began a ballad while the bride walked from the house on the arm of her father.

Julia's dress was simple and elegant, the bustle swaying as she took the steps to her groom. She carried roses, brought in by train, Callie was sure. There had been no expense spared for this wedding and Callie was glad she was able to stay.

The Methodist minister was fairly young but had a strong tenor voice that lent somberness to the moment. The ceremony was over in a short time and Callie realized this was the first non-Catholic wedding she had ever attended. Well, short or long, the Gregg's seemed just as married and just as happy.

The chairs some of the wedding guests had sat in were being pulled back to the edge. A small group of musicians were gathering at the opposite end of the platform from where the minister had stood and where the newly married couple started a set with three other couples joining them. Soon a country reel had formed and the musicians and dancers both looked as if they were having a good time.

Callie tapped her foot to the happy music and was startled when Seth's breath moved the soft ringlets that she had made on both sides of her face. He said quietly, "May I have this dance, Miss Callie."

Callie immediately remembered the evening before and how she had let him do all those things and felt herself flush from her neck to the roots of her hair. She started to turn away.

Seth stopped her frantic flight by laying his hand on her lower arm saying, "Darlin', you've got nothing to be self-conscious of. Nobody can tell anything about you and me if you simply treat me in the normal way. Now come on, I don't see how your limp can keep you from dancing. Just follow what the other ladies do and you'll be fine."

And she was. Callie took the position Seth pointed to and the other three couples smiled their welcome to her and then the music began. Callie had watched dances before but hadn't realized how many different movements were really involved. But Seth was right, her limp didn't get in the way of the dance and no one commented on it.

She left the dance area out of breath as Seth led her to a chair. "Would you like a cup of lemonade or something stronger? They might have sangria," he teased.

Callie exclaimed, "Oh no, just lemonade." Then realized he was only trying to get her to relax about her lapses of good behavior.

When the band struck up a waltz, Seth leaned down towards her. "I believe this dance is mine." And put his hand down to take hers.

Callie grasped her own hand close to her breasts and said, "Oh, a waltz is completely different. I couldn't wa…"

Seth pulled her into his arms and began slowly waltzing her around the room. The limp was more noticeable but neither of them fell or stumbled and no one paid any attention to them. Everyone else was busy with their own life. Callie began to relax and enjoy having a handsome man, strong, tall and actually very nice, dance her around in front of all his friends.

There was food, of course, and Seth brought back a plate with fried chicken, some kind of German potato salad, a pickled bean salad and little dumplings filled with pork sausage.

Ever the inquisitive cook, Callie said, "I'm going to have to get some of these recipes. I can figure out some of them but others are completely escaping me."

Seth picked up a chicken leg from his plate stripping it of meat in one swift movement.

Callie looked at him and asked, "Missed breakfast?"

"No, just ravenous whenever I'm around you, I guess. Just can't get enough." He gave her his wolfish grin.

Flustered by the expression on his face and the message he seemed to be sending her, she stood and quickly walked into the house saying, "I've got to go and thank Julia and wish them happy one more time before I leave."

The joyous couple was busy, like bees, flitting from guest to guest laughing and talking. Callie caught Julia's attention and indicated she had to leave to fix supper for the hands.

Julia took her aside and whispered, "I hope we can get together when I get back. I wanted to begin a quilting bee with some other ladies who live close enough. And I wanted to ask for some of your recipes. I can't boil water and Ben knows but I don't think he realizes just how much I don't know about cooking," the new bride confessed.

"Don't worry a wit, Julia. I'll write some of the more basics down and have them here waiting for you when you get back from your wedding trip. I also have a cookbook I can lend you written by a chef from the Delmonico restaurant that will come in handy."

"Thank you so much. And thank you and Seth again for such a lovely wedding cake. It was beyond anything I would have expected. My sister was green with envy."

Seth met Callie out front with a new black buggy she had never seen before.

"Where did this come from?" She was impressed with the quality of the leather seats and foldable flaps that would keep out rain and wind in bad weather.

"I drove it over after picking it up from town. I ordered it the day you told me you didn't ride. I can't have you bounced around in a buckboard every time you want to go to town," he said as he helped her into the trim front section.

"I sent Jamie on ahead, so it's just you and me, Darlin'." He pulled himself up into the seat beside her.

Callie looked around quickly to see if anyone had overheard the endearment but no one was close and Callie let out a relieved breath.

Seth slapped the reins against the horses' haunches lightly and they responded to the command instantaneously. They drove out of the gate and turned toward Harrison ranch. Callie looked straight ahead, shy now that she was alone with Seth. Finally, Seth pulled the horses to a stop and turned toward her.

"Darlin', look at me. We've been talking all afternoon and I thought you were enjoying yourself. I was enjoying myself."

"I just...I don't know. I keep thinking about what I did. I mean what we did, or you did, and I feel just awful." Tears started to fill her sad eyes.

"Now don't cry. You're making me feel like the lowest critter. I don't know what you want me to do. I didn't do anything any other red-blooded male wouldn't have done in my place. I enjoyed being with you but I don't want you to feel bad about what we've shared," he explained quietly.

Callie wasn't able to meet his gaze. "Other people do what we, umm, did? Women let men touch them and make them feel, feel…I don't know what but it couldn't be right," she finished quickly.

"Darlin' it was more than right. When a man and women are attracted to each other they're allowed to touch and enjoy one another, give each other pleasure. It's all part of making love."

"If it's part of making love, then what does that mean? Do we love each other? Does that mean we should marry and have children?" she asked seriously.

Whoa there, thought Seth. Is what they have been doing making love? This seems to be going too fast.

"Men and women don't always have to be married to enjoy each other," he said reasonably.

"But then you end up with children, babies, left at church doors or foundling homes," she accused. "That's what happens, isn't it? If we keep doing these things, I could have a baby. I could be one of those women people whisper about." She almost ended in a whimper. "You think I'm like my mother." Feeling trapped out in the open with him she began to panic. "I want to go home. I mean to the cookhouse. I think I understand now. I'm sorry I didn't think this through sooner. I feel like such a fool. Please, take me back home," she said, her eyes shimmering with unshed tears.

As he got the team moving again, Seth thought, damn, Matt was right. It breaks your heart when she cries.

Jumping out of the buggy as Seth pulled it to a stop in front of the cookhouse, she went directly to her room to change into her uniform. She still had a supper to put out and the hands would be back to the compound soon.

Callie looked in the mirror and knew anyone could tell she had been crying. Well, if anyone mentioned it, she would tell them that weddings always made her cry. Pinning the watch on her shirtwaist, she went into the kitchen to get the meal ready for the men.

Jamie kept up with a litany of chatter while they finished preparing the supper. He repeated how beautiful the cake looked and how everyone remarked that Callie could open a bakery in town. Then he added his thought that the town was big enough to need a bakery, especially with so many unmarried men in the district. Desserts would go over well since they were more difficult to prepare. Maybe some of Callie's meat pies, too.

Callie let the talk wash over her as she worried over her future. Once a person who never planned her life, she was now focused on what would become of her if she kept feeling uncomfortable around Seth. He had said she didn't have to step out with him but could she actually tell him no and still remain on his ranch? Possibly see him with another woman when his attention was drawn that way? She wasn't sure she could do that. She was attracted to him and he was the only man she ever met who made her feel the way she did around him.

The men would hate for her to leave but possibly if she taught Jamie enough, he could continue on his own. He was young but had already picked up much of how she thought a kitchen should run. And the idea of a bakery didn't seem out of the question although she didn't have any money to start one up. Would that be something a bank would lend toward? A business loan she could repay over time? That wasn't something she was experienced with at all and she had no one to ask. Except possibly Matthew. She would write him and ask what he thought of the idea.

Knowing Matthew would want her to join him where ever he was setting up his headquarters, Callie hesitated to write about her doubts of remaining on at the Harrison ranch. She didn't want to encourage her friend in thinking anything could be between them. If becoming closer to Seth had done one thing, it had proven to her that she and Matthew didn't have the right feelings for one another to make a marriage. A strong connection, certainly, but not close enough physically for a marriage. That would require much more between them.

After breakfast, Seth was down to the cookhouse to speak with Callie. Jamie was out taking care of the animals so he knew they would be alone.

"Callie, I know I didn't make myself very clear yesterday. You know I say the wrong things or don't know what to say at all, especially about emotion and feelings like that. I don't know what I feel about you except I need to see you and I need to touch you and I need you to want me to do those things, too. Am I making any sense?"

Callie nodded but kept washing the plates and leaning them against each other to dry.

"Don't do anything rash. Don't leave or anything, until we talk more. I need you to help me figure out what we have together but there isn't time now. I have to take a couple of the men and ride out to the pasture the horses are in. Something's goin' on and we're down a good many of the stock according to Jeb. It may be predators. It may be a rogue stallion starting up his own herd. Won't know till we get out there and cover the whole area. Can I go knowing you're going to wait for me?" Seth asked to her back as she kept washing dishes.

"I'll be here. What do you need me to do while you're gone? How many men are you taking with you?" she asked as the practical side of Callie snapped into motion.

"Just three more besides myself should do it. Possibly gone for a couple of days."

"Do you have cooking gear, food and water?" asked Callie as she began a mental list of their needs.

"We always travel with our own tin ware and coffeepot with fixins'. Water is plentiful but we can grab some jerky and…"

Before he could finish Callie had taken one of the smaller pots and filled it with the leftover lunch packages containing biscuits with ham and cheese. Going into the pantry, she returned with several jars. "There is some beef and barley soup and chicken with rice. You could heat them in the jar with the lids off but use the pan, it will be safer."

Moving back into the pantry she added, "I just wrapped up this ham to put away but you should take it and a dozen hard boiled eggs." She placed the items in a cloth bag that had once held sugar.

Seth laughed, realizing what a whirlwind he had. "What no dessert?" What in the hell was holding him back from declaring himself? He wanted to kiss her so badly but knew they could be seen through the windows by the men waiting for him.

Standing in front of Callie blocking her from the windows, he cupped her small face in one hand. "I'll be back in a couple of days." Then he did bend down quickly and planted a kiss on her startled lips. "Remember, Darlin', I always kiss the cook." Then left with that wolfish grin.

Seth and the three ranch hands reached the pasturelands that had been set aside for the horses that weren't needed except for round ups and at branding time. The yearlings were too young to start training yet so they ran loose as well as some of the older mares. That wasn't to say that they weren't with foal out here, just that Lothario's mares were vetted and selected for their breeding potential and all those mares were kept closer to the ranch.

There wasn't a horse in sight and nothing was evident that would make a rancher worry, except for the vultures circling overhead a few miles away.

"We'll try over there first," said Seth indicating the large, dark birds using the air currents to glide over whatever it was of interest below them.

The four men kicked their mounts into a canter and soon were overlooking the carcass of a mare that had evidently fallen and broken a leg. The carrion had been at her for a couple of days, at least.

"What do you think could have caused her to break a leg like that, here? Doesn't look like a rut or log or anything to trip her up." Will gave his view of things.

"Think one of the stallions tried to mount her and she got skittish? I guess she could have got spooked and the whole herd ran and she fell during the stampede," pondered Jeb.

Seth had been going in ever-wider circles from the carcass and then got down and studied the ground. "I don't see any sign of predators. At least not the four-legged kind."

"What did you find, Boss?" asked Will.

"There were shod horses here but not any of ours. The shape of the shoe is a little different and nothing I've seen before. We may have to contact the Sheriff if there is rustling going on. I don't want anyone to think we won't protect our stock," Seth told them.

Seth motioned for the men to follow him as he kept his gaze on the ground. "I think all the horses went this way. Away from the river which seems like the opposite of what the herd would have done if left on their own."

The group followed the tracks through the undulating hills, sometimes losing them in the tall golden grass then picking them up again when they crossed a sandy spot. There was always a mix of the two types of shoes along with some that were not shod. Most of those were the younger horses that would stay with the herd. Dusk was approaching so Seth called a halt to the search and chose a spot to set up for the night.

Sitting on the ground leaning against their saddles, the men watched the sparse fire. They were glad Seth had stopped in to see Callie. The food had warmed them enough so that they all thought they would sleep and they still had food to get them through the next day.

Morning came too soon but hot coffee and a couple of hard-boiled eggs got the men up and ready. Seth was already walking toward the direction the horses had been heading. The men mounted and followed the signs that led them, kept leading them, westward.

Just as Seth and the men were thinking they knew where the horses were going, Jeb called out so all would hear, "I think some of the horses headed a different way. Broke off from the group. There aren't as many tracks. Look how many fewer there are now."

The others slowed while Seth went out and started circling back to his starting point. "I think Jeb's right. They're either driving them two ways or have separated the horses they want from the rest of the herd and let the herd go on their own," ventured Seth.

"The main group went this way but there are still those strange shoes with this group," shouted Will.

"Do you think we should split up, Boss? Two follow each of them?" asked Jeb.

"No," Seth called back to the man. "I can't decide how many there are. I think the four of us should stay together until we see what we're up against."

The four horsemen continued to follow the tracks that had veered to the north, skirting the property line between Seth and his neighbor, O'Malley, an older rancher who had pretty much given up on maintaining cattle or anything else. Seth's men had been tending the fence between the two properties for a couple of years now and Seth had thought about offering to buy him out.

Noticing Lothario pulling on his bit, Seth gave him his head. His mount's pace increased and soon left the other three riders behind. Seth thought his stallion had picked up the scent of the herd and was racing towards it so he wasn't surprised when he came up over the rise to see almost the entire herd fenced into the corner of the property.

Jumping off Lothario, Seth saw that someone had added two wooden fence lines to corral the now agitated animals. Lothario was snorting and pawing the ground as Seth pushed first one then another of the railings to the ground.

Seth never heard the rifle shot but felt a splintering pain to his head as he fell next to the now open fence. He saw Lothario jump the lowest railing into the corral and circle the herd, which turned to follow in his wake as he led them all back the way he had just come.

The three riders heard the shot and rode past the departing herd, seeing the still saddled Lothario at its head. They all had their rifles in their hands when they spotted Seth lying in the grass and went to his aid. Will told the other two men to keep a look out for any other shooters as he knelt down to tend to Seth.

He wet a clean bandana and held it to the wound that scraped along one side of Seth's head, tying it there with the one that had been around Seth's neck. The cut didn't seem to be deep but was bleeding profusely and Will was thinking about the logistics of getting Seth back home to medical care. He didn't like the fact that his friend was still unconscious.

The others came back from their scouting mission to say the shooter must have jumped onto a horse and ridden out as soon as he saw Seth wasn't alone.

"I'm not sure how to get him back to the ranch," Will said to the others. "He's too big to put on a horse with any of us." Making a decision, he continued, "I'll put him up on mine and I'll start walking back. You men don't waste any time along the way. Just get Seth back as fast as you safely can. Send someone for me with another horse when you get to the ranch."

It took both Will and Jeb to lift Seth over the saddle and they debated whether to tie him on or hope he would stay on by himself. They decided a little rope wouldn't hurt. Once finally in place, the four horses began the return journey leaving Will with a bedroll, food, a full canteen and his Winchester.

CHAPTER 11

Callie was awakened by the shouts of the men across the compound. She was just pulling on her shirtwaist and skirt over her nightgown when Jamie came running into the cookhouse yelling her name.

Running, she cried out, "What's wrong. Is there a fire?" Her first thought of the ever-present danger for a rancher.

"No. Seth's been shot and ..." But before Jamie could finish Callie was running with her ungainly gait out the front door in time to see a horse with a body slumped over the saddle reach the ranch house.

Callie got to the men before they barely had Seth's body untied and Jeb was trying to lift Seth off the horse. One of the other men grabbed Seth's legs.

Callie said, "Wait, let me look at his wound before we move him too much."

"It's his head and Will bound it up but he hasn't said anything since he was hit. Hasn't even moaned in pain," volunteered Jeb.

Callie noted the blood-soaked bandana and neckerchief and told the men to continue getting Seth into the house. "Can you get him to his room? It's upstairs."

The two men grunted and began carrying their dead-weight burden into the house, trying to be gentle.

Callie ran into the kitchen and grabbed a stack of clean towels then looked for any medical supplies. She found them in Seth's office and took what she thought would be helpful.

Climbing the stairs, Callie started wondering how Seth had gotten shot. And if the wound wasn't serious, why didn't Seth wake up?

The two men had placed their patient on the bed, on top of the covers and backed away. They seemed confused as to what to do next and both looked relieved when Callie came into the room.

As Callie unwrapped the seeping bandanas and let them fall into the pan she held, both men turned pale and scrambled to get through the door first. She asked, "Would you tell Sully I may need him?"

Both men answered, "Yessum." And left to do her bidding.

Worriedly, Callie looked over the injury. The wound didn't seem deep so that was good, she thought, but then Seth's skull was just beneath the surface. It didn't look as if it needed stitches since the skin was simply missing, scraped or burned off. Callie took a clean cloth wet with water from the pitcher and dabbed around the wound to insure there wasn't any other damage she was missing.

As she leaned back with a sigh, the bleeding seemed to ebb and the dry cloth placed over the wound wasn't soaked with fresh blood.

Sully came clomping into the room looking pale, his eyes a little sunken and the smile gone from his face. "How's my boy?" he asked.

"The wound doesn't look too bad and the bleeding has stopped. He hasn't said a word and the men said he's been that way since they found him," Callie told him worriedly.

"Must be concussed. I sent for the Doc. He lives just outside of town, this side. Sent for the Sheriff, too, since it seems we got us some rustlers. Had to send two men out to the horse pastures to pick up Will. He gave up his horse so they could bring Seth back faster," Sully explained.

He gazed down at Seth laying so quietly on the bed. "Jamie's gettin' coffee and an early breakfast goin' for the men. No one's gonna get any more sleep tonight. I'm just trying to figure out what the Boss would want me to do now."

"Well, I know he wouldn't want anyone to put themselves in danger. He cares more for any of you than he does a whole herd of horses," Callie said emphatically. "Help me lift him a little, Sully. I've got to get this blood-soaked shirt off him and then his trousers and boots. If we get him into bed, I'm sure he'll be more comfortable."

"I can send someone for Maria. She wasn't planning on coming to the ranch until Seth sent for her but I know she won't mind comin' back early."

"I can do this. I've nursed dozens of orphans through epidemics at St Michaels. He simply weighs a little more than they did."

Sully helped Callie roll Seth unto one side as they removed the dirty, bloody shirt and gently rolled him onto the other to pull it off his other arm. Then they pulled off his boots and socks. They both looked worriedly at the belt at his slender waist when Callie turned and picked up a bath towel off the railing on the washstand and held it discreetly over the controversial site.

Grunting his approval, Sully commenced unbuckling the belt and trouser buttons. Callie went to the foot of the bed and started tugging the pant legs. First one and then the other until the trousers were down to

Seth's ankles.

Callie and Sully smiled at one another upon reaching their goal with everyone's sense of propriety in place. Pulling the blankets over Seth, they left the pillow off the bed so he remained flat. Callie had thought the doctor would have been there by now then realized it had barely been over an hour and a half leaving at least another hour before the doctor could be to the ranch. And then only if the doctor was at home and available. She didn't think a buckboard ride into town would do Seth any good and could cause more damage so that seemed all they could do for now.

"I've got first watch, Sully. Tell Jamie he's in charge today. He knows what we were going to fix. It's nothing he can't handle on his own and I'm here if he has any questions."

Sully looked at Callie and knew he wasn't going to have any luck with talking her out of staying and, heck, she was probably the most qualified to take care of Seth, so nodded and left the room.

Callie picked up the dirty clothes and boots and put them near the armoire in the far corner of the room. The wet rags she placed in the slop bucket and then she sat to watch her patient.

Seth was breathing regularly, eyes closed without any sign of movement behind the lids. Was that good or bad? She couldn't remember. Head wounds were few and far between at St Michaels even though the children took spills and falls throughout their childhood. She felt his forehead and it was still cool to the touch, which she knew was a good sign. She sat back in the chair that Seth probably used to put his boots on and off and waited for the doctor and for Seth to wake up.

The doctor finally entered the bedroom with Sully following about daybreak. She had heard them come into the house and up the stairs. Shouting for them to hurry at that point would not change the outcome. Callie was anxiously waiting, standing on the far side of the bed as the doctor sat his bag down and looked sternly at his patient.

Removing the bandage, he grunted, felt around the wound and down around Seth's neck and back of his head. Taking a stethoscope, he listened closely to Seth's heart. Then he began feeling every bone starting from Seth's shoulders down both arms. When he lifted the blanket and saw the discreetly placed towel, he looked up shrewdly at Callie who was blushing to the roots of her hair. He said nothing and placed his hands down both legs the same way he had the other parts of Seth's body.

The doctor finally felt content with his physical. "The good news is I don't think there is any other damage done to this young man. Doesn't seem that he hit his head on anything when he fell and since you say he was standing when he was hit, I don't think we're looking at any long-lasting effects."

Sully asked the question Callie wanted to. "If that's the good news, what's the bad, Doc?"

The doctor tilted his head and answered, "Seth is going to take his own time to wake up. The head is hard and protects itself in many ways but each injury seems to take its own time before the patient is up and back to normal. Sometimes there is some memory loss, especially about what happened right before the incident or they can be more serious and have slurred speech or be missing words. Sometimes that gets better over time and other times they become a new person all together.

We won't know until he wakes up. Either way, he should stay at home and rest, no riding and that includes in a wagon."

"But he will wake up?" asked Callie who wanted a more definite prognosis.

The doctor answered as he closed his bag. "I've never personally known anyone not to but there are articles in the medical journals of patients who have been unconscious for years."

Callie swallowed and bravely lifted her head saying, "I understand, doctor. Thank you very much for coming. Should I be doing something in particular with his care?"

"Keep him quiet and when he wakes, give him liquids and light foods until he seems able to move around. Watch for any unusual activity or if he seems disoriented, send for me immediately. Just keep him from getting agitated until I can get here. Otherwise, I'll be back tomorrow evening. I've been up all night delivering a set of twins and need to sleep if I'm going to be of any use to my patients." The doctor left with Sully leading the way.

Callie's mind went wild, imagining Seth waking up and not knowing who she was or what they had done together. What if he didn't know or remember any of them? Would he be frightened being surrounded by strangers? Would he still love training horses and being a rancher?

Wiping her eyes, Callie remembered Sister Theresa saying, 'tears, have their place, but only when sorrow is the only outcome. If there is hope then there is no need for tears, so pray for hope.'

Callie dropped to her knees and did as she had always done when faced with insurmountable fear - she prayed. She prayed for Seth's recovery, anything else she needed or wanted didn't matter if Seth didn't fully recover.

Getting up from the floor, she laid down on top of the bed. She was afraid she might fall asleep and wanted to be close enough to know if he moaned or moved. That is where Jamie found her a couple hours later.

"Callie," he whispered. "I-I brought you some food and I'm making broth, is the Boss awake?"

Callie gazed up at Jamie. "He hasn't woken up yet. He has to be watched and I don't want to leave him alone."

Jamie said, "No, I-I don't want you to leave him either. I-I can fix dinner, it's already started. I'll leave the food and come back later."

"Stay with him for a minute. Yell if he wakes up." She took a last look at Seth and went down the stairs to use the privy and returned with warm water from the stove's reservoir. After sending Jamie back to the cookhouse, Callie tucked her hand under the blanket to make sure Seth's chest was rising and falling in even breaths. Once ensured that he was no worse than before, she ate the meal Jamie had brought.

Taking a washing cloth, she soaped it before wiping it over Seth's face, which had the stubble of more than two days of beard. She washed his neck again and then both ears and rinsed the cloth. His chest was lightly covered with soft blond hair that stood at attention caused by the chill of the evaporation. She wiped and rinsed, progressing down first one side then the other.

When she met the area covered by the towel she hesitated and then began the ablutions on the far side of the towel with first one leg, then the other, one foot then the other. Soaping, washing and rinsing each part, slowly, lovingly taking care of the only man she would ever love this way.

Seth was beautifully made. Muscles covered by smooth skin golden hued in areas that were kissed by the sun. Callie had seen him shirtless even in this cooler weather when working with the horses so his muscular chest and arms weren't a surprise. His thighs and calves were well muscled, as well, probably from all the riding he did. Even his feet were strong, completely masculine and Callie responded to his masculinity in ways she didn't understand. She knew, though, that anything he wanted to do with her when he was awake again was going to be eagerly anticipated.

Callie thought about her relationship with Seth, the things they had done, the things she wanted him to do, and feared he didn't feel the same way, would never feel the same way. But at this point it was the least of her worries. Getting Seth awake was the most important thing right now.

Jamie stopped back to see how Seth was two more times without a blink as to finding Callie lying next to him on the bed. Jamie told her he would pass on the information to the hands because they were all worried about Seth. He asked if Callie needed anything and she told him no, just for Seth to wake up.

Darkness was falling again, and Callie lay back on the bed. Still exhausted from being woken in the middle of the night and the worry over Seth robbed Callie of much needed sleep. She needed to rest if she was going to be any help at all and she worried when she realized the doctor hadn't returned as he had promised. Her eyes grew heavy and soon her even breathing joined Seth's in the quiet night.

"Darlin', Callie Darlin', you're gonna havta move, honey. Nature calls. I gotta' get up," a raspy voice whispered into Callie's ear as she snuggled into the man that meant so much to her.

Callie woke with a start. "Seth, are you, all right? Do you feel, all right?"

"I'm fine. What happened to the horses?" he asked. "Hell, I got a heck of a headache." He reached up and found the bandage the doctor had applied.

"You were shot trying to find the missing herd. Knocked you out completely and the men brought you home but you hadn't gained consciousness. Out cold they said from the time they found you," Callie informed him in a rush.

"Are the horses still missing? Did we catch the rustlers?" he asked bewilderedly.

"I'm not sure. They said they saw Lothario running with the herd. Later Sully came in to see how you were and told me Lothario came back with the saddle and rifle still intact. Will got picked up and is back, too."

"What happened to Will? No, never mind. I gotta' get up and, well, I just need to get up."

Callie swung her feet over the side of the bed saying, "I'll get a chamber pot for you." She lit the candle so she could see.

"Oh, no you won't. I'll, er-r, relieve myself like a man in the great outdoors. I will not do so with a woman holding a pot for me," he told her firmly.

As Seth spoke, he pulled back the covers swinging his legs to the floor and stood up. The towel dropped to the floor and Callie looked anywhere but at a now very naked Seth.

"What the hell was that?" he asked as he kicked the towel out of the way.

"I was trying to protect your modesty."

"Darlin', I lost my modesty with you a long time ago." Then unconcernedly turned toward the doorway.

Callie ran to his side and tried to wrap her arm around his waist to keep him from falling. Seth looked at the diminutive woman attempting to give aid to a man that weighed more than twice what she did and smiled affectionately.

"I am afraid that you will get light-headed from blood loss. Please let me help you." Glancing around the room she asked, "Um, don't you want to put on some trousers?"

He smiled down at her and her flushed cheeks and said, just to be contrary, "No, I'm fine as I am." And proceeded out to the hall and down the stairs while not using the railing.

Callie stayed close to his side, at least she could break his fall if need be. They walked slowly to the kitchen's back door and Callie handed Seth the candle as he said, "This is as far as you go. I can make it to the privy on my own. I feel fine, really."

Opening the door, he went down the steps on his own as Callie watched his bare cheeks descend into the night.

Callie was about to head out to the privy to check on Seth when she saw the light from the candle coming back toward the house. She didn't look too closely since she was finding it difficult not to soak up every inch of him, she could. She convinced herself she was simply trying to make sure he was all right and that there wasn't any residual damage from his injury.

"All right, Darlin', I'm sorry I teased you. I'm thinking you have a lot to tell me about what happened and I know I probably owe you for taking good care of me." Leaning down, he kissed the top of her head.

"You were brought in shot in the head and unconscious and I was so worried you wouldn't wake-up or if you did that you would have memory loss."

"Darlin', I could never forget you." He hugged her to his naked side as they walked back to the stairs.

When they reached the steps, Seth gave a little bow saying, "After you. Or if you would like to follow me up so you can admire my attributes, I'll accommodate." And he went to take a step toward her.

"No, ah, no, I think it's time you got some clothes on so you don't catch cold," Callie told him reasonably.

"I'm not cold, believe me, but maybe I best get dressed to prevent both of us from being embarrassed."

Once back to his room, Seth dressed in clean trousers and shirt. Callie tried to get him to lie back on the bed explaining that the doctor wanted him to take it easy for several days once he did wake up.

"Okay, I will if you will. Come back and lay beside me and I'll rest," he said, patting the mattress beside him as he leaned back against the headboard.

Callie climbed up beside him, snuggling into him as his arm came around her.

"I really was worried about you. I haven't made a meal for two days. Jamie has been great about taking over. We owe him."

Soon the stroking of her hair and the loss of fear over Seth's health helped Callie fall asleep. That is how Sully found them. Seth woke first when he heard the boots on the stairs but didn't move so as not to disturb Callie. She had seemed so worn out he wanted her to get as much rest as she could before their life went back to normal.

Sully looked from Callie to Seth and said rather gruffly, "I have to talk with you. The Sheriff's been out and we have more information."

Seth carefully removed his arm from around Callie and slid off the bed.

"You really, all right?" asked Sully. "You worried all of us but that little girl mostly."

"Besides a murderous headache, I'm okay. What did Mason say?" Seth asked about the sheriff from town.

"Can you make it downstairs? To the office, maybe?" asked Sully.

"Told you I was fine. But we won't disturb Callie down there and I don't want her hearing some of this anyway."

Once seated, Sully began. "Well, the Sheriff and the hands have been over both our pastures and O'Malley's. There are signs that the rustlers have been all over his place and cut wire to get into ours. Looks like they boxed in the horses and were coming back for them. Seems like they were going to drive them to the train spur to be taken to auction." He shook his head at the truth as if unable to believe it. "Them big cities are still feeling the loss of horses after that equine flu outbreak a while back. There's a market for any healthy animal, even unbroke ones."

Seth absorbed the information and asked, "Did they catch any of them? The fella that shot at me?"

"Not the shooter, yet. But the Sheriff thinks that the two he has will turn on the man who did. Horse stealin' is still thought a serious crime and those men will be trying to make a deal. They're facing significant punishments for rustling, too. Maybe even more than for taking a pot-shot at you."

"Well, the horses are probably worth more," Seth said chuckling then continued. "What do you think our chances are of getting these guys? I don't like the idea that they would use violence to protect their stolen goods. The ranch hands might fall upon them by mistake when they're out on regular rounds for the cattle. I don't want to chance anyone else getting hurt."

"Can't say for sure. Losing the horses to Lothario probably hurt their plans, some. That damn horse hid that herd so well we haven't seen them since they ran past Will and the others. I know they didn't get taken onto O'Malley's because we went out that next morning and fixed the cut wire and then ran that whole line."

"No other cuts, no place where they may have taken horses through before?" asked Seth still rubbing the back of his neck.

"Nope, but we didn't have time to really ride over all of O'Malley's lands so that will be done tomorrow in teams with the Sheriff in charge. He's talked about making us temporary deputies or some such but we'll probably just ride out with him and keep the hands out of any shooting if we can. They all want to catch the feller that shot you but they're ranch hands. No one signed up for more than that," Sully reminded his boss and friend.

"I'll go out with you tomorrow and Lothario will take me to his herd. Probably put them in some valley and you've been riding right by them."

Sully asked bluntly, his protective instincts kicking into play. "Now what about that little girl upstairs? What are you planning to do now that you've basically been shacking-up for the last couple of days?"

"What do you mean? I just woke up a couple of hours ago. I can't be held responsible for anything she chose to do. I didn't ask her to stay," he said defensively, allowing the pain in his head to drive him to speak roughly.

"Maria isn't back from visiting her nephew. You told her she wasn't needed while you were out on the range so she left. I'm not sure when she's coming back. There wasn't any need before now," Sully reminded Seth.

"I don't need anyone to watch over me. I appreciate Callie looking out for me but I'm fine now and I plan on riding out with the men in the morning." Seth was defiant. Not allowing the head wound to dictate his actions or limit his ability to protect his property.

"That doesn't deal with the problem of Callie being here alone with you. I saw you both on the bed together, myself. It's not right, Seth. She deserves more. I warned you to stay away from her if you weren't gonna be serious about the girl. She just wants to be part of a family, wants someone to love and be loved by."

Seth, fighting to see through the red blur of pain beginning to cover his vision and trying to find some relief from the ache that was now one long throb, snapped back at Sully. "Look, I've told her to stop looking toward me for family or love or anything more than what we have. I can't help it if she threw herself at me while I was out cold and couldn't send her away. I'm not husband material. I never will be and I will never be able to love her." With that he stood and went out to the hall - and ran smack into Callie.

Her stricken expression told Seth more than words

ever could that she had overheard his hardened comments.

"The doctor is here to see you," she said ignoring everything that she heard and then limped out of the kitchen door.

She gave no indication if she heard Seth's softly whispered, "Damn."

CHAPTER 12

Callie went directly to her room. Brushing her braid, she re-wound it in the usual bun at the base of her neck leaving the little strands of hair that always curled on both sides of her face. Retrieving warm water from the stove, she cleansed herself of the past few days before dressing in a clean uniform and apron. Pinning the gold watch on the front of her shirtwaist, she was ready to be the cook again. A position she knew she was good at. A position she knew she was made for. Maybe the only position she should have tried to have.

Walking out to the kitchen, Callie smelled the soup simmering on the stove. Jamie had set out the vegetables for the evening meal and was just entering with more wood.

"Everything looks like you have it under control. I'll make the applesauce cake before you need to put the roasts in. I want to thank you for doing everything while I was gone. You can have the next couple of days off to make up for it," Callie told him.

"I-I just followed the plans. You had it worked out already," he said modestly dropping the firewood into the box next to the stove.

"I told you, you would be good at this," Callie reminded the young man.

"Hands said I d-didn't cook as good as you but they licked the plates clean so I-I couldn't have been too bad." Standing a little straighter, he grinned with pride.

"I am sure you did fine or I would have heard them complaining all the way up to the ranch house," she

135

teased as she got out the ingredients for the cake.

"I-I need to make butter though," Jamie told her. "I was doin' other stuff."

"That won't be a problem. I'll get the cake in and then I'll get the butter jars. I need some exercise since being cooped up inside for the past couple of days." She turned to the pantry and anything that would prevent her from thinking and remembering Seth's harsh words. She felt if she kept busy then she wouldn't remember the words overheard in the back hallway. Nothing Seth said had been incorrect or opposite of anything he had said directly to her. He simply made it very plain he wasn't the marrying kind and that he knew it. Had come to grips with it and was happy with his decision. It simply wasn't a decision Callie could live with. Not on the ranch with the possibility of seeing him every day.

The afternoon went quickly with many little jobs to catch up on and preplanning food use that Jamie wasn't trained to do yet. Dinner ran smoothly with many of the hands welcoming her back, complaining about the poor replacement she left them with, and other teasing comments made at Jamie's expense. All in friendly banter with Jamie giving them grief as good as they were giving him.

Sully told her he and some of the other men were heading out the next day and asked if she could put some food together for them. They may be gone overnight so that would mean fewer men left at the compound for meals. Callie told him that she would have provisions for ten men for two days unless he thought there would be more.

"No, that should be enough. We'll come back either way. If we don't catch them SOB's, then we'll come back to rest and go out agin'." Noting her quiet demeanor, he asked, "You all right, Callie child?"

"I am fine, Sully. Just thinking about what I can put together that you can eat with the least amount of cooking or needing to stop and setup camp. Will you need coffee or water?" At Sully's negative answer, Callie said, "I'll have it ready by breakfast."

Callie welcomed the distraction of fixing the food for the hands to take with them. While boiling eggs, she made up some soup to put in mason jars. Then baked another spice cake and made up meat pies from the left-over roast and vegetables that could be eaten cold.

She had set dough to rise for onion rolls and nearing dawn, she placed them in the oven and baked them off. Later she split them in half and spread them with freshly churned butter. She was wrapping the sliced ham and a good hunk from a wheel of cheddar when the hands arrived for breakfast.

Callie called for them to come on in. She had made eggs and thick sliced bacon kept warm in the oven, buttermilk biscuits with sausage gravy and the usual pots of coffee. Some of the hands were leaving with Sully and some were headed towards the cattle herd. The horse training had been put on hold until the rustlers were caught.

Jamie came in with the milk bucket and Callie covered it with a cloth and took it to the cold room. She would work with it later after the men were fed and gone for the day.

Sully was one of the last ones in and nodded his good-morning to Callie on the way to the table. He looked worried but tucked into the food as if he hadn't had the weight of the world on his shoulders.

Coming over to the counter after he had eaten, he helped Callie pack the food into several cloth bags. They balanced the weight between the five bags as Sully said he was impressed with the amount of food and told her he knew the men would be appreciative.

"Anything can be overcome - sleeping on wet ground, cold wind and even snow if a man has a full belly. The men will truly be thankful come the end of the day to know they have this good food waiting for them. I really appreciate you going to so much trouble but I can't say as I'm surprised." As if weighing his words carefully, he continued, "Callie child, you give too much of yourself for others. You need to toughen up and take what Callie wants. You know what I'm sayin'?" he asked her, watching her expression to his questions, hoping she would stand up for herself before becoming run over.

"I'm fine, Sully. I learned a lot in the last few days. I am tougher than I look. I always have been underestimated because I'm small. Don't worry about me. I'll get on with my life and Harrison ranch will simply be a pleasant memory for me. Now you better get out there before they come in after you," she told him, smiling encouragingly when he hesitated.

Jamie helped Sully take the bags out and gave them to a few men to tie on their saddles. Callie started the cleaning up and rubbed her eyes that were finally showing her tiredness. She poured some coffee and added sugar hoping that would help since she didn't have time for sleep and there was a long day in front of her.

Later that afternoon, Jamie came into the kitchen and was concerned at how tired Callie looked. "Why don't you lie down and get some rest. I-I can fix dinner or whatever you need doing. Not expectin' any time off."

"No, I won't be able to sleep. I mean, I'm really not tired." And gave a weak smile trying not to let the boy see her weariness or the fact she didn't want to be alone with her thoughts. Not yet. Not until the hurt in her heart eased a little. She felt too raw to make decisions and she didn't want to make the wrong ones for the wrong reasons.

"Yeah, I know. It's hard to know that someone is out there shooting at the hands. It could have been so much worse with the boss. I-I wanted to go with them to help but the Boss told me my job would be watching over you. That would help him the most."

"I don't need more help, Jamie. There's going to be fewer men to feed here for the next couple of days at least. You can take time for yourself while we wait this out."

"I-I got somethin' to show you," he said rather shyly.

Callie had hoped he had gotten over being shy with her but it seems whatever this is, it had brought out his self-consciousness again.

"What's in the box? Not something that needs burying, is it?" she asked hesitantly.

Jamie laughed as she had intended. Removing the lid, he slid the box toward her across the counter. It was filled with several small birds made for women's hats like the one she had on her own.

"Oh, they are darling, Jamie. So perfect they each have their own personality. How clever. How did you get the feathers to look like they grew there? The little rings of color around this one's neck and the way the wings fold back. I almost expect it to take flight," she said smiling with delight.

"I saw the little bird on your hat and then I knew why I had been saving all those feathers. I made this one first and then the others just kept coming. I'd finish one and then another idea for one would just come to me," he explained excitedly.

"I would love to have a hat with one of these little gems on it," she confessed.

"I was hopin' you'd take them into town. Maybe see if the lady that makes hats would buy some from me. She paid me for turkey feathers once but I don't want to try to talk with her. She's a stranger and I-I-I d-don't...."

"That's all right, Jamie. I can see if she has a need for them or I can write to Lizette and see if there is a milliner she buys hats from who may be interested. With two grown-up daughters she buys a lot of hats." Callie picked up another bright-eyed bird to admire its perfectness.

Jamie smiled his thanks and began packing the little birds back into their box.

CHAPTER 13

Sheriff Mason, a big man with blond hair and blue eyes rode in on a large horse as tall as Lothario. He had a packed saddlebag and rifle along with a leather belt of extra bullets. Turning his steely gaze to Seth, he said, "I thought you had a concussion or something. What are you doing here?"

"My horse knows where the herd is and I want to get a crack at the sons of bitches that shot my good hat." He grinned at his friend to let him know only half of that was the truth but he wasn't letting him know which half. "Besides, I have part of the food."

"All right, but if it gets too much for you, stop and rest or take yourself back home. It may take a few days to cover this much ground and now we only have a couple of horses to look for instead of a herd," Mason said to Seth.

"We have the advantage that we don't need to hide our tracks and we have a lot more man power than we had the first time out after them," Seth replied indicating the posse of ranch hands.

"Let's go and I'll show you where we found the last trail of rustlers." Mason started off while the group rode after him.

It wasn't going to be a quick find. There were a lot of bushes and dips and swells that could hide a few men on horses. They all had to be searched. Days later the group finally ran to ground the three horsemen they were seeking.

Will, roping one of them right off the horse, pulled

the man to the ground as he would a calf to be branded. The sheriff fired a shot over the heads of the other two and they pulled-up raising their hands into the air, showing that they weren't going to die over a few horses. As the sheriff took their weapons and tied their hands, they all were eager to blame their non-present gang member as the one who shot Seth.

Seth and most of the ranch hands started back to the Harrison ranch. The rustlers, tied onto their horses, were escorted by several riders from town who made-up the posse to the nearby county seat of Preston to stand trial.

Giving Lothario his head, Seth urged his horse to find his family. Lothario stepped up the pace and soon was cantering over a hill and joining his herd, bringing Seth with him. Several of the yearlings were running next to their sire, trying to gain his attention. Seth grinned as he rode over the swelling hills and finally the herd was closer to the river and the ranch where Seth and, evidently Lothario, wanted them for the winter.

Unaware the men had returned, Callie turned and there he was. Seth. Tall, handsome, long strong legs still wearing his trousers and chaps, the same gear as he rode out in days ago, only now covered in a film of dust and who knew what else. Smiling as if he just saw a gold nugget, his eyes sparkled with humor. And then that grin that always got to Callie, deep down in her womanly parts.

Callie's heart skipped a beat and her instinct was to run into his arms and tell him she was glad to see him. To say she was relieved that he hadn't been shot again. To tell him how happy she was he wasn't hurt and now safely back at the ranch. But she did none of those things.

Instead, Callie ignored him.

Disappointed at his reception, Seth gave a little grunt as he stood up from the edge of the table where he had been watching Callie as she prepared dinner. He sauntered over to the stove and picked up one of the clean tasting spoons as he had seen her teach Jamie to do and took a little sample from the pot simmering on the stove.

Callie saw him out of the corner of her eye but was too late to stop him from placing the sample into his mouth taking a nice, big spoonful. He swallowed with difficulty and at her inquiring expression said, "Not your best effort, Darlin'."

Callie returned her remark with a deadpan look, saying, "I'll apologize to the chickens. I'm making a warm mash for them so they'll keep laying on these colder days."

He smiled, showing those sharp white wolfish teeth. "Well, that relieves my mind. I was afraid you had lost your touch while I was away. Or you were just out and out going to poison us all."

"I will think about that last bit but the hands didn't do anything to get in my bad graces."

"I know, and I still want to talk about that. But right now, isn't the best time and I have a feeling I smell more like Lothario than I should. Talk with me later tonight?" he asked with one eyebrow raised.

"I think we have talked enough, Seth. I think we want two different things and I don't think either of us can change what we are. What a lifetime has made us. I'm sorry I can't be what you want but I can't abandon all my principals and beliefs," she told him sadly knowing years of being taught by the nuns had ingrained certain convictions into her. She couldn't ignore the voices inside her head any longer. She would need to find a way to leave Harrison ranch.

Turning away, she heard him say, "I didn't realize I was asking so much." Then he left by the side door toward the ranch house.

Seth was thinking about the conversation he just had with Callie. The conversation he swore he would hold off having until they were both relaxed enough with each other to talk rationally. To share with one another what it is they feel between them. He should have waited and approached her after he had time to clean up, to shave this stubble off his face, to look the part of a prosperous rancher searching for a wife.

Instead, he rushed his fences as usual when he had any dealings with Callie. He tried to tell himself it was a bad idea to walk in without warning. That she may need to prepare herself before facing him. But he couldn't wait to see her, needed to know for sure she was still there because she wanted to be and not because he ordered every single one of the hands and Jamie not to let her step foot off the ranch. Seth didn't feel good about the way they had left things and had wanted to be sure she was there when he returned. There wasn't anything keeping her on the ranch and he still feared Matthew would return for her – or at least write to her and lure her to another town. Possibly with the promise of a marriage. The one thing Seth knew would move Callie enough to abandon her commitment to the ranch and to him.

He hadn't been in too good of a mood when he had to leave with the sheriff. He hadn't even said goodbye to her in case he couldn't stop himself from begging her for forgiveness for the things he had said during that raging headache. That he hadn't meant what he said. He just wanted Sully to shut up so he could think but instead he ruined the bond that he and Callie had formed. He had to start all over and do a better job of showing his feelings, such as they were.

Maybe they were too far apart as Callie had said. It didn't feel that way when Seth thought about how much he missed her when he was out on the range. How at every meal he thought about the small, soft hands that had prepared the food they ate? How he worried about her and about Jamie's ability to keep her at the ranch until he could get back and talk with her, explain why he thought he could never love her, love anyone, the way she needed him to. But that didn't mean he didn't want her, that he couldn't see them as a couple, maybe even with children.

Callie's mind was a blur. They were back. He was back. Nothing bad happened, her prayers had been answered. She had not asked if they got the rustlers or if more horses were missing. She had been so glad to see him yet she had held herself back from leaping into his arms. Telling him she loved him enough for the two of them and that she would stay on the ranch until he changed his mind and turned her away or she died a withered-up old lady. Was she regretting not showing him she cared? But if she ached because she didn't hold him against her breast now, how bad would it be if he rejected her again? When all hope had been extinguished? And what happens when she realizes it already has been?

CHAPTER 14

Seth and Callie rode silently side by side in the buckboard. She had been expecting Sully to pick her up that morning but Seth arrived in his place and she really couldn't refuse to travel with him. She had told Jamie she would make sure the dressmaker got the little feather birds and to negotiate a good price for him. This extra money was going toward buying his cowpony so it was important to him to sell as many as the proprietor would take.

Seth pulled the horses to a stop in front to the milliner's but Callie was off the seat and standing on the boardwalk holding the small box before Seth could get down to help her.

"I'll be down to Thompson's picking up some nails and shingles if you need anything," he told her.

"Thank you. I'll be fine," she said curtly and entered the neat little storefront. A bell tinkled lightly as Callie closed the door.

A pretty brunette woman with hazel eyes and bright smile came through a curtained doorway. "Good morning, I'm Miss Abby White, the proprietress. How may I help you?" she said in a friendly breezy way. She was much younger than Callie expected although she had known the woman was unmarried. Quite the conversational topic among the hands during dinner some nights.

Abby was dressed sensibly in a white shirtwaist with full upper sleeves and then small buttons securing it tightly to the lower arm. There was a cream and black cameo pin at the lace trimmed collar. The skirt was brown hounds-tooth with a wide waistband that peaked under the breasts emphasizing her womanly proportions.

"I am Callie St Michaels, and I brought some darling little birds that you had indicated an interest in viewing. Jamie is very talented and I think they would look ever so smart on some of your creations." Callie opened the lid of the box and took out one of the little birds and turned it around so that it could be viewed on all sides.

"Oh, they are sweet, aren't they? And clever. Is this real jet for their eyes? Oh, and here they are pearls. I do like them very much. And you said the artist was Jamie? He sent me some feathers that I used in some of my hats. I sent his money back with the ranch foreman, Sully. Will you give me a minute to figure out a price to offer?"

"Certainly. Jamie works with me at the Harrison ranch. I'm the cook there," Callie told her.

"I have to admit, I know. Not much happens in a small town that everyone doesn't soon know about. Makes life interesting for us single females," Abby said with humor.

"May I look around? The items in the front window caught my eye. Not that I have much spare money. I only have this one dress other than a couple of shirtwaists and another skirt. I wear uniforms most of the time when I'm working," Callie explained.

"Oh, take your time. I don't have anything readymade for someone your size but most of my designs can be cut down to fit you."

Callie picked up some embroidered bed sheets with matching pillowcases trimmed with crocheted lace. "These are lovely, Miss White. Did you do these as well as sew?"

"I was the fourth daughter and I think my mother gave me all the sewing and knitting duties to keep me out of trouble. The fact that I loved doing it simply made me more proficient. I find I do more embroidery, crocheting and tatting than anything else. My designing and sewing are mostly for younger women and there aren't very many of us in the district, I am afraid."

"Mrs Gregg was saying the same thing but she plans on starting a quilting bee so there is a place for the younger women to go to socialize. I have to admit, it is difficult to meet other people, especially other woman, out on the ranch."

Then Callie continued, "I probably shouldn't have but I have fallen in love with this dress and jacket. It is more daring than I usually wear but I am tired of being so conservative. And I can always wear the jacket if I feel it is too immodest. Do you think it will suit? I am so short that sometimes the dress looks like it is wearing me rather than the other way around."

"That can be a problem with petite ladies but I think I have the perfect material that will keep the dress light enough that it won't weigh you down." And with that Abby pulled a bolt of fabric in gold and greens, the small print just keeping the material from appearing plain.

"Oh, I like that," said Callie smoothing her hands over the fabric. "Is it very expensive?"

"Actually, no. I have to keep in mind my customer's needs when I purchase so I make sure it is affordable and much less expensive than what it would cost in the bigger cities."

After Callie got the price of the dress, she smiled in relief and agreed to the purchase.

"Well, let's get some measurements and I can have

this done by Friday if that is acceptable. Any final adjustment can be made then," Abby said grabbing a tape and leading Callie into the back room through the curtain.

Callie was helped to remove her dress and stood under Abby's scrutiny in her camisole and stockings.

"I see you do not favor wearing a corset," Abby said as she began to take measurements.

"Well, my work is fairly physical, lifting heavy pans and cutting meats so I haven't worn one for quite some time."

"For the lower neckline, I would recommend wearing one. Not that your waist needs cinching in. Simply something to lift, to emphasize the bosom. You have one so you should show it off."

Callie giggled. "I never really thought about having a bosom. They just always seem to get in the way but you are probably right. I shouldn't really go around such a 'loose woman' even if it is more comfortable."

"I'm going to have you try on one of these. They are made for women who really don't need one, if you know what I mean. A little lift but not made as if it was holding up the Grand Tetons." Both young women laughed.

While Abby was kneeling, writing down measurements, she asked Callie. "How is it, working out there with Seth Harrison? I always thought he was a handsome devil." She smiled conspiratorially up at Callie.

"Handsome is as handsome does," she quoted a nun proverb. "And my work doesn't bring me in contact with him." Which was the truth, they simply seemed to keep running into each other in non-work times.

"I can see that. He always seemed like a lone-wolf

sort to me. But still attractive with it," Abby said as she finished making notes. Telling Callie, she could re-dress, Abby put all the measurements and material behind the curtained doorway.

Abby came back calculating on a small pad of paper. "I can buy these birds but I would rather place another order from Jamie and then send these on consignment to my friend in St Louis. She is the one who taught me the business and has need of more inventory than I do. She can also pay more for this type of thing. Do you think Jamie would agree to that?"

"I think he will see the wise business sense in that. He's a bright boy."

Callie looked wistfully at a beaded reticule for eveningwear and sighed at its beauty and probably pricey cost. Next to it was a leather coin case and a small perfume bottle cloaked in leather to protect it from damage while being packed or carried.

"These look familiar," said Callie trying to remember where she had seen them.

Abby blushed prettily. "A travelling salesman showed me a brochure and I ordered them from him. I recently got them in. He had a lot of other items, mostly for men, but I was hoping he would stop by again when he comes through."

Callie looked closely at Abby and said, "Don't worry, he'll come back. I could almost bet on it."

The two women said their farewells and Callie went to walk down the street to where Seth had indicated he would be.

As Callie exited, the little bell tinkling behind the door, she looked up to see Seth waiting down the street. He pulled the wagon up and Callie apologized, "I am sorry. If I had known you were ready to leave, I wouldn't have taken so long." She climbed into the wagon without his aid again.

Seth turned the team around in the main street since there wasn't any traffic to speak of and headed back toward the ranch. This was not how he thought this trip would be. He thought he would say a few words to break the ice and Callie would do her share and take up any slack. Instead, Callie seemed content merely to sit out the ride without any conversation.

He didn't like it when Callie was mad at him or just out and out ignored him. He had apologized for intruding into her bath, he had apologized for just about everything he ever did or ever said to her. What more did the darn woman want? Seth knew that his communication with women lacked a little couth but really, he was always honest and up-front. That should count for something. He would try again now that the business with the birds was out of the way.

"Callie, are you feelin' all right?" he asked in a conciliatory manner.

Callie didn't want to talk to the so handsome wolfish Seth Harrison that has women swooning and lusting after him. "Fine," she said sharply.

"Umm, I've lived on a ranch my whole life so I understand about certain functions." He asked tentatively, "Is it a female thing?"

Callie turned to him with eyes glaring and a look that said 'oh, no, you did not really just ask me that'. She said distinctly, "It is not a female thing. It is a male thing. Men are idiots!" And she didn't say another word all the way back to the ranch.

Seth reviewed his plan in his mind over and over on

the quiet trip back to the ranch. What the hell did she mean it's a 'male thing'? Men weren't moody or grumpy, they didn't withhold physical contact when they got miffed. He was going to have to seriously improve his communication skills or this wasn't going to bode well for his plans. I mean, how can he marry a woman if he can't even get her to talk to him?

CHAPTER 15

Sitting in front of the large desk in the jail house, Seth watched his friend Mason across from him. He wasn't comfortable spilling his guts to his long-time friend but no one at the ranch was in his good graces or he in theirs.

"I mean, you've never felt the need or desire to marry? Right? We're the same age and no one is treating you like you have the plague for staying single." He looked closer and said sharply, "Mason, you're supposed to be my friend. Help me out, here."

Mason gave a grimace saying, "I met Callie while I was there hunting up those rustlers. She was so dedicated to making sure you were going to pull through that bullet wound she gave up everything else to care for you. And the other men, they couldn't say enough about how grand she is about everything. Things she didn't have to help with."

"I know, it's not about that. She is wonderful with the ranch hands and all the things they miss being out on their own. Some of them are just boys in my mind. She has helped them sew and learn to read and write. I know she's wonderful but does that mean I should marry her?"

"Not if you don't love her. I'm a great believer in love in a marriage – and a goodly amount of lust. That's what came between Abby and me. I liked her and she is a great girl but we just didn't have that special feeling between us. We both knew it and now I see her in the street and we stop and talk. I would help her with anything she asked of me but we weren't marriage material."

"See, that's what I'm talking about. You still see her and no one says anything. Why can't that work for Callie and me?" Seth said eagerly.

"Because it was mutually agreed and although she is one of the few single women our age in town, I would never do anything that would make other's think of her in any poor light. She is a friend and only a friend."

"I don't think I can leave Callie alone – not in that way. I really like her," Seth said as if he forgot about his friend sitting across from him.

Mason shook his head in sorrow. "Seth, my friend, you love this girl and you better figure it out. After all, most of the rest of us have. Can you tell me you could watch her walk down the street with some other man? I mean, I found her attractive and she sounds like she is kind and generous. Maybe I should come on out to the ranch and visit with her some night."

Seth looked at his friend through narrowed eyes and said, "If I find you on my ranch with my cook, I'll call you out. I have enough competition with every love-struck cowhand. You - I would really have to worry about."

"Seth, if you feel that strongly about her, you better go over to Abby's and buy a ring because if you don't, someone else is going to."

"You think it has come to that? If I don't 'stake my claim' as Sully puts it there may be other fellas looking to take her on as a wife?"

"Think? Do you know how many unmarried men we have here in town and nearby ranches? I happen across them all the time and one thing they all have in common is that they would much rather be married. Abbey is one of the few unmarried women but it isn't for lack of trying by the men here about. She simply knows what she wants and so far, no one has come up to her standards. I don't think your Callie falls into that same category. I think she wants a family and to her that means a husband first."

Grumpily Seth grouched, "She ain't 'my' Callie. She simply works for me and she hasn't even been here all that long when all's said and done. Why do I need to put a ring on her finger so soon? Why can't I get to know her better?"

Narrowing his eyes, Mason asked, "Do you think you'll like her more or do you think you'll like her less, if you were given more time? Is it time you want or are you trying to have your cake and eat it, too?" Mason shook his head as if facing a losing bet. "I'm simply telling you that men are about to descend onto your ranch once news gets out about her being out there. I think your hands haven't said too much about her so as to keep her as their cook for as long as possible but the Gregg's ranch hands have been spreading the news. Says she baked the best cake they ever saw or tasted for the wedding. I was there so I agree with them. A woman with those kinds of accolades isn't going to stay single for very long, my friend. Time to put up or shut up."

Letting his boots fall off the desk, Seth stomped out without telling his friend goodbye. He was tired of being told what he already knew. His time with his feisty, beautiful ranch cook was coming to an end. If he wanted time to make up his mind about keeping her, he had already had it. Word was out and every randy cowpoke within fifty-miles would be coming a courtin' and keeping his ranch hands' cook occupied when she should be doing other things. Like taking a bath in his six-foot long tub.

Seth was sitting in his office, ignoring his urges to run down to the cookhouse and take Callie in his arms and carry her back up to the ranch house just to be alone with her. He knew he couldn't do it but the urge to do so was still strong.

Opening the outside door to the office, Sully entered without preamble so used to the room being a second home. "Well, boy, what have you been up to today? Missed you around the paddock and the mares were uneasy until you brought Lothario back."

"The mare's do not miss my damn horse when I take him to town. So, what did you really come up here to tell me?"

"I thought maybe you'd like to bounce a few things off me. You know, take advantage of my aged wisdom," Sully said more serious than he wanted to sound.

"You are the last man I should confide in. You're trying to keep us apart."

"No, I'm trying to keep that little girl from running and maybe running into trouble. A girl like that out there on her own can be in harm's way. I won't let that happen no matter what there is between the two of you."

"Hell, I don't want her hurt either. I don't want her to leave and if I could figure out a way to make her stay, I would. I mean, I practically asked her to marry me," Seth finally admitted.

"What do you mean 'practically'. Either you did or you didn't. What is it with you all of a sudden you can't say what you want?" Sully asked completely confused.

"I mentioned marriage and she didn't seem interested."

"In this 'mentioning' did you mention that you loved her?"

"Not exactly but I'm willing to marry her, so isn't that the same thing?"

"I don't know," Sully said sarcastically. "I know she has gotten letters from that St Michaels friend of hers regular like and he's been in town. I think he's just waiting for her to let him know when she's ready to leave with him."

Seth looked up worriedly. "Do you think she'll go with him? I mean, he said as much when he was here but I didn't know he was back."

"He's back and I don't know what the boys and I will do when she leaves us. I don't know what you'll do, either, since I think that you'll wake up one morning and find out you did know how to love. You just didn't know you knew."

"You say that as if it's a done deal. Like she has already made up her mind. She's only been here a few weeks," Seth argued.

"I know that and I'm surprised it happened so fast but I knew it the moment I saw her on that train platform. I knew she was going to be the best cook we ever had and I knew she would be taken up by a good man."

"So, what you're telling me, Sully, is that it's too late? I waited and she's chosen another?"

"No, I don't think she has or that she wants to. She loves you, son, and I know you love her. What you have to do is understand your feelings for her before someone makes the biggest mistake of their life."

Seth spent the rest of the day thinking that Callie's assessment of men being idiots might not be far off the mark. He was an idiot for not making Callie listen to him when he had the chance. Once she got her feet on the ground, he hadn't been able to get her to himself and everyone seemed to be watching him like a hawk. If he didn't know better, he would think they were purposely keeping him from speaking with her alone.

The ranch hands seem to need to speak with Callie or need help with a sewing problem or she was teaching reading or writing every time he went into the cookhouse. It was like having a damn school going all day long. The men were going to have to realize that she had other duties to attend to. She had to spend some time with Seth. But Seth was the only one who understood that.

Finely, after supper one night, Seth stomped into the cookhouse and said loudly, "All of you, out!" The three youngest ranch hands looked at each other for support and each of them failed the other. They all shot an apologetic expression at Callie and grabbed their books hurrying out of the front door, practically trying to squeeze through in mass.

Laying down the book in her hand, Callie turned politely toward where Seth stood. "You wished a word with me, Mr Harrison?" She never called him boss.

"Yes, but not here." He looked pointedly through the windows toward the bunkhouse that now had several of the hands standing on its porch. They were all watching the drama unfold, waiting to see if their Miss Callie was going to need their aid. Seth knew it and Callie knew it. Their unasked-for support made her sit a little straighter and confront Seth head-on.

"If it is not about my job, Mr Harrison, then I do not think we have anything to say to one another," she told him firmly.

"It's not something I want an audience for. Its personal and I want to talk with you alone, personally," he repeated unnecessarily.

"I don't think that is a good idea. We always end up in an argument that has no end. We have to learn to ignore our feelings for each other and go on with our lives. Since this does not seem to have anything to do with my work, I will have to ask you to leave me so I may return to my reading." She leaned to pick up the book.

"Callie, you may be right about doing this in a public place. This way there will be no doubt as to my feelings and no way there can be any miscommunication between us." Then he continued, "All right, it has to do with your work. I'm firing you. You are no longer my employee."

Callie looked up him, hurt and accusation in her eyes. "You said whatever happened between us you wouldn't use it against me. You wouldn't hold my job over my head."

"I'm not. I'm offering you another one, one where you will never feel alone again or be afraid of me or want for anything." Seth dropped down to one knee and took her hand in his. "I'm asking you to marry me. I'm asking you to be my wife."

There was a little enthusiastic yelling from the bunkhouse. Callie heard, "Finally" and "Hooray, he did it!" As the ranch hands returned to the bunkhouse and closed the door, she had trouble focusing on the man right in front of her.

"Oh, Seth, you didn't need to do this. I was getting used to us as we are. I don't want you feeling pushed into marriage by the hands or Sully. I want you to be happy," she said gazing straight into his eyes.

"But this is what I need to be happy. I'm miserable without you. Sully's the only man here that will talk to me voluntarily. The men say I'm worse than a bear with a hang-over." He smiled shyly. "Darlin' if that ain't love, what is?"

"Oh, Seth, I think there's more to it than that," she said quietly.

"There is, but I think I aired my personal feelings enough for the time being. I know I don't show it sometimes and I don't know how to explain it, but I love you. I'll spend the rest of our lives proving it to you, if you'll let me," he told her earnestly.

Callie leaned forward and rested her head against his forehead whispering, "I have prayed for this moment. When we were as one in mind and spirit and I am afraid it will be crushed as it has been in the past." One small tear rolled down her cheek with others brimming in her eyes waiting their turn.

"It took a couple of smarter men than me to show me I have loved you from the first time I caught you in my arms. I was just too stupid to put a name to it. No one told me about love, not any kind of love. I thought I knew what it was but I just knew about lust and that scared me. I knew that lust fades but with you I loved first then lusted. If the lust is gonna' fade, it won't be for the next couple of decades or so. But the love will just keep getting stronger. Do you understand what I'm trying to say? Do you understand that I know love now? I want everyone to know I love you and that I'm a better man for your loving me in return. You still love me, right?"

"Yes, I still love you. Love is not something that stops and starts on a whim. Once you love someone, they are always part of your heart. I will always love you," she pledged.

"And you'll marry me? You want to be my wife?" Seth almost pleaded.

"Yes. And yes. Always." She sank onto her knees to welcome his caresses and kisses. Seth slipped the ring onto her finger to claim her as his own.

Seth had extinguished the lamps and sat with his legs stretched out in front of him. Callie sat crosswise on his lap with her arms around his neck and her face snuggled into his chest. "I don't want you to leave me but I know you're tired and I have to make breakfast in the morning," she whispered into his shirt.

"Let 'em starve for all I care. Why don't you go and get some of that sweet smellin' soap and we'll go and have a bath," he growled into her ear.

"Oh, Seth, as inviting as that sounds I don't think there is a ranch hand out there who isn't listening for you to go up to the house - alone so that they can get to sleep. I think they all took an oath to protect my honor and they are taking it seriously," she answered him with a smile in her voice.

"My own damn fault. I told them to watch out for you while I was gone but I didn't tell them to stop when I got back." Nuzzling her hair one last time, he swung her to her feet.

"I could make a lot of noise leaving and then sneak back in here later, while you're in bed." He tried to kiss her into submission.

Shaking her head slowly, she said, "I do not think that is a good idea. You will get the nuns all up into my mind and then neither of us will get what we want."

"Okay, but plan on one more for breakfast." He gave her one last kiss on the lips before leaving.

Her comment of, "I'm counting on it." hung in the air behind him.

CHAPTER 16

Callie stared into the long mirror in the corner of the room that would be hers from today on, hers and Seth's. It seemed surreal. Less than five weeks ago she had been a wide-eyed young woman getting off the train in Sweetwater excited to start a new job at Harrison ranch. Now she was starting a whole new life. So much change in such a short time.

Her regret was that Matthew wouldn't be able to be at the wedding. She knew there was no way the letter she sent would reach him since he was on the road and wouldn't be home to the City of Kansas for another week or more. That was all right. She knew he would wish her well. When he was here, he had almost given her his blessing if she decided to marry Seth. Evidently, he could see something was there between her and Seth before either of them had.

She smoothed the lace that bordered the small pearl buttons down the front of the dress Abby had sewn for her in time for the wedding. The pretty, little cream shoes peeped out from the scalloped hem that showed an under dress of white and pink stripes. Instead of clashing with her 'red' hair, the pink trim made Callie's skin glow.

Callie was very happy with her dress and little box-like hat with its white bird sitting in a nest of white netting veil, made just for her by Jamie with the help of the Harrison ranch chickens.

The dress with its short-waisted jacket had hung in the armoire next to two others Seth had ordered right after their trip to town. Abby had remembered every item

163

Callie had admired and every fabric she had dreamed over. So, when the boxes and packages arrived from town, Callie was charmed by the elegant style of the dresses and touched by the thoughtfulness Abby put into each of the articles.

She was also touched by Seth's wanting to please her. To make up for what he considered his personal short-comings. To Callie, he was perfect and had nothing to compensate for. Seth had been alone for so much of his life he didn't realize that the love he knew when he was young was still there inside him. Callie was going to help him realize how strong his love was and how to show it to others when he needed to. Love wasn't a weakness – it was a strength. Many people lived their whole lives without knowing it but Seth wouldn't be one of them.

Pulling on the cream lace gloves, she picked up the little beaded reticule and took one last look in the mirror. The last time she would see herself as an unmarried lady.

Sully drove the buggy up to the ranch house and then helped Callie onto the front seat. He handed her a bouquet of white and pink flowers, some roses, of course, with white and pink ribbons hanging down. He was dressed in a suit jacket over a vest and ironed shirt. She realized it was the first time seeing him in anything besides denim trousers with suspenders and plaid shirt. Sully climbed up into the buggy seat and looked once more at Callie.

"Callie child, if I had a daughter, I would have wanted her to look just like you." He picked up the reins, made a clicking sound, and the horses moved toward the gate.

The hands and Jamie had ridden off to town earlier. By waiting, Callie wouldn't end up riding in the dust stirred up by the horses and Seth wanted to be to the church in time to see to the last-minute details.

The church was on the closest side of town and it didn't seem to take any time at all. Callie was nervous and excited and hopeful. Seth had made a promise and they were about to make those same promises and vows in front of God.

Sully was to walk Callie down the aisle and turn her over to Seth, much like he had those few short weeks ago. Callie looked at the front of the church to see Reverend Walters and Maria's nephew, Father Manuel, who had been recruited to perform a Catholic ceremony. The good Father had been out to the ranch to take Callie's confession earlier that morning.

Then she saw Seth dressed in a suit with white shirt and black tie, standing to the side and looking so loving Callie's heart tightened in her breast. Sully led her towards the man she loved and turned her over to Seth at the minister's instruction. Callie hadn't even noticed Abby standing there ready to take the bouquet from her or Jamie standing up as Seth's best man.

She only had eyes for Seth. Her husband to be, the man who woke her from a girl to a woman, the man who had Callie making plans for the next ten, twenty, thirty years, had her full attention. Her eyes roamed over his features as she made a mental picture of him so that she would remember this day forever. The man, who now she had met him, she couldn't remember how she had lived before knowing him.

Reverend Walters proceeded with the ceremony and then Father Manuel administered the sacrament and performed part of the Catholic service. The few wedding attendees, the ranch hands and Maria and her husband, sat quietly and prayed when asked to and responded when they were able.

Since the Catholic service was shortened, the total time for the ceremony was soon over. Seth gave his bride the much-awaited kiss. The look of total love in his eyes made up for all the pain and misunderstanding that brought them to this point. The newly married couple walked down the aisle as the guests threw rice and good wishes after them.

Seth, laughing at some of the comments that seemed to be getting a little too graphic, announced, "I am taking my wife home. I do not expect to see or hear from any of you. Jamie knows where the champagne is and will set out some food for you all to enjoy in celebration. As for Callie and me, we will celebrate alone and will see you in a week."

Slapping the reins lightly on the horses' rumps, the team took off at a fair pace taking them home to Harrison ranch.

Seth removed Callie's wedding dress, taking each pearl button carefully and un-doing it so that more and more of the muslin under dress showed. He pulled it off over her head only to be faced with the underdress which he pulled up over her head, too. Then he found a short corset trimmed with pink ribbon and he said, "Hmm, this is new. Something Abby felt you just couldn't do without, I take it?"

Callie said shyly, "She seemed to think I needed a little, lift, push up…"

"She thought you needed something to lift up your

beautiful breasts? I think she's crazy. Your breasts are just perfect. A little large for your body but then I'm not complaining."

Callie stood there in her stockings and camisole, again new and trimmed with pink. Prettier than anything she had ever owned before.

"Now here we are again." She splayed her hand open and made a wave over the big copper tub, wooden bench and handpump. "I am almost naked and you are fully clothed. Now this cannot be right. This isn't how it's done, is it?"

Seth laughed saying, "No, you're right. We should both be in the same state of undress. You may help at any time."

He unwrapped the tie from around his neck and was shrugging out of the tailored coat and vest. He heeled off the short dress boots that would have had Matt jealous and put his hands to the buttons at his waist.

She laughed. saying, "Well, that didn't take long. I'll have to learn to speak up more often." She looked at him still in his shirt, now unbuttoned and trousers undone while he bent to pull off his socks by their toe.

Pulling the ties loose on her corset, Callie could soon remove it and pulled her camisole over her head. Seth stopped in mid hop of removing his last sock and his mouth went dry. "Oh, Callie, I have a good imagination but I never imagined you could be so beautiful."

Callie smiled shyly. "You have seen me without clothes before. We were even in this room."

"No, the bath water hid most of your attributes, believe me. You are breath taking and I am the luckiest son of a bi…." With that he tore off what few items of clothing he was still wearing.

Callie turned toward the tub and sat on the edge then swiveled to lower herself into the warm water. A second later, she felt Seth enter the tub and slide down behind her, his legs sliding past on both sides.

"This is what I wanted to do last time but we weren't at that point yet," he whispered into her neck as he wrapped his long arms around her and cupped each breast.

Laying back onto him, Callie enjoyed his body as it slid against her in the silky water. Seth took the little sponge again and soaped it and began washing the rosy tipped breasts barely peeking out of the sudsy water. After thoroughly washing her breasts, Seth's hands and sponge disappeared beneath the water and found the intimate areas that had brought such a pleasurable experience the last time.

Seth was breathing quickly but so was Callie. He had only been able to kiss her neck and ears and was frustrated in his inability to really make love to Callie as he wanted.

"Darlin', we're gonna' dry you off and I'm gonna' continue this session in our bed." He helped Callie dry off with a warm, soft towel. Then quickly dried himself and wrapped a towel around his waist and another around Callie's body. Lifting her into his arms, he carried her up the front stairs and into his bedroom that they would now share. He set her down on her feet and Callie looked at the big bed with new eyes.

Seth unwrapped her towel and opened the bed, folding the blankets back as he placed Callie on the cool sheets. She enjoyed the smooth feel against her heated skin, which was still singing from Seth's ministrations in the bath.

"Is this part of it?" she asked.

Seth pulled his towel off and lay down beside Callie. "Yes, this is part of it," he answered patiently. "Some of the best part."

Leaning over her, he covered her lips with his mouth, sucking lightly and coaxing her lips apart. He sent his tongue into the moist opening and danced with hers. Seth's hand was cupping and kneading one of Callie's breast and then he lowered his head and took the other nipple into his mouth.

Callie arched with the desire that shot through her. She wrapped her arm around and cradled his head as he drove her to new heights of wanting, not even knowing what it was she craved. Just knowing she wanted him closer, his weight on top of her, his body close to hers.

Giving a final kiss to the pouting nipple, he slid further down Callie's body kissing his way, subtly licking secret spots until he found his way to the downy cover of her feminine mound. He felt Callie stiffen as he kissed her and quieted her by stroking her breast and then finding the moist center of her being. Seth moaned and sunk his tongue deeper, becoming one with her in the most cherished way. Enjoying being this intimate with Callie escalated Seth's desire to almost breaking point. He had never done this with any other woman, never wanted to, but with Callie he wanted this experience. He wanted her to have this, to enjoy this moment with him. It was his gift to her.

Seth continued rubbing his tongue against the nubbin he found there and as it increased in size, Callie's lifting of her pelvis, her arching into him increased in intensity. Callie had her hands in Seth's hair, pulling him into her. Putting his hand between her legs, he added stroking with his fingers to her fulfillment. Loving her with all his being, he wanted to bring that expression of amazement to her face again.

He needed her to reach her peak while he was so close to her. He felt a subtle change in her, the tensing and stiffening of muscles that clenched around his fingers and then the shuddering of the aftermath spasms as he slid his fingers into the smooth female channel one last time.

Callie was still trying to catch her breath when Seth returned to kissing one breast and stroking the other, loving the soft feel of it against his palm.

"Was that part of it?" Callie asked.

Seth answered between kisses, "It is now." And continued the attention to her breasts he was stroking with his tongue.

Pulling Callie into his side, Seth stroked her hair. "Come on, Darlin', you need to sleep." Callie snuggled against Seth but didn't close her eyes.

She said quietly, knowing he wasn't asleep, "That's not all of it. There is more. Something to do with your…your manhood."

"My manhood is just fine. Now relax and go to sleep," he answered sleepily.

"Seth, you are not telling me something - something important," she accused. "There is more. We are to become as one. We join our bodies, making as one a wife and a husband. Why don't you want to make me your wife? Did I do something wrong?" she asked with a catch in her voice.

"It's not anything you did. You're perfect and I feel like the luckiest man in the world," he prevaricated.

"I know there is more to making love. I know it is supposed to hurt the first time for the woman and I know we are supposed to join together."

"Look at you, Darlin', you're small and beautiful and perfect. I'm not. I'm afraid of hurting you, really hurting you if I, we, fit together. I'm too big for you, I didn't think about it before. I didn't see myself up against you but I don't think we should go further," he tried to explain his fear. He didn't want to hurt her. He would rather remain celibate than cause her an injury.

Callie thought about what he said. She looked down between them and realized to what he was referring. It was the first time she had seen a male member in full erection. He did look huge. At least in comparison and a little fission of fear went through her thinking of him inserting something that large into her.

"A stallion is much bigger than a mare, right? Yet they fit together. God would not have said that husband and wife is as one if it wasn't possible. I don't think we are a mistake. I don't think God makes mistakes." Callie allowed a few minutes for her words to sink in. "Make love to me. I will tell you if you hurt me and we will figure something else out," she said emphatically.

He began to deny her but then Callie said, "Please Seth. Make me your wife. Help me."

Seth lay over Callie supporting his weight on his arms and Callie spread her legs to give him access to the womanliest part of her. Pushing slowly into the tight opening, he waited for Callie's cry for him to stop. She didn't cry out.

Feeling a small resistance, Seth stopped worried he would hurt her. Callie put her hands on his backside and pulled him into her. Suddenly he was up to his hilt in his wife. And then she was moving, undulating, trying to urge him to pull out and push in following the ancient rhythm of making love.

"You're really, all right?" he asked in her ear.

"I am fine. I cannot explain how much I love feeling you in me. This is better than anything we have done so far. I am going to love making love."

She began a series of little moans that built and he felt the same muscles enclosing his engorged member that had tightened on his hand. Callie stiffening with another orgasm sent Seth spiraling into the strongest climax he had ever had.

"Oh, Darlin', I told you not to moan. It totally un-mans me." He kissed her till she fell asleep.

Seth looked up at the bedroom ceiling, his heartbeat finally back to normal and feeling completely drained. He had dreamed of lying beside her, kissing her unheeded by clothing and interruptions. He wanted to savor the reality. He'd sleep when he got used to having Callie with him all night long.

Now, after being part of that emotion of well-being, of being carried along as it swelled to a peak and then broke against the tide of sensations, Seth knew he had been made for Callie and her for him. It wasn't a mistake that she had been sent to Harrison ranch, it wasn't a mistake that he had been attracted to her from the first time he saw her and it wasn't a mistake that she was in his arms right now satiated with his loving her.

Callie woke up snuggled against Seth's chest. She felt a little shy, but after starting to remember all the personal and intimate things they had done, gave a secret smile. She was now a very married woman and so happy. And curious.

Last night she had been too wrapped up in the sensations and desires that Seth created in her to think or question what her part should be. She thought she may have been disappointing, not enough of a participant. It seemed the whole night had Seth giving and her receiving and she didn't think that lovemaking should be all one sided, but what was she supposed to do exactly?

She enjoyed looking at Seth naked, his arousal last night somewhat intimidating but not frightening. And the feelings it provoked made her shiver merely thinking about them. Delicious might be a good word for them. She certainly wanted to repeat the procedure only this time paying more attention to Seth and what he needed or liked.

Looking at her still sleeping husband, Callie placed little kisses along his chin and jaw with their raspy stubble. She let her hands roam over his chest, covered with a nest of masculine fur. She found he was a sensual paradise as she felt his male nipples pebble hard with her discovery.

Becoming braver, she spread her hand lightly over his manhood and innocently felt up and down the hardening shaft but was most intrigued with the soft velvety crown. What a contradiction in one male appendage.

Seth murmured with an early morning raspy voice, "Darlin' you're playing with fire. I planned on letting you recover before we, ahh, sinned again."

Callie smiled, pushing her breast into him, asking, "What if I want to sin again? Besides we are married and it isn't a sin, in fact, it would be more of sin if we didn't."

"Darlin' you make me want to thank those nuns for bringing you up Catholic." He pulled her over him so she was resting on top of his chest with her head against his heart.

"Seth? Husband? Can't we make love again? It was the most earth-shattering experience, really. I felt filled with you and with your love." She was making little circles with her finger in his chest hair as she spoke.

He clasped her hand tightly to his body. "God woman, I'm only human. I really thought we should wait. I can keep my hands off you, I think, but not if you keep tempting me. You must be sore."

"My breasts may be a little sore but I think the rest of me is just fine." And she squirmed to get her feminine mound in touch with his now fully aroused member.

"According to those nuns of yours, I can't say 'no'. Ain't that right?" At her murmured agreement, he rolled Callie under him and began to kiss her neck and mouth thoroughly.

The second loving coupling was easier than the first and more than satisfying. Callie had taken some time to touch and encourage Seth to let her know what he liked, which was pretty much everything. But Callie was beginning to note a hitch in his breathing when something in particular caught his attention and she worked on repeating those things. This making love was going to be a lot more fun than either one of them realized.

EPILOGUE

Callie stood by the kitchen doorway of her home looking over the Christmas Eve party that was going to be an annual event from now on at the ranch. She felt her heart swell simply knowing all these people touched her life and made it better in some way. All the ranch hands and their unwavering trust in her ability as their cook and teacher. Ben and Julia Gregg, for their friendly welcome to the community, Maria and Carlos for all their help around the house and Abby who introduced her to beautiful new clothes and style. Reverend Walters for being there during the wedding. Father Manuel had to hold mass at the mission but had blessed the group earlier before he left. Jamie for opening her eyes to the wonder of childhood again and, of course, Matthew, her lifelong friend and confidant.

The decorated tree was beautiful. Seth had cut it down and Jamie and she had decorated it. Of course, there were little feathered birds on almost every branch adorned with red ribbons. The fireplace was garlanded as was the stair rail and the entire house smelled of cinnamon and nutmeg.

Callie's eye swept the room stopping on her good friend Julia and the pronounced bump heralding a new generation and a smile formed on Callie's lips. Next year at this time Callie would have a small bundle to hold, as well, and their two children would grow up as close friends. She still had to inform Seth but she knew he would be happy and excited and scared. All good things considering the newness of all this family business to him.

The dining room table was covered with the good food Maria, Jamie and Callie had prepared. Candelabra with multiple candles graced each end of the table and between were petit fore' frosted and decorated with a pink rose, candied walnut meats, pecan tartlets, small powdered cookies, along with savory cheese sticks, pickled herring, Stilton cheese, and fruitcake with a brandied raisin sauce. Callie's traditional egg nod was present as well as an added Sangria which Seth had insisted upon.

The table practically groaned with the variety of food that the three had considered necessary to their guests' enjoyment. It did not seem to be the wrong approach to having a happy relaxed gathering.

Seth stood by the fireplace looking over the Christmas Eve party that was a first for this house. His heart swelled simply knowing all these people touched his life and made it better in some way. Mostly, though, his attention focused on Callie. She was in her element having decorated the house bringing in more greenery than an atrium.

She had been baking and cooking enticing edible delights for days. The house smelling of peppermint, cinnamon, nutmeg, wintergreen, and chocolate – it had been a myriad of scents for the past week.

But for him, Callie's scent stood out as vanilla, spice and warm, inviting woman. Seth was waiting for his little mare to inform him of the most important change in their life. He didn't know if he was ready to be a father but with Callie as a mother, his child would be blessed.

The two hosts of the party drew closer together without a conscious thought. They were soon side-by-side and Callie smiled up into the face of the handsome cowboy who stole her heart. Seth smiled down at the woman who showed him what love is and they both thanked God for their good luck in finding one another in this big western territory.

Macgregor's Mail Order Bride

SWEETWATER, KANSAS 1874

CHAPTER 1

Mavis Miller refolded the letter for the final time - she promised herself. Gazing guiltily into her companion's face, she said, "I know. It doesn't change anything. We've made our decision. We've been on this train for days and could have gotten off at any town and taken a train back to where we started."

Emily Johnston, her confidante, was a pretty, young woman much the same age with calm grey eyes and light brown hair pulled into a neat bun. "Mavis, dear, you know it's simply nerves getting to you as we get closer to Sweetwater. If you and Mr Macgregor do not suit, we will return to Chicago and try again." At Mavis's stricken look, she amended, "Possibly I'll try it next time. Don't worry, you won't need to make a decision directly upon arrival. Mr Macgregor wrote that he would give you ample time to decide. He sounds reasonable and mature and steady."

These were the same arguments Emily had used when they had discussed the various letters sent in reply to their advertisement for a husband. Whichever one of them found a letter from a gentleman they thought was exceptionally appealing then that was the man they would pursue. The two women were very satisfied with their choice. That is until they quit their jobs, let their room go, and got on the train that would take them to Sweetwater, Kansas.

Emily bent toward her friend patting the hand holding the letter. "Now put that away and enjoy the trip.

I, for one, have never been on a train or out of the city in my life. I'm getting two dreams fulfilled at once." She smiled warmly at her friend of three years.

"I'm sorry, you're right. Mr Macgregor seems like a fine man and it is simply nerves. I mean, what if he is disappointed with me? He could tell us to get back on the train at first sight," Mavis said worriedly.

"I don't think that's a possibility. After all, he sent the money for both our tickets. It was even his idea to send enough for round trips to ease any concerns we might have about being stranded in Sweetwater. A man who thinks of relieving our possible fears has to be as considerate in other matters." Both women nodded together understanding the meaning behind the words.

Mavis put on a strained smile to reassure Emily she felt everything would be fine but she knew Emily wasn't fooled. Then she went back to worrying about their future.

The train pulled into the depot in Sweetwater and the young women searched about their seats to make sure they had left nothing behind. Looking at one another, they squared their shoulders, and walked pointedly toward the steps as brave as any soldier going off to war.

Mac Macgregor waited impatiently for the train to disgorge its passengers and baggage making their last stop Sweetwater. His long hair and bushy beard tugged in the slight breeze relieving the day of some of its heat. Green eyes searched the platform for two women dressed in city clothes and then he spotted them. He took a couple of minutes to look them over before approaching them.

The women were similar in size, with the brunette being a little taller but both shapely. The brunette had her back to him, shiny curls cascading from under her hat and a maroon colored dress, which even he could tell was very fashionable. As smart as any Abby would have in the front window of her dress shop in town.

The second woman was facing him. Her face was lit with a smile and the dress, a golden peach color, was more stylish than most women wore around here but with less fussiness than the brunette's. And both of them had hats that were more feathers than head covering. Mac took a deep breath stepping up onto the platform and heading toward the two women.

"Mrs Miller? Mrs Johnston?" he asked in that deep rumbling voice that had most people looking at him warily. The same look the two women in front of him had on their faces. "I'm, Mac. I mean, Joseph Macgregor. I've come to pick you up and take you out to the ranch. Can I take your bags?" He held out his beefy hands to take the cloth bags they both clutched to their breasts.

"Thank you. I'm Emily Johnston and this is, Mavis Miller." Emily felt she had to make the distinction early on. She smiled and gave Mavis's sleeve a little tug to get Mavis's feet moving and then they followed the big man to a buckboard at the end of the platform.

Mac helped both women unto the wagon's bench and went to collect the trunks that held everything the two women owned in the world. He lifted the largest one up onto his brawny shoulder and grabbed another that he tucked under his other arm and strode toward the buckboard. Then returned for the last two cases.

Emily took this time to note not only Mac's height but the length of his legs incased in the blue denim trousers tucked into scuffed work boots. A wide leather belt with brass buckle encompassed his lean waist. His shirt was plain white long-sleeve but the Stetson he wore with panache.

Climbing onto the seat, the buckboard suddenly seemed small. He snapped the reins and the team was on its way. They rode right through the main street of town, which was larger than either woman had expected. Emily noticed the dress shop and nudged Mavis to make sure she had seen the windows filled with highly styled hats and accessories. Opposite there was a mercantile as well as a dry goods store, both of good size. Most had two stories and it appeared as if there were rooms or apartments above them. Emily thought they would find something of interest in all of the stores and looked forward to returning to town. The plan was that once Mavis was settled, then Emily would find work until, she too, found a husband.

Mr Macgregor, or rather, Mac had described it as small with a few stores but nothing like they had in Chicago, even after the Great Fire. Not that they had money to spend in all those stores in Chicago, anyway. They barely had enough extra money to pay for the newspaper advertisement looking for a husband and the postage for the letters sent after finding one interesting enough to write back to.

They passed the last house in town and the neat white church with a bell tower and well-maintained cemetery. Then it was open land, a few trees lined the road giving them shade as they passed but otherwise there wasn't much else to stimulate conversation among the three people.

Mavis was still frozen in place, an expression close to terror on her face. Since Mavis was between Mac and herself, Emily didn't see how she could help a conversation proceed so it was up to Mavis to hold her own with her intended. She would need to learn to talk to the man at some point.

Instead, Emily took the time to think now they had met, Mac. The man wasn't anything like she thought he would be which meant Mavis was thinking the same.

Emily hadn't imagined Mac would be so large - all over, big hands, big feet, and big fuzzy red beard! A red head? And what a mane of hair, red, there is no other name for it and curly. It would be adorable on a young boy but on such a masculine male, it was incongruous. Then there was that orange, almost glowing mustache and full beard billowing out from his face, practically hiding his eyes. What was the man thinking? Didn't he look in the mirror each morning? Emily smiled at the thought when she realized that without shaving, he had no need to look into a mirror.

Deciding she had worried about Mavis's fiancé long enough, she inhaled deeply then leaned back to enjoy the openness of the terrain. She gazed at the green fields with grass tall enough to wave in the breeze, dotted by trees, signs of blue bells and several other spring flowers growing alongside the road. Emily hoped that she would have time to collect some on walks. She planned on leaving the two other people alone to get to know one another as often as possible. Even though Mac had given Mavis as much time as it took to become comfortable with him, Emily knew any man had his limits. A month at most would be needed for Mavis to build up the courage to marry the man she had agreed was the right one from the others who had written to them.

Mavis kept running conversations through her mind that she should be having between Mac and herself.

Questions she thought she should ask faded as soon as she thought of them. Bouncing on a buckboard seat wasn't the best time to hold an important conversation that would influence the rest of their lives. She couldn't even talk with Emily because anything she said could be heard by Mac and if not, it would seem impolite to have a conversation he was unable to contribute to. He might even think they were speaking about him and she didn't want that either.

Mavis didn't notice the scenery as they passed it or Mac's easy manner handling the team or his bright green eyes that darted towards her, as they must be getting closer and closer to his home. Her new home but she didn't want to think about that right now either.

How did she explain that she wasn't usually this tongue-tied? That she usually had interesting and bright conversations with anyone she met? That she really wanted to get to know him so she could accept his proposal fully? How did she find herself in this position?

It was a redundant question even to herself. She knew why she had thought sending out an advert for a prospective groom seemed like a good idea. She needed to move on with her life and to do that she needed to be married once again. A married woman had so many more options, so many more ways to be content. She wanted that again. And as Emily had convinced her, Mavis deserved to have it again.

Mac looked over the heads of the team of horses and thought about the two women sitting beside him on the buckboard seat. They each sat straight and held their heads high. Their cute little hats with the lifelike birds bobbed every time the wagon hit a rut that had hardened into a ridge. Their small lace gloved hands clasped together in their laps held attractive cloth reticules. He would have accepted either of them although his intended was the more attractive and better dresser of the two. Even so, the other was pretty in her own right and seemed very proper. A good indication his prospective bride was of the same nature.

Earlier, Mac had been regretting ever letting his younger brother, Jamie, talk him into this but after meeting Mavis maybe it was going to turn out all right. After all, mail order brides have been coming west for years and this was similar. Only he had replied to her advertisement.

Heck he had put his best foot forward in every letter, letting Jamie read them to make sure there wasn't anything in it that might scare off the woman. Mac knew that communication wasn't his strong suit and allowed himself to be guided by Jamie. At thirty-three, all three of Mac's younger brothers thought it was beyond time for him to get married. That and the fact they all thought him grumpy and felt a female would be a soothing influence.

Mac thought it was just time to start a family and Mavis had already been proven fertile. She had lost both her husband and young son during a diphtheria outbreak a few years back and felt she could now remarry. This marriage was her chance to have a family again. They would both benefit from their union and that's why Mac had agreed to sending the money for the tickets. Mrs Johnston accompanying Mavis was fine with him. It actually showed Mac that Mavis was smart to protect herself from a possible scoundrel preying on women putting advertisements in the newspapers.

He was pleased with the agreement so far. Mavis

seemed pleasant if a bit shy, and Mrs Johnston was protective of Mavis, and he liked that about her. Mac smiled with the good deal he thought he had made. The only problem was his beard was so thick no one could tell.

Mac growled out that the next ranch they saw would be his and the women sat up leaning forward as if to see the first glimpse of their future home. At least for Mavis. It was still to be decided where Emily would end up.

When the ranch house came into view both women's mouth dropped open. It was beautiful. Everything about it was beautiful. The house appeared to glow as the sun began to set. The windows of both stories reflected the rays making it appear as if there was a welcoming lamp waiting in every room.

The large two-story ranch house had a porch wrapping around two sides of the structure, furniture spread out over the painted deck. The front door was off center and painted a bright welcoming green, as was the rest of the trim with the main portion of the house a deep tan. A large stone chimney ran up the far side of the house with another near the rear indicating a well-heated comfortable home. Both women were excited to see the interior. The well-kept yard surrounding the house boded well there would be beauty inside.

Helping the women down from the buckboard, Mac allowed each to climb the four steps to the porch. Mac's long strides got him to the front door first as he swung the wide door open and waved the women inside. He was worried they would find fault with his home since they had lived in the big city their entire lives. He knew his was more countryfied and made comfortable for a bachelor household of him and his three brothers even though two were still away at university. They returned at certain times of the year. This had all been explained in his letters and Mavis seemed fine with them living with them after she and Mac were married. She even said it would be nice to have a ready-made family and Mac took that as a good sign. His brothers were important to him and this had been their home. He didn't want it to become a conflict between him and his new wife or her and his brothers.

Mavis took a few steps in followed by Emily. Their gazes roamed over the long leather sofa and the four other large chairs sitting on an Aubusson silk rug. Some heavily carved tables holding various painted globe oil lamps were set about the expansive room. The large stone hearth and beam mantle took up one full wall. Antlers from various animals were dotted across the stone but not in an abundance. They seemed right against the roughness of the native material. It was all natural and part of the life out west.

An archway led into a formal dining room and the woman continued through a swing door leading to the large kitchen with a table and chairs to seat ten. The bare windows opened out to the covered porch and there was a door accessing the rear yard. The kitchen was clean if a little cluttered and there was a delicious aroma rising from the oven.

Mac said, "I made some supper since I thought you might be hungry when you got here. I'll show you to your rooms upstairs and then I'll get the table ready."

He turned and strode across the dining room and living areas to the front hall eating up the space easily while the women hurried to keep pace with him. They caught up with him on the upper floor standing in front of a clean neat bedroom with a beautifully handmade quilt consisting of pink and white materials.

"There's this one and the room directly across from it. You can decide which one each of you wants. I'll have supper on in half hour or so." He left them alone as each woman searched the other's expression for confirmation.

'You don't need to go to so much trouble. I can handle supper or help with the table," said Emily.

It seemed his green eyes burned through her when he looked directly at her but she wasn't aware of any animosity with the gaze. Just an intenseness that must be part of the man's make-up. She remained gazing back at him waiting for his response.

"You're guests. I'll get supper." Then he left without another word being spoken.

Mavis pulled the hatpin out and set the pretty straw hat with the little brown bird and spring flowers on the top of the dresser. "Well, what do you think?" she asked worriedly.

"I think it's too soon to make up your mind about anything. We're both tired and there's been no time to get a true sense of the man, really." Warily, Emily asked, "Do you have an opinion of him?"

"No, no you're right. It's much too soon to make up my mind one-way or the other. Now let's go downstairs and test out what kind of a cook he is." She put her arm through Emily's as Emily left her hat alongside Mavis's.

Supper was as quiet an affair as the trip from town had been. Emily kept trying to draw Mac out by asking questions, which probably sounded banal to Mac, simply to get him to open his mouth for any other reason than to put a spoonful of stew into it. Not that he ignored the two women or that he was actually rude in any way but he was definitely a man of few words.

The two women offered to clean up but Mac turned them down and told them to go and settle in. Which of course meant the two women would go upstairs and talk over their day and fears in one of their bedrooms.

CHAPTER 2

Emily had heard Mac get up earlier and then clanking in the kitchen as the stove was stirred to life. Finally, unable to wait any longer for Mavis, she tapped quietly on her door. Emily didn't want to be the one to greet Mac feeling Mavis should meet her potential husband first this morning. Emily would try to give them as much privacy as possible so they learned more about each other without a third party getting in the way.

Mavis came to the door without opening it, asking, "Who is it?"

"It's me, Mavis. Did you get any sleep? You sound terrible."

At that, Mavis opened the door looking a little pale with dark shadows under her eyes. "You know how to build up a girl's self-confidence, don't you?"

"I told you to give it time last night. You were already tired from the train trip and then you just expect to find all the answers in one day. Go back and rest, and stop fretting," Emily told her friend. "I can keep myself occupied and explain things to Mac. About how excited you are and how difficult it was to get to sleep after meeting him and seeing this beautiful ranch house."

Emily could find no way around it. She would need to face Mac and explain that his intended wasn't feeling well after her trip yesterday. She couldn't tell him Mavis was a slug-a-bed or that she had stayed up all night worrying. Emily would simply need to keep him occupied until Mavis felt better. Brushing her hands down her neat shirtwaist and plaid skirt, she took a deep breath before descending to the main floor.

Emily pasted on her friendly meet-the-bear-in-the-morning smile and entered the kitchen to see Mac bent over removing a pan from the oven. He did fill out a pair of trousers well and his feet were just in socks making him appear very much a homebody. The man turned around and Emily's breath caught in her throat.

He was tall and broad like Mac but there the resemblance ended. His hair was auburn, and cut short on the sides and left to wave on top. Startling blue eyes twinkled and a smile bookended by dimples were prominent on a clean-shaven face with a cleft in the strong chin. It was what Emily thought of as an open face, no subterfuge or deception, and she found it very attractive. He stood facing her in his stocking feet, which she found attractive, too.

Smiling widely, he said, "Welcome, I'm Jamie and you would be…?"

"Emily, Emily Johnston. It is nice to meet you. Are you cooking breakfast?" she asked trying to calm her erratic heartbeats. Her face felt warm and she hoped she wasn't looking as bemused as she felt. This had to be one of the bachelor brothers Mac wrote of sharing the house with.

"We alternate cooking duties and try to make things like stews or soups that will hold if one of us is late. It works out and there is always cheese and crackers to fall back on. I won't lie to you. We burn a few meals but the house airs out after a day or two." He smiled that dazzling white-toothed smile with the dimple quotation marks.

Emily laughed as he meant her to and then offered, "I was a hotel cook back in Chicago. Nothing big and important but we had twenty rooms and it was treated like a boarding house with breakfast and dinner included. It was open to the public so we had the occasional drop in customers as well. I found I actually missed it while we traveled by train here."

"I couldn't ask you to do that, Mrs Johnston. You're a guest after all," he began trying to be polite although she could tell it wouldn't take much to sway him into allowing her to cook. At least the meals he was usually responsible for.

"It really wouldn't be a problem. I am used to working sixty or more hours a week. I'll get fat and lazy if I don't have something to do while I'm here."

Her comment had Jamie looking over her body from foot to head, which wasn't her intention. Emily often opened her mouth before thinking how it was going to sound to others.

Blushing, she heard him respond, "I don't think that you could ever get fat or lazy." Then he turned to the stove just in time to keep the eggs from burning.

Emily pointed to the back door saying, "I, um, I'll be right back." She headed for the privy wishing her fair skin didn't respond to a blush so hotly.

When she returned, Mac was sitting at one end of the long table and there were two place settings to the right of him and one to the left. The food was served family style and Jamie remained standing to seat Emily before walking around to his own chair. Mac handed Emily the basket of biscuits and pointed to the honey in the center of the table along with the butter and salt.

Feeling she needed to explain why she was the only guest at the table, said, "Mavis is a little tired after our trip and apologizes for missing breakfast."

Surprisingly Mac responded, "Long trips take a lot

out of you. I hope she feels better by dinner." Then went back to concentrating on his meal, sopping up the egg yolks with half a biscuit before popping it into the space through his beard which appeared when the man opened his mouth.

Emily was hoping Mavis could accept Mac as he was for her sake because Emily didn't think he was capable of changing at this point in his life. They finished eating and Mac stood when Emily asked to be excused but not out of politeness.

Turning, he said as he was leaving the room, "I'll see you all at dinner. Have a good day." Then grabbed a Stetson off the hook by the door, shoved his feet into his boots and went outside.

Emily leaned over stacking the plates and then grabbed the coffee cups almost clearing the table in one trip. Jamie looked impressed and went to clear the rest while Emily took the dirty dishes to the sink. There was hot water in a reservoir on the back of the stove and a handpump on the end of the sink. It was efficient and well thought out for anyone needing to work there.

Emily would make short shift of these dishes. She shooed Jamie off to his daily jobs and said she would prepare dinner, which he leaped at since it evidently was his day to cook the meals. On his way out, he told her he had planned on ham so Emily let herself into the storeroom to see what else was available.

Mavis came down halfway through the morning. She had fallen back to sleep after speaking with Emily but there were dreams, or nightmares, that weighed heavily on her mind. She found Emily in the kitchen, which has always been Emily's safe domain.

"Is there any tea? I think I would kill for a cup of

tea," Mavis said as she sat down at the table.

Emily stopped wiping down the counter area saying, "I'm sorry. I looked because I knew you would need a cup but it will have to be coffee. How about I add a lot of sugar and cream. Will that do?"

"Is there any whiskey?"

Emily looked worriedly at her friend asking, "Is it that bad? Are we there again?"

Shaking her head, Mavis admitted her real feelings. "No, not really. Just my attempt at humor to lighten my mood," she said rubbing her temples. "I can handle it."

Coming closer to Mavis, Emily said quietly, "You don't need to go through with this if it is going to be so stressful on you. We can tell him you do not suit and get back on the train and go home. We can save up and send Mac the money he put out for our tickets if that would make you feel better." She confessed reasonably, "It would me,"

"Ladies, excuse me," Jamie said from the dining room doorway. "I couldn't miss some of your talk, at least the gist of it. Please give Mac more time. It takes a little to have him warm up to people but he really would make a great husband and father. He has wanted a family for years. When Da died, Mac, being the oldest, picked up the pieces and continued as the head of the family. It hasn't been easy and he focused everything on the ranch while the rest of us took time off to go to college and travel. I think he's lived alone for so long he's become somewhat a recluse. Could you stay a week and give him a chance to open up a little?"

Both women looked guiltily at one another, and Emily let Mavis take the lead since it would affect Mavis's life the most. "Of course, we'll stay. I was merely allowing my unfounded fear and nerves overcome my more rational self. I must assure you I am not as weak and sniveling a person as I must appear at this moment. It really has nothing to do with your brother as much as it does with my own memories. Please forget what you may have overheard. I'm not that person anymore and I will never go back there again," Mavis told them.

Jamie smiled in relief. "I'm Jamie, by the way. It's been good to meet you, Mavis. I've read all your letters so I feel I know you." Then looked worriedly between the two women and asked, "That was all right, wasn't it?"

"Perfectly all right and completely normal. Everyone needs counsel when making this big of a decision," Mavis replied as she smiled and her face bloomed into beauty. "I am glad Mac had someone to help him make decisions just as I have Emily. Everyone needs someone to lean on in times of change."

Jamie smiled back, locking his gaze with Mavis, saying, "I feel so much better knowing you'll be here when I get home tonight." Then as if coming out of a dream, continued, "Ah, both of you. I look forward to seeing both of you tonight." He turned quickly and left the house by way of the front door.

Emily looked over to Mavis but she seemed unconcerned with what had just happened. Then Mavis said, as if there was never an interruption of their previous conversation, "I guess I will take that coffee and is there an egg left?"

Mavis spent the rest of the day investigating the house, which if plans came to fruition would be her home for the rest of her life. Her family's home so she went into every room except the brothers' bedrooms and the office off the living area. Mavis felt those areas would be considered private areas to the men.

Each room was clean enough but had a kind of lonely, desolate feel to it. Mavis couldn't fault the furnishings or over all upkeep. Everything was used but hardly worn and it had the same feeling in every room. It just wasn't a happy house. Mavis smiled at her personifying the rooms of a house. Perhaps it was simply Mavis who wasn't happy.

She had tried to tell herself not to put too much hope into this meeting. That despite the letters, only six of them, she really didn't know Mac. That was what this time together was supposed to solve. Getting to know one another. But then she sleeps the day away and Mac evidently went out to the range. Of course, why should he stay at home and kick dirt while Mavis got herself together?

Making up her mind as she headed back to the kitchen and Emily, Mavis made a decision she would treat this like a job interview. She was applying to be his wife and the mother of his children and would need to show him she was serious in her intentions. And she was. She was tired of working merely to keep a bed to sleep in and food in her belly. Her whole life spent worrying about having enough money to pay the landlady even while sharing the room with Emily.

Having a successful husband would relieve her of all that worry and both Emily and she could benefit from the marriage. If Emily found a husband nearby then the two women could remain close friends, as well. There wasn't any reason their plans wouldn't work out. The only thing jeopardizing them was Mavis's inability to see herself as Mac's wife. As any man's wife.

Now why did the younger man, Jamie, come into her mind? Yes, he was handsomer than Mac and less taciturn but was that all? Mavis's first husband hadn't been all that good looking although he had been a good man and an excellent father. As usual, thinking of her family brought the feeling of loss over her so strongly she wondered if it wouldn't have been easier to let it all go. Let herself disappear into that abys that seemed so welcoming at one time. A time she had promised herself and Emily she would never get close to again. And she wouldn't. The decision to remarry had been her own. The yearning for what she once had and lost. The need to be a mother – again. And Mac was the way back to the life she should have had all along. The life that she knew she wanted and deserved.

Emily put back the stack of plates she had just removed from the cupboard, then opened the next door and extracted the cups and saucers from it, so she could wipe down that shelf. Cleaning, especially in a kitchen, always calmed Emily. The repetition of doing the same motions made her feel under control and she knew when the day was over, everything would be back in order.

Since cleaning was such an integral part of her nature, Emily didn't need to put a lot of thought into it. She had time to think and much of that time was spent thinking about Mavis and if this was still a good idea for them both. They, Mavis and her, felt that with such a lack of marriageable aged females in the territory, Emily would find a man to share her life with as quickly as Mavis had. The city wasn't that place so they had decided to try further afield. And they had been right. Mavis had seemed ready for a change, ready to move forward while they were reading letters from prospective husbands back in their lone room in Chicago. Had Emily's enthusiasm at having her friend looking forward to the future blinded Emily to reality? Was Mavis still too fragile emotionally to remarry and possibly have another child that could be lost to illness or accident as so many others had early in life?

It had been Mavis's idea – or at least, Emily remembered it that way. The two had been walking through the park last fall and there were several families also enjoying the last of the warm weather. One small boy had caught Mavis's attention and she stood watching as if mesmerized. Emily knew the child was about the same age Mavis's son was when he passed. She could see the pain and then longing in her friend's expression. That was when Mavis turned to her and said, "We are wasting our lives like this. We were meant to have families. Children to love. Emily, I want to get married and I think you need to have a husband, as well."

Emily remembered the warm feeling that rose from deep down inside her. It was like a living thing growing and swelling her heart until she thought it would burst from her chest. She knew Mavis was right. That they both needed to move on to more than a subsistent way of living and to do that, they needed to live somewhere they could find husbands. Spotting a news stand and seeing advertisements for wives in several of the territories had both of them realize how their dreams could be fulfilled. Write an advertisement asking for what they wanted. Then sit back and wait for the right letter to reach them. Mac was one of the first and Mavis thought he sounded like the right man for her. Now Emily hoped her friend would remember all they went through to get to

Sweetwater and the reason they thought Mac was a good match for the once married woman.

Standing with the damp towel wadded in her hand, Emily's mind returned to what she was doing. The pantry had been a total disaster, mason jars of preserved food lined the shelves with no semblance of organization. She would not put it past these men to simply grab the first jars in sight and that became supper. There certainly was no rhyme or reason to the placement of items although it was clean and Emily had seen no sign of rodents or other infestations. Emily didn't allow any pests in her kitchen.

With that thought, she caught herself up short. This wasn't her kitchen. It was never meant to be her kitchen. She had to remember that. She and Mavis planned this as a way out of their lives of living hand to mouth, not having any reason to continue other than to keep themselves alive. A lonely existence even with the two friends sharing everything they had in life. The goal was to get Mavis married to a good man and then Emily would get a job and maybe a room in town and find a husband she could love and have a family of her own with. Someone to love her no matter what her past.

Mac was more reserved and single minded then he had seemed in his letters but they hadn't really had time to talk, get to know each other. Jamie was right to have asked that they stay and at least try to get to know Mac. They could always go home if they had to. Only there really wasn't a home any longer. Well, they would cross that bridge when, and if, it became necessary. Emily smiled as Mavis entered the kitchen and the two women discussed what they should prepare for supper since Jamie had given up his turn as chef.

Emily and Mavis paced the living room waiting for

the men to descend from the upstairs. The dinner was complete and the table set with the good china Emily had unearthed in one of the cupboards and a centerpiece made up of early spring flowers Mavis had found in the herb garden.

They had both taken advantage of a bath in the large copper tub they found in the room off the kitchen. It had been like manna from heaven having the ability to cover their entire body in the warm water and the pleasure of having clean water poured over their hair was exquisite after those days on the train. Even the boarding house where they rented a room didn't have such a luxurious bathing room. Of course, the one here was simply a room once probably used by a housekeeper or perhaps as a sick room off the kitchen. But that made it close to the hot water and the tub drained itself through a pipe in the floor just as the kitchen sink did. Emily could see it was also the room used by the men, or rather Jamie, for shaving. The mirror and shaving gear were off to one corner near the window and natural light.

Now they stood nervously waiting to be tested and graded on their appearance and their wifely capabilities. Both of them, although only Mavis's life was the one crushed if they failed.

"Mavis, stop fretting. You've checked your hair in that mirror ten times in the last ten minutes. You look beautiful. That color is lovely on you and you know the style is perfect since you designed and sewed it yourself. Now sit down and try to look less harassed. This isn't your execution," Emily admonished her friend in a loud whisper.

"I know but this is the first time we've had to talk to Mac without having the excuse of being tired from the trip. He'll really be paying attention this time, I think. I'm afraid I'll freeze again and he will think I don't like him or something and then he'll send us away," Mavis answered worriedly.

"Stop thinking like that. He will not send you back. He would not reject such a beautiful, caring woman as you. And if he does, I'll slap him so hard his head will spin." Seeing this sort of conversation seemed to have Mavis smiling, Emily allowed her imagination free rein. "But my hand will probably bounce off that wiry beard so I'll kick him in his shins…no his man parts!" As she finished her fearsome statement, she saw Mac in the reflection of the mirror standing on the bottom step of the stairs.

Emily's cheeks immediately turned a fiery red that would have won first prize if there had been a competition between Mac's beard and her face. She wasn't sure but she thought Mac might have been laughing – at her! How dare he listen in on a private conversation and then laugh? Mr Macgregor had a lot to learn about manners. Emily wasn't going to examine her own too closely. She needed some sort of armor to survive tonight as well.

Both women turned from the mirror as Jamie noisily stomped down the stairs and smiled at them both. The men had changed into clean trousers that fit like gloves and clean blue shirts, making Jamie's eyes show to their best. And their best was pretty damn good. They were wearing shoes - the boots being left in the kitchen on a mat there just for that purpose.

"Well, ladies, what a welcome. Two beautiful women and a house that smells deliciously. What more can a hard-working man want, right, Mac?" Jamie said passing his brother and entering the living area stopping in front of the two women.

Mac followed at a slower pace than his brother and Emily still couldn't tell if the glint in his green eyes was due to anger or mirth. Either way, he winged out his arm at Mavis, which she accepted and he walked her into the dining room and helped her into a seat to his right. Jamie smiled at Emily and mimicked his older brother but Emily told Jamie to seat himself as she brought in the meal which was plated and sitting on the warmer. He offered to help but she assured him she had it under control and then had the food on the table in less than a minute.

As Jamie helped himself to seconds on the ham and potatoes, he asked, "What did you do to these potatoes? I've never had anything so good." He looked between Emily and Mavis for an answer.

Emily answered, "They're called potatoes au gratin' from a recipe I received from Chef Charles Ranhofer of the Delmonico restaurant. He does magical things with foods. One of my favorites is eggs Benedict. But, right now, I'm holding room for Mavis's cream Brule'. I've been dreaming of it ever since I smelled the vanilla custard cooking on the stove."

Jamie showed surprise saying, "I wouldn't have thought you could make any such thing from what's in our pantry. Isn't that right, Mac?"

Mac politely looked up from his plate that was also filled with seconds of everything and responded, "Yes, everything is very good. Tasty. Very good, ladies." He continued eating his meal while ignoring the other three. They would have to take satisfaction in the fact the man seemed to like what he was eating although he may eat everything with the same single mindedness. A man his size was used to fueling it in some manner and perhaps it didn't matter with what.

Emily gave an encouraging look to Mavis and then Mavis took a deep breath placing a question directly into Mac's lap. Turning toward him, she asked, "And was your day interesting, M-m-mac?"

Mac stopped with his fork midway to his mouth and looked nonplussed but then answered, "There were a couple of dead calves found in the western range so we went out and took care of them. Can't leave them to bloat or they draw carrion and coyotes." Taking a breath, he finished bringing his fork to his mouth.

Mavis was unsure how to continue so looked down at her own plate and pushed a little of the potatoes and sauce around. Emily looked at Jamie for help and she didn't think she rolled her eyes but she was sure Jamie did. They caught each other's gaze and began to giggle. Emily quickly brought up her napkin to cover her mouth but the giggles weren't stopping. Jamie was also covering his mouth, put his hand out to reach for his glass of water then thought better of it.

Then, and Emily was sure it was Jamie who started it, a rumble of suffused laughter began. Emily couldn't help herself and her giggles turned into laughter, too. Mavis looked chagrined but then her lips started to tremble and turn up at the corners and she too was laughing until tears streaked down her cheeks.

Mac, looking at the rest of them in complete consternation, didn't crack a smile.

Finally, Mavis got herself under control and that brought Emily and Jamie into a more decorous mood. The three finished their meal under the unspoken rule of not looking into one another's eyes.

Emily and Mavis cleared the table quickly and Emily brought the coffee pot around as Mavis dispersed the small dishes of dessert. The other three of them were very complimentary of the dessert and Mavis accepted the compliments graciously.

Mac stood up. "Ladies that was a very good meal, the best since I was to Kansas City. I apologize for Jamie. He's not used to having polite company at supper so I ask for your forgiveness of his lack of decorum." With that, he placed his napkin to the side of his dessert plate and left the room heading to the office off the foyer close to the front door.

The other three glanced at one another, breaking the unwritten rule, and each burst out laughing again with Jamie even holding his stomach since he had eaten so much supper. It was a much lighter mood that ended the meal than the one that began it. It took longer for the three of them to clean-up than it would have taken Emily alone but the camaraderie was too valuable to lose. They decided to take some lemonade out onto the porch to enjoy the mellow evening.

They had each selected a rocking chair on the porch off the kitchen. The rhythmic squeaking and sound of the rockers wearing on the porch deck was soothing. Of course, all that laughter had been an icebreaker in and of itself. Emily smiled merely thinking about it.

"Thank you for your efforts tonight, Jamie. I know you were instrumental in getting Mac to open up." Emily began easily.

"I know you can lead a horse to water and all that but to lead out with dead calves…." He shook his head and Emily could see the grin on his lips.

"It's simply his way, his life. You said yourself he spent a lot of time alone. Talking during meals is probably hard for him. Let's give him some time to get relaxed around us. Besides, it wasn't what he said that got me laughing. It was merely pent up stress and it took that way as a release. I feel so much better, lighter, I guess, since supper. Mac was simply answering a question. That is his life. He wasn't trying to be offensive, and it is what he lives every day. What did you think, Mavis?" Emily tried to draw out her friend's opinion of Mac and supper.

Mavis said un-accusingly, "I was laughing at you. Both of you but you most of all, Emily. It has been ages since I heard you laugh that freely. It lightened my heart to hear it. I'm glad we came. I think it will work out after all."

And the three of them became quiet again simply rocking and listening to the night sounds but Emily caught sight of the large bear-like silhouette withdrawing into the shadows of the front porch.

CHAPTER 3

In the morning, Emily ran smack into Mac as he added wood to the cook stove. He seemed a little surprised to see her and Emily asked, "Didn't Jamie tell you of our agreement? I said I would cook for the time I am here, kind of singing for my supper so to speak. I'm used to being active, well, so is Mavis, and we don't mind keeping ourselves busy. If you don't mind, that is." She brushed her hands down the clean white apron covering a simple day dress with white collar and cuffs.

"I don't mind. I've got no complaints of the food so far and can't see that I would. If it gets too much for you, though, just let me or Jamie know and we'll go back to normal."

"Is that what you want? For things to go back to normal, Mac?"

"It's different." He gazed directly at her which didn't make her as uncomfortable as she thought it might. "I don't know. Strange to have other people in the house…besides my brothers, that is," he told her honestly.

"When I was alone, it was the lowest point in my life. No one to care for, no one to care about me…" She let the sentence die off as she fell into her memories.

"Was that after your husband died? Must have been a hard time for you, being so young an all," he said trying to commiserate, show compassion which she found comforting.

Emily stood up straighter feeling guilty at the assumption of a dead husband but now was not the time to tell Mac that Mavis had lied to him, even if it was for a good reason and for a good friend.

"I don't like to remember those times. I met Mavis and she saved my life. She offered to let me share her room at a boardinghouse and helped me get a job washing dishes at a hotel. From there, I began cooking and the rest, as they say, is history. Now what do you men like for breakfast?" She slipped into the position of cook that was such a comfort to her.

Mac left the room going to his office until she was ready to serve. She made a substantial breakfast including flapjacks, sausage, ham fried up from the night before and eggs. Jamie waited for her to sit before taking his own chair while Mac sat after them. Probably knowing the others were down and he needn't have to hold a conversation with Emily.

Conversation centered between Emily, Mavis and Jamie with furtive glances toward Mac to see if he seemed to want to add anything. His gaze rarely left his plate unless it was to search the table for butter or syrup.

The three of them released a large communal sigh when Mac stood, thanked Emily for cooking the meal and informing the room at large that he would see them that evening.

At supper that night, Mac tried to participate more in the conversation. He complemented the ladies on how well they looked. Complimented the table settings and centerpiece, noting that he enjoyed seeing the flowers inside since they could only be seen on the way to the privy otherwise.

Emily did not dare glance Jamie's way and noted Mavis was seriously contemplating Mac's every word and nodding sagely. She was impressed at her friend's dedication to keeping the meal on a more adult level this evening.

Mac became quiet as the food was placed in front of him and Jamie took this opportunity to tell the ladies of his visit to town. "I ran into Abby. She owns the dress shop on the main street and, of course, she knew we had two guests. She invited you ladies to a quilting bee, whatever that is." His grin and sparkle to his blue eyes told Emily he knew it was another term for gossip group. "If you want to attend, she's planning on stopping by the day after tomorrow about noon. She'll drive you over to the Gregg's ranch and bring you back before supper."

Emily looked to Mavis to give her preference and Mavis answered for them both, "That sounds lovely, doesn't it, Emily? We'll get to meet some of the local ladies and gossip."

There was a distinct expression of fear in Mac's eyes at that last comment which Emily noted with interest. Now what information was this quiet man panicked about coming to light at a quilting bee? Interesting. She would need to think on that later. She nodded her head in agreement to Mavis's plan.

"Good," Jamie said. "I'll have a couple of chickens ready to fry up when you get back."

"Jamie, Mrs Miller and Mrs Johnston are not here to be your personal chefs. They are guests," Mac said pointedly.

"That's all right, Mac. It's not a problem. Jamie knows I enjoy cooking and it isn't work to me. More like a hobby - like knitting. It keeps me busy." She smiled at Jamie to let him know she was indeed happy to cook his requested foods.

That night while talking over the day's activities, Emily said, "I'm really impressed with your ability not to even smile at some of the inappropriate things Mac brings up at meal time. I think you're getting to really understand him and it's good to see you interested in what interests him."

"I was biting the inside of my cheek the whole time. I try to concentrate on something else like a pattern I'm working on or a problem I'm having with a sewing project," Mavis confessed.

"Oh, Mavis. How are you going to be able to live with the man if you find it so difficult to sit through a dinner with him? Is he so different from his letters, really?" asked Emily. She found the man taciturn but not frightening or unintelligent. In fact, she thought there might be a great deal more to Mac than Mac allowed others to discern. She had a glance into the office he always disappears into and it had shelves of books. Someone must have read them.

"No, I guess not but there is a difference. He seemed…. I can't put my finger on it but he seemed friendlier in the letters. Less guarded more open." Mavis sat on the bed pleating her skirt through her fingers as she spoke. "I'm not sure how much we do have in common and I'm remembering how it is to be married. How it was the first time and I can't seem to put Mac into that role in my life." She seemed to be pleading for Emily to understand. "Am I making any sense to you?"

"Well, he was trying to let you know what he really felt but now being face to face he's finding it difficult to speak with you. He seems to have an undercurrent of shyness I find kind of attractive in a man as large and powerfully physical as Mac is," Emily admitted.

"Are you attracted to Mac?" asked Mavis skeptically.

"I think there are a lot of things attractive about your future husband and I know you will be a happy couple," answered Emily honestly to her best friend.

"I hope so. We have both invested a lot to make this work and after I'm settled, we can concentrate on getting you married, my friend." Standing, she hugged Emily and left for her own room.

Just after twelve o'clock on the appointed afternoon, the women waited in the doorway as they watched a double buggy pull through the gate and stop at the steps to the front porch. A beautiful young woman dressed in very fashionable clothing was smiling a greeting, her hat something that could only be purchased in New York or Paris with ribbons and feathers piled high.

"Hello, I'm Abby. I take it you got my message. I must say I was excited to hear of two more ladies joining our community and I became even more excited when I found out one of you was a professional seamstress and designer, too. We will need to get together and swap horror stories about impossible to please customers and vendors who don't come through with the materials as promised," said the bright-eyed brunette with a wide smile lighting up her perfectly balanced face. She had high cheek bones and narrow chin, a smooth brow with winged eyebrows over wide, hazel eyes. Full lips, seemingly always turned up in a smile framed even, white teeth.

Emily pulled herself up and took a seat on the rear bench leaving the space beside Abby for Mavis so they could talk shop. Perhaps having another female friend will help Mavis commit to Mac and settle here. Emily hoped so. She wanted Mavis to be happy now after grieving for so long. It was time to heal.

Mavis and Abby kept up a continual conversation as some women do who immediately feel a bond. They would politely throw a question over their shoulder at Emily but Emily was content to sit and ride and know her friend was beginning to let herself feel again.

Too soon, it seemed for the front passengers, Abby turned into a gate on the opposite side of the road from Mac's. It must be the next ranch because Emily hadn't seen any other roads or drives turning off from the main road.

Upon their descent from the buggy, feminine squeals of delight surrounded them as well as a lot of hugging. Even Emily and Mavis came in for some hugs as they were introduced over the chaos of removing hats and needless shawls. Soon the women were sitting around a quilt laid over a wooden frame and the appropriate colored thread was dispersed to each. Serenity reigned as each woman took their needle in hand and began the project in front of them.

The quiet did not last long as Abby, evidently the boldest of them all, said "Well, Julia, you look about to burst. I'm not counting on my fingers or anything but I think you can go ahead and let it out. It's been more than nine months since the wedding."

Julia, their hostess and the most obviously pregnant woman there, looked up with a mock reproving expression on her face and replied, "Why Abigail, whatever are you trying to infer? My reputation is beyond respectable."

"You forget, I've been here longer than you and I know that handsome devil of a husband of yours. It's his reputation I was referring to." That comment brought giggles from several of the others sitting around the quilt.

Emily had been reminded of the hesitant expression that appeared on Mac's face when Jamie had passed on Abby's invitation. She took this time to collect information for Mavis. "It seems like a close community with all the ranchers. I suppose you know of all sorts of skeletons in the closets?"

Julia, and Callie, was it, passed a look between themselves as Julia answered, "Well, the female population has been growing by leaps and bounds it seems." Then looking down at her own stomach started laughing which, of course, spread around the circle of women. Holding her large belly, she continued, "I didn't mean it like that but I guess in that way, too." She looked pointedly at Callie who was smiling widely and in the family way, as well.

Julie tried to explain between the giggles, "What I mean is Callie got here just before my wedding last fall and then she brought these two into the group." Indicating the youngest of the women and obviously unmarried. "Before that it was only Abby and myself. I think the more the merrier. There are plenty of bachelors for all."

That comment made the youngest two girls blush and giggle and whisper to one another so the others couldn't hear their comments.

"But we don't press for information from one another. Their past life, their history, is just that. We start a clean slate and each woman is welcomed," Julia said pointedly and continued to sew having laid down the law as to what anyone should or should not ask about.

Emily had heard it was the same with men. No one asked which side of the war they fought on, which side of the law they participated in. When they reached a new state or territory, life began again from there. Then they had to prove themselves but were accepted as they seemed. She had heard of criminals becoming well-respected lawmen and visa versa. At least the dime novels seemed to make it out that way.

Emily considered what she had been told and then realized that Julia and possibly all of the others thought she was trying to get gossip to spread about other women. In complete mortification, she blurted out, "Oh, no, I didn't mean that. It's just that, well, I wanted to make sure Mr Macgregor was honorable, true to his word. You know, safe to leave Mavis in his care. I-I would never attempt to pass judgment on any one's life. It is simply that this is so important. We came all this way and he is like a clam."

She saw the two women, the leaders as Emily had decided, relax again and Callie said, "It has to take a great deal of courage to come so far from home to marry a stranger."

Mavis entered the conversation at this point. "So, you know? I wasn't sure if Mac had said anything to his neighbors." She sounded relieved she didn't need to keep secrets from these nice ladies.

"Well, if you get more than two sentences out of Mac at one time, my hat's off to you. The man must be deep if the myth about still waters and all that," offered Abby. "But nothing goes on in Sweetwater than it's around the whole town within twenty-four hours."

"I've only met him a couple of times in town," added Callie. "But he was always polite and quiet."

Julia interjected, "I only see him when he rides over to talk with Ben about livestock or something like that. Never accepts an invitation to dinner. Just has his say and then leaves. Sometimes he doesn't even get out of the saddle."

"So, there are no signs of heavy drinking or bad temper?" asked Emily embolden to ask outright for her friend's sake.

Abby shook her head emphatically. "No, nothing like that in the entire family. Mac has always been a very responsible man." Then grinned conspiratorially. "Now those brothers are an entirely different story!" And that comment brought smiles and laughs from around the group.

Callie stopped her stitching saying, "Mary Margaret, Mary Elizabeth, why don't you go out and look at the horses in the paddock. I know you've been dying to see which of the ranch hands are working there. Just remember Sister Mary Ruth's rule, both hands on your own body and both feet on the ground." The two young girls left with their heads together issuing whispered notes.

"Now there are only mature women left so we may discuss things a little more freely," said Callie.

Julia picked up where she had left off. "The brothers are a little, um, enthusiastic but good at heart. Always willing to come to the aid of any of us. It's just that they're young men, with, umm, needs, and this is a small town and, um...."

"What Julia is fumbling around with telling you is that the younger brothers have been known to visit Miss Lily's to let off a little steam. Nothing all that much. I used to live in an area that if I told you what went on, your ears would burn off from your blushes," Abby relayed. "Besides, Lily is a great hairdresser. She did this for me." She turned her head in several angles so the rest of the ladies could admire Miss Lily's work, well, her daytime work anyway.

Mavis surprised the ladies by saying frankly, "Well if that's all, I feel more confident sleeping under his roof. Perhaps I can unload my gun, now."

All the women except Emily that knew of the weapon and carried one of her own, gasped and asked, "You have a gun? A pistol? Do you have a holster under your skirts?" The questions became hot and heavy as wide-eyed ladies issued their requests for information.

"I've been asked to sew a hidden pocket in a petticoat to fit a derringer for a lady who did a lot of gambling," admitted Abby. When a couple of the ladies looked curiously at her, she continued, "Oh, not in town. Back when I was in Kansas City."

Emily patiently tried to answer each question as it was asked saying, "I didn't bring it with me today since I was told it was a short trip and I was going to be surrounded by other women. When I do carry it, I put it in my reticule. It's really quite small, smaller than a derringer. It was made by Reed and it fits in the palm of my hand." She held up her hand to show them how small that actually made it. The rest of the women were suitably impressed.

Emily tried to get back to the subject at hand. She didn't want Mavis to tell the others that Emily did indeed have a loaded Reed on her person at this time. Emily felt justified since one never knew when a snake was going to show up on the road and Emily was a relatively good shot - at close range at least.

To get back on track, Emily said, "We, I mean Mavis, asked for a personal recommendation from the minister in Sweetwater but the letter seemed stilted, as if written under duress."

"No, that's simply Reverend Walker's way. Mac doesn't go to church so I'm sure Reverend Walker didn't wish to say anything about Mac he didn't know personally," explained Julia.

"Well, if you are willing to support his intentions to be honest then I'm more than reassured," Mavis answered sounding the most relaxed she had since coming to Sweetwater.

Callie had gotten quiet and finally very softly said, "My husband, Seth, is a very big man. Not as broad as Mac but as tall and powerful. All muscle like a cowhand needs to be and I want you to, ah, know that it, umm, it fits." She finished in a rushed whisper.

Everyone looked questioningly at Callie, except Abby that is, who continued to sew her square. So Callie, brighter than her own red hair, said a little louder, "It fits. You know, even if it looks too large, it fits."

There was a moment of complete silence followed by whoops of laughter and, "Oh, my."

When the laughter died down, Callie reiterated her comment, "It fits, no matter what size." Then held up a hand to prevent any more chaos and finished, "I merely thought I should let Mavis know in case it was a concern. It was for me but everything worked out fine." Then the whoops of glee and pointed looks at her protruding stomach brought more crimson color to Callie's face.

Julian stepped in to save her friend, saying teasingly, "You ladies are impossible to hold a serious discussion with. I think it is time to get some refreshments in the kitchen."

As they all inserted their needle at the point they had stopped stitching, Mavis leaned over to Callie and quietly said, "Thank you. The thought crossed my mind but I had no one to ask. My first husband was as inexperienced as I was so there was no talk of sex or anything personal. We merely struggled along making it work, I guess is the best way to say it. I appreciate your concern for my welfare. I look forward to seeing you again after today."

Callie said, "Seth is allowing me to travel short ways from the ranch but when I get further along, he probably won't let me out of his sight. He breeds horses and has seen too many accidents occur during the most normal of births, so he won't take any chances of my not being with him if I go into confinement."

The ladies enjoyed tea, which was much appreciated by Mavis, to the point that Julia put some dry leaves in a jar to send home with her. Mavis tried to refuse and Julia told her to think of it as a welcoming present so then Mavis graciously accepted.

The two unmarried women had returned so the conversation around the quilt became banal. Emily asked how Julia had met Callie. "Callie made a beautifully decorated cake for my wedding. She was a chef at one time in a fancy hotel in St Louis."

"Sous chef," interjected Callie.

And without missing a beat, Julia continued, "And then she put together an easy to follow recipe book for me. I didn't know how to boil water. I do not lie. Callie sent me some of the best meals and all I do is follow her directions and things come out perfectly."

"You were not that bad to begin with, Julia. The pot roast last week and custard pie was divine. Most recipes are simple, at least the ones these ranch hands favor. Sully told me a hunk of meat and a plate of beans would keep them happy," added Callie speaking of her ranch foreman.

At the puzzled looks on Emily and Mavis's faces, Julia entered to explain, "Callie first came here to cook for the ranch hands on the Harrison ranch but she won Seth Harrison's heart instead." And she nudged her friend with her shoulder bringing a shy smile to Callie's face.

Blushing, Callie admitted, "I was a little frightened of him at first but you can't keep a St Michaels' girl down. Right girls?" She looked over to the two youngest there. They nodded and sat up straighter in their chairs. Evidently, St Michaels added pride to their girls.

Abby explained, "Callie was from St Michael's Foundling Home in New York City. She's been bringing others from there to work and make their lives out here in the west."

"Speaking of St Michaels, how long has it been since you've seen Matthew?" Callie teasingly asked Abby raising her brows in question. "He doesn't seem to make it out of town to see me anymore when he visits."

"He hasn't been to town all that much. And most of the time only gets an overnight stop before he has to head out again," Abby answered. At the raised eyebrows all around the quilt, she stated, "And he takes a room at the hotel."

"Yes, but does he occupy said room?" teased Callie, since Matthew was practically her brother. She was hoping Matthew was serious this time about Abby. She would be good for him and he needed something good to happen to him after so many years living on the streets of New York.

Some of the ladies started to put their needles and

thimbles away. Their section was complete as was Emily and Mavis's areas. Julia announced the quilt finished and thanked them all for their hard work. Julia had wanted it finished before the baby came even though it was for a full-sized bed. She wanted to have the child grow into the quilt, to be stable, solid evidence that its mother had loved and cherished it even before it was born.

On the ride home Emily again took the back seat but was invited to join the conversation of the two front passengers more often. It seems that Matthew was another former member of the orphanage. He came to Sweetwater to make sure Callie was safe and then became interested in Abby when he stopped in to her shop to sell her items from his catalog for resale.

It seemed all children who came to the orphanages too young to know their names were given the last name of St Michaels as had Callie. So, Mary Margaret was a St Michaels but Mary Elizabeth was Cooper. Abby filled them in on who was who in town and who they would probably run into at some point.

Emily tried to keep the names straight so that she would know them when she went to town for a job. After Mavis was secure in her engagement or possibly even already married. Either way, Emily was keeping her thoughts on after the wedding. What she would do and where she would go. Regardless of the fact she knew Mavis would urge her to stay at the ranch, Emily thought it best the newlyweds be alone. Or as alone as possible considering there were others calling the ranch home, as well.

The names of store owners and the fact there was a hotel restaurant buoyed her hopes for a future remaining near Mavis. Even if they didn't see one another daily as they were used to doing, town was only an hour away. Certainly, better than being left in Chicago without any close friends. Emily knew what it was to be alone in the world without anyone to ask for help, anyone willing to help.

It wasn't long before Abby was pulling around to the front of Mac's house. Emily and Mavis thanked Abby profusely for taking them to the quilting bee and hoped to have many more of these visits. Abby assured them she would do so and would send messages by way of Mac or Jamie who both ventured into town weekly.

At supper that evening over fried chicken and mashed potatoes with gravy, Mavis was much more animated. Talking of the quilting, meeting Abby, the food and the tea. Emily sat back and enjoyed her friend's reminiscence of the day. Allowing Mac to see the real Mavis. The Mavis who had written the letters, the Mavis who befriended Emily when she was at her lowest point.

Jamie seemed mesmerized by the change in Mavis, too, and watched her more than ate. Usually his appetite was unending, eating until the bowls were empty but this evening, he had one piece of fried chicken even though he had told her it was his favorite. Mac ate four so it wasn't that the chicken didn't taste good. Emily looked back at Jamie and made a mental note to ask him about tonight's dinner when they were alone.

As usual, Jamie helped with the cleaning up. Both Jamie and Mavis telling Emily to go out on the porch to enjoy another mild evening since Emily had done all the cooking. Sitting on the side porch, as it was called, Emily heard before she saw Mac walk up to her by way of the front porch.

"It sounds like you had a good time at the Greggs,"

he said in that deep baritone that made goose bumps form on Emily's arms and neck.

Emily tried to quiet her heartbeats before replying, "Yes, the ladies were more than welcoming. It kind of looks like there will be a population explosion in a few weeks."

"Yep, those men didn't let any grass grow under their feet," he said as a matter of fact.

Emily suppressed a smile. Of all the comments to make about two newly married men that was the one Mac chose.

"What all did you talk about? I mean being strangers and all. Not much in common," he continued.

Emily tried to hide her surprise, since this was more conversation at one time from Mac than she had been witness to. She thought about what they did say and thought that Mavis had pretty much touched on every subject. That is except one. Mac was fishing to see if he had been discussed. Emily was sure of it.

Emily replied rather nonchalantly, "Well, you know women. When we get together, we discuss men."

There was a choked sound from somewhere high above Emily's head as she asked, "What do men talk about when they get together?"

A moment of silence was followed by a grunted, "Cattle." Mac left the porch the same way he entered.

Emily was eager to get Mavis alone in her room later that night. The day's information had to be taken out and thoroughly studied, not much new to learn about Mac although he feared something coming out, even yet. Mostly it was new information about Mavis's potential neighbors. Nothing bad there. The women had circled the wagons and formed a protective society around themselves. That was good for when Emily had to leave Mavis, leave the Macgregor ranch. The chance was always there that Emily would find a man in another town or even need to return to a city where jobs were more plentiful for women.

Mavis sat cross-legged on the pink and white quilt, brushing then braiding her hair. She had discussed all the points of concern of the day's conversations. Mavis blushed saying, "I'm very intrigued with seeing, I mean, meeting Callie's husband."

Emily, she thought without blushing, replied, "I know there is always teasing about that…size, I mean. In the hotel the servers and other kitchen staff would forget I was there and begin completely inappropriate conversations." Emily remembered talk of female anatomies, male anatomies, street talk that she heard but didn't always understand. Something an innocent unmarried girl should not understand. But the secret had to be kept if Emily wanted to continue her work.

Now that it no longer mattered it was still not safe to tell people she was just plain old, Miss Emily Johnston. The widowed state gave her credibility as an experienced cook and the rooming house where she and Mavis shared a room didn't allow single women to lodge there. Only widows because the landlady didn't have to put up with all those men 'sniffing around her front porch' which Emily hoped was just a euphemism.

Mavis was quiet and that meant she was thinking about disturbing things, like her lost husband and baby.

"All right now, let me in," said Emily. "What are you worried about? Did seeing those expectant mothers bring back memories?"

"No, I'm glad that they both are so happy. It gives

me hope." Then said quietly, "I was trying to tell Mac about today, you know, but I couldn't tell if he was entertained or bored. That beard completely hides any expressions and he didn't really reply to anything so I'm at a loss. Can I live the rest of my life with a man that says maybe five words a day?"

"I know. I haven't been able to read him either. Why can't he be more like Jamie, so open, so willing to share himself?" asked Emily sadly.

Emily yawned and told Mavis goodnight returning to her own room. Looking down the hallway towards the men's rooms, she didn't hear any sound, not even snores coming from under the doors.

CHAPTER 4

The next morning after breakfast was finished, Mavis excused herself to go upstairs and make the beds. Jamie pushed the last of his biscuit into his mouth and mumbled he had to get going, too. That left Emily and Mac and an uncomfortable silence.

"Did you need more coffee?" she asked knowing he had been nursing the partial cup in his hand for the last fifteen minutes.

"Can you help me?" he rumbled.

"Can I help you? What do you mean? How can I help?" she asked confused by his request.

"I think Mavis is frightened of me. I don't think I did anything to make her afraid but she shies away from me." Emily heard the hurt in his voice and her heart melted.

"Of course, I can help you. I think it is that no one can read your expressions. Anyone speaking with you has to guess your responses because we can't see your face and you don't say very much." She tried to explain gently so as not to hurt his feelings or anger him. Again, not being able to read his emotions was causing confusion – for her.

"You think I should trim my beard? You think that will relieve her fears?" he asked incredulously.

"It would go a long way to allowing people to see your expressions." Emily encouraged, "At least think about it."

Mac grunted, neither in agreement nor in disagreement, and stood draining his cup of coffee and left by the side kitchen door.

Dinner was quieter than the previous night. Emily kept trying to engage Mavis in the animated conversation like the evening before and Jamie seemed slightly subdued, too. Mac gave his usual compliments for the meal and table settings then excused himself to go into the office and closed the door.

Jamie excused himself, too, and that left the two women cleaning up the dinner dishes and then sitting out on the side porch. Not speaking, just enjoying the late-night critters making their spring mating sounds. Finally, they stood and went upstairs to bed.

Emily had been unsure as to whether to tell Mavis about the short conversation she and Mac had earlier in the day. Would it help her friend to know Mac did notice Mavis' fear of him? Or would it cause her to be even more self-conscious around him? Would it be best not to say anything and that way Mavis wouldn't inadvertently tell Mac anything? Emily didn't want Mac to think what he told her in confidence would be spread around. With him, she recognized another who likes to keep private things, private.

The next morning Emily felt Mac behind her as she took the biscuits out of the oven. She set the biscuits down and turned to ask him what kind of eggs he wanted.

She wasn't sure if a gasp escaped her but she knew her mouth fell open in shock. She quickly tried to hide her amazement but was having trouble doing so. Mac stood in front of her - but an entirely new Mac. A tall handsome stranger stood there looking hopefully at her for approval.

"Oh, Mac. You are beautiful," she said as she expelled a breath.

Mac went crimson from his overly white neck to the

top of his now closely cropped head of hair.

"I'm sorry," she said. "You are almost breathtaking. Why in the world would you hide that handsome face?"

Embarrassed at her praise, he shrugged, replying, "It started one week after I had to be out on the range with sick cattle keeping the coyotes away while they were too weak to protect themselves. By the time I got back, it just seemed too difficult to cut through the undergrowth so to speak. Even the barber refused to shave me, saying it would take all day and dull his blades."

"Then who helped you?" And immediately a name popped into her mind. "Miss Lily," she whispered.

"How the hell do you know about Miss Lily?" he demanded.

"I, I, it doesn't matter does it? I understand she is very good at styling hair. Abby highly recommended her," she finished lamely disclosing her source of knowledge.

"Good God. Someone save me from women!" He fumed and stomped off till Emily heard the office door slam.

Emily took the respite to rethink what had just occurred. She had not been lying when she said he was beautiful. Emily had always thought Jamie had gotten all the looks of the two brothers but that was not the case at all. While Jamie was attractive in a charming, boyish sort of way, Mac was all man. His green eyes seemed to glow with life, twinkling with humor. Although the skin under the thick beard did not show the sun kissed gold evident other places, he had devastating dimples, etched deeply on both side of his wide, erotic mouth. A smooth jawline with a cleft in a strong chin completed the overall handsomeness. Emily had trouble reconciling this handsome man to the Mac she knew. Oh my, she has to warn Mavis before she sees Mac. Mavis will need to be more collected than Emily was when she first sees him.

Emily quietly ran up the stairs to warn Mavis that the good-looking man she finds downstairs is really Mac. Finding her making beds, she told her friend she didn't have time to explain. Just that Mac had shaved and not to look shocked no matter what. Mavis merely nodded dumbly as Emily ran softly back to the kitchen and continued preparing breakfast.

Mavis walked calmly though the swinging door and spied Mac immediately. She kept her mouth from falling open but stumbled a little with her compliment. "Why, Mac. You look so different. I mean, you look very handsome without your beard and hair." She sort of fell unto her chair hoping she didn't look as flummoxed as she felt. This man she could believe was Jamie's brother.

Thankfully, Mac took her words at their intent and said, stroking his now bare chin, "I thought it was time for a change. Getting married and all, I should look more human." He laughed at his own little joke. Then picked up his fork attacking his plate of food with relish.

Jamie had already seen his brother earlier that morning and besides, he knew what Mac looked like beneath that fur encased face so he wasn't as surprised as the two women. Mavis ate in silence, chewing slowly and thinking. Emily offered more coffee. Breakfast progressed as usual.

Mac barked out orders to Jamie, which was also part of the morning routine. "Get one of the men to bring over more lye for the privy. It's going to need extra with more people using it."

Jamie acknowledged the order without a blink. "I'll

get right on it."

"And check on that heifer I brought in. I didn't like the look of that boil. We might have to lance it to get the puss out of there," he said between bites.

"Yep," agreed Jamie.

Emily had become immune to the 'work talk' as she thought of it occurring during the meals but glancing over at her friend, she noticed Mavis had stopped eating, even stopped bothering to push her food around her plate.

Mac was up and wiping his mouth on his napkin saying, "I'll see you all at supper." He went toward the office. Jamie headed out the kitchen door after thanking the women for breakfast.

Mavis said, "I'll start upstairs." And left without saying anything about Mac's change in appearance. Emily was at a loss. She thought Mavis would at least acknowledge the fact Mac had gone out of his way to please his wife-to-be. Did her friend not understand what a big step that was for Mac to take? That Mac had altered himself merely to appease Mavis's show of distancing herself from him. Something he wanted to alter enough to go to great lengths of riding into town and presenting himself at the local brothel for a shave and haircut. Probably not something most men did and would be well known around town within a few hours of his doing so. Abby had made that quite clear when they were talking. Nothing happened in a small town that wasn't fodder by noontime.

Smiling, Emily thought of the handsome man her friend was about to marry and hoped this meant more to Mavis once she thought about things. Emily was impressed and Mac wasn't even her husband-to-be. That the man proved to be as attractive as his younger brother was a bonus in her mind. It should be in Mavis's mind, as well.

A few minutes later, Mac walked in and strode to the cupboard to get a cup and filled it with the leftover coffee. Leaning back against the counter, he let his long, muscled legs encased in blue denim trousers stretch out in front of him. "Do you think it worked?" he asked eagerly. "Do you think she isn't frightened of me anymore?"

"I haven't really spoken with her but I am sure this has gone a long way to making her more at ease with you," Emily replied reassuringly.

Confusion showed on his face as he asked helplessly, "What more should I do?"

Emily searched her mind. Where to start, she thought. "Well, you need to practice dining. I mean, you sit down and then you rarely say anything and when you do it is usually work related. You gulp down your meal and then wait impatiently for the rest of us to finish."

"That's because I don't waste time chit chatting about nothing. It's supper. I'm there to eat," he finished belligerently.

"It's dining and that requires a little thought on your part to contribute to the conversation going on at the table," explained Emily.

"What should I talk about?" he asked trying to find some common ground.

"Well, like at breakfast, you could ask Mavis about what she plans to do with her day. You can offer to show her the cows, er, cattle, or simply take a walk together. You can join us on the porch after supper and not be so reclusive," Emily suggested now that she had gotten into the possibilities.

"Jesus!" Mac swore. "Do I do anything right? You sound like I'm a completely untamed animal that shouldn't be allowed in the house."

Emily reached out and touched his arm to stop his leaving the room. "I'm sorry, that came out badly. You are a good person. A good man. I never meant for you to think anything else. I was focusing on the areas we need to work on to make Mavis comfortable but there are many more good points to you than bad."

Mac looked at her silently pleading to state the good points, needing to hear some positive comments about himself and that's when Emily realized how long it had probably been since anyone acknowledge Mac's positive attributes to his face.

So Emily began quietly. "You are a good man, Mac. You take care of everything and everyone around you. You wake up in the morning making sure the cattle, the ranch hands and Mavis and I are all safe. You make sure we all have food and the things to make our life easier and a secure place to sleep at night. You think of our comfort, our needs above your own and I am sorry if we haven't shown you the appreciation a man in your difficult position deserves."

Mac stood up and placed the cup on the counter. Emily looked up to see that the worry lines were gone from his forehead and eyes. He looked like he wanted to say something in response but couldn't find the words. He simply patted the hand that Emily had placed on his sleeve and went back to the office.

Emily hoped he knew how heartfelt her words had been. Jamie, Mavis and Emily had all been trying to mold Mac into a more socially acceptable person when all along they should have been admiring the strength and endurance that made him the man he is.

Supper that evening was not as quiet an affair as usual. Mac was newly shaven, if with a few nicks due, she was sure, to not having any practice. He wore clean tan trousers, white shirt with ribbon tie. Helping Mavis take her seat, he then stood waiting for Emily to bring in the hot dishes from the kitchen. When that was complete, he pushed her chair in for her before seating himself. Jamie looked on with surprise but wisely said nothing.

Mac complemented the meal but mentioned what he liked about each item. Right down to the pickles. Jamie added his approval of Mac's comments but let Mac take the lead.

"How was your day, Mavis?" he asked without a knife or fork in his hand. He was looking toward Mavis with polite interest.

Mavis, caught off guard by this unexpected question from Mac, answered, "Fine."

Undaunted by the brief reply, Mac again asked Mavis, "Would you like to walk with me after supper? Maybe go and see the paddocks and barn?"

"I-I have to help Emily with the cleaning-up," Mavis said weakly.

"Don't worry about that. Jamie will help me, won't you, Jamie?" Emily said brightly.

"There, that's settled," said Mac who then returned to eating his supper and ignored the other three for the rest of the meal.

Jamie was distracted helping Emily do the dishes and kept looking out the window but there were only fields in the horizon. The barn and paddocks were on the other side of the house, downwind she had been told and for the most part, that was true.

"Don't worry." She felt Jamie was still worried about Mavis and Mac making a go of their engagement. "Mac seems to be really trying to make this work. I think Mavis is able to be more relaxed, more herself around him, now. I think everything is going to work out for them." And Emily smiled to let him know he didn't need to be concerned about the couple any longer.

"Yeah, it looks like it will work out as planned." Slapping the towel down on the back of a chair, he said, "I'm going to my room. I've got a letter to write and book I wanted to finish."

Emily told him, "Have a good evening. I think I'll sit out on the porch and crochet as long as I can see. Ham and eggs in the morning all right with you?"

"Sure. Sounds good." He left with a thoughtful expression on his face.

Emily was on the porch when Mac came up the back steps. He looked like he was in deep contemplation. Looking down at her he asked, "How long did it take to get over losing your husband?"

Emily was at a loss. She either continued the lie started all those years ago or be honest with Mac and hope he understood the reason for the subterfuge. But before she came to any conclusion he said, "I feel Mavis is holding back, not telling me something because she doesn't want to hurt my feelings or something female like that. I would understand, though, if she felt she wasn't ready to marry again. Losing your husband and child…it must be hard to pick up the pieces and begin again. Open yourself up to the hurt."

Emily was surprised at the empathy Mac was able to have with Mavis's situation, the pain and heartache that is with her daily. But Emily didn't want Mac to think Mavis wasn't ready, because Emily knew Mavis had passed that milestone.

"I know she thinks of them every day. The baby, only three, was her pride and joy. She had placed so much hope on him, on making their family work. It was hard on her, to go on living afterwards, I know, but before she put the ad in the paper, she had said goodbye to her past. Not completely, she'll always be a woman who suffered a great loss but she has acknowledged she wants to be a woman who has more to live for. Getting married, having a family will give her a future. And I know she's ready for that. She has always been a little shy, withdrawn, modest in her manner. But I do know she wants to be married and a mother again more than anything else," Emily told Mac, wanting him to understand he wasn't going to replace a dead husband but have a new life with Mavis.

"What about you? Do you yearn to be married and be a mother?" Mac asked.

"Yes, I think I would like to be married and have lots of babies. It seems kind of sad to end your days with no one to mourn your passing. No one left behind to prove you ever existed."

"How long were you married for? I mean was it several years?" he asked casually.

Feeling uncomfortable with the direction of the conversation, Emily stood gathering her hooks and thread saying, "It was a long time ago and I don't wish to discuss it." This was her standard answer she gave in which case most people backed off with their probing. She wasn't sure it would work with Mac so she said good night and quickly went into the house.

There wasn't a light showing under Mavis's door so there wasn't going to be any talk about what happened that evening till morning. Emily went into her room and shut the door. Undressing in the dark, she climbed beneath the pink and yellow quilt. She tried to sleep and tried not to think about Mac. There was more to the man than either she or Mavis ever thought. His letters said more about him and his thoughts than the few words he said to them on a daily basis.

Perhaps he wasn't used to verbalizing his feelings. The questions he asked tonight told her more than anything he had deeper thoughts than what to have for supper or if the cattle needed to be taken to water. Now how did she show Mavis that man? And why did her thinking to do so cause a pain in her chest?

Mavis allowed Jamie to sit on the bed next to her. She knew they couldn't keep meeting in her room since Emily often used the time right before bed to speak with her about the day's events. About what Mavis was feeling and what Emily was feeling. They had been so close for so many years that it was second nature to share everything. Everything except her feelings about Jamie and how much she wanted to be with him.

The same argument between them began again as Jamie tried to understand her reluctance to tell Mac she couldn't marry him because she loved Jamie. "This time was supposed to be for you two to decide if you would suit. Tell him you don't. I can rent a place for you in town until things die down and then we'll become engaged. It can happen by the end of summer. We could be married by then and live here or in town. Mac always said this would be our home. For all of us and our families. I could build us a separate house away from here if you don't want Mac around."

"It's not that I don't want him around. But knowing I am here to marry him makes me realize how wrong he and I are for one another. I had those thoughts before I met you so I shouldn't feel guilty but I do. I also feel I owe Emily the truth. She has been so supportive in my search for a husband. My marriage was supposed to lead to her getting married as well." She gazed into his eyes. "I owe Emily my life."

He wanted to understand everything about Mavis. Wanted to understand why she felt her wishes, his wishes, were less important than someone else's. "Tell me. Why do you feel you owe Emily so much?"

"After my family died, I wanted to die."

He interrupted her, picking up her hand to show he supported her, that he wanted to help her as well. "That's normal, I would think. I can't say I understand your pain and loss but I sympathize with your grief."

"No, I really wanted to die but was too cowardly to face doing so right away. At first, I spent my time at the cemetery lying next to the fresh graves but was chased out of there by the caretakers every night. So, I went home and found a bottle of alcohol my husband had and drank that hoping it would make me forget. It seemed to help so I got more and drank it. Then more and so on. By that time, I didn't really care. I wasn't working as a seamstress any longer and I lost my apartment from not paying the rent. I slept in alleyways and behind stores. I would help at a laundry once in a while until I received my wages and bought another bottle. I was drinking the cheapest I could find and one night took a long look at my life…."

He pulled her closer. "Oh, Mavis, I wish I had been

there. I wish I'd been able to help you through all of that."

"No, it was something I had to do for myself. Hit bottom before I could climb up again. I was standing on the top of a bridge deciding how to climb over the railing when I first saw Emily." She actually smiled at the memory. "She was the only person I could say actually looked worse than me. I turned away from the river and asked if she needed help. She said, 'not as much as you do, I bet.' I told her she was wrong. That at least I had a decent pair of shoes and my dress fit."

"My God, what did she say to that?" He was amazed at what he was hearing. How did these two women ever become such close friends after a meeting like that?

"She told me, 'Then sew me a new one. Somehow, she knew I could, well, I could if I had been sober. Her excuse had been she had lost so much weight from not eating, that her clothes hung on her. And she was sickly thin. I felt sorry for her. In her state, no one was going to hire her. Even I, as drunk as I kept myself, knew that. I could still find enough work to feed myself and buy booze. Emily, on the other hand, looked so weak no one would take her on."

"So, you helped her? How did that save your life? I don't understand."

"Maybe it's a female attitude like a mothering instinct but having to take care of her made me clean-up my life. It gave me someone to care for and about. If I didn't care for myself, I, at least, cared about what happened to her."

"And now you still feel you owe her? Doesn't she owe you anything for saving her, as well?"

"Yes, and she has repaid me more times than you'll

ever know. For three years she kept me sober and learning to live again. I helped her recover from losing her father and her home in one fell swoop. She was young and had nothing to call her own. The landlord locked her out of her house while she was at the funeral and she had no one and nowhere to go for help."

"I hope the bastard rots in hell to do that to anyone. So how long had she been on the streets when you found her…or she found you?"

"A month, at least. She still had nowhere to go and I had a little money and a room. I took her under my wing and made plans. It was those plans that saved my life, as well. If someone has something to look forward to, something to wake up and head toward, then there is hope. Hope makes all the difference. I gave her hope and she gave me hope. If you don't think too closely about it, it works."

"For how long do you owe her? I mean, I have as much money as Mac has and own one fourth of this ranch. If it's money you feel you owe her or a new start, I can do that as well as Mac can. I'm a working owner and Mac wouldn't begrudge me my fair share if I told him I needed it."

"I don't think she'd take your money. Not Mac's or mine, either. It is a matter of pride, I guess, and only someone who has once lost their pride can understand why it's so important. Emily wanted me to get my pride, my sense of self back and she knew becoming a wife and mother again was what I needed. I think she needs the same thing for almost the same reasons. She lost her only family followed by devastating suffering. She needs to find the right man for her and it begins the day I marry Mac."

"Why can't it begin the day you marry me? Mac will understand. I know my brother better than either of you and I know he won't want to marry a woman I want. He isn't as committed to any one woman as he is to the idea of marriage and getting a family."

"Possibly you're right but I can't take a chance of breaking the family up by changing my mind now. We will need to break off our relationship and I will have to honor my commitment to Mac. And to Emily."

CHAPTER 5

At breakfast there was no talk of work, there was little talk at all, and Emily was too tired to enliven the small group since she hadn't fallen to sleep till after midnight. Standing up, Mac asked, "Mavis, what are your plans for the day?"

Again, Mavis was caught off guard. Emily looked with a hard glare at her friend trying to get her to respond to Mac's simple question. My god, was the woman going to pieces on her now after all this time and planning?

Then Mavis broke the silence saying, "I was going to do a little laundry and maybe sew on some buttons. Jamie brought down a couple of shirts." She looked to Jamie for confirmation.

"Just a little sewing," he said, in collaboration.

"Good. I'll see you at supper." He grabbed his Stetson off the hook and left through the side door.

But Mac missed supper that night. The three others decided to eat in the kitchen and there was lively chatter while each reminisced about their childhood. Jamie related his first kiss, which earned him a switching from his Ma because it was right outside the kitchen window and the little girl involved had cried afterward. He said it made him aware there were two people involved in a kiss and that both of them had better be in agreement or the outcome could be not being able to sit down comfortably for a week.

The women commiserated with him over the event but he did concede he had recovered both his dignity and his desire to kiss pretty girls. The women in turn told him of their first kiss, a neighbor boy for Emily and a distant cousin for Mavis. No one cried but they admitted to being a little older than Jamie in his first attempt at romance. Then the group broke up. Jamie to finish a letter and Mavis was turning in early. Emily thought it would be a good time to take a bath and started heating water on the stove.

Emily, wearing her nightgown and heavy cotton robe, looked around to make sure she hadn't dropped a pair of drawers or anything else embarrassing in the bathing room. She turned with her arms full to head back upstairs. As she opened the door, the moist air escaped into the kitchen. She glanced up in time to see Mac come into the kitchen from the porch, his shirt flapping open and untucked from the loose waisted denim trousers he favored while working encasing his muscled thighs. His feet were bare.

His eyes widened when he saw her and he cleared his throat but was having a hard time saying anything. His eyes traveled up and down Emily's body practically devouring her with their hungry heat.

Emily went to pass him saying, "Excuse me. I, I'm done with the room if you want it."

"No, I want you." He pulled Emily to him and wrapped his arms around her. Pressing her up against the back wall of the kitchen he pushed his hips into hers as he held her easily suspended above the floor. Nuzzling the warm area beneath her ear, he murmured little words that Emily couldn't identify. She stretched her head up giving him more access to continue his explorations of her neck.

Sensing her acceptance, Mac bent his head and covered Emily's mouth, searching for a response, asking for entrance to her inner warmth. Her hands were pinned between them but she wasn't sure if she would have tried to push him away if she could. The kiss stopped immediately at a shout from behind them.

"Mac!" yelled a shocked Jamie.

"Go away," growled Mac, acting like a dog protecting a tasty bone.

"Not until I find out if Mavis is all right with this," he said stubbornly. Evidently refusing to yield the room thinking Mac had Mavis up against the wall like this.

"Go away. Now!" Insisted Mac trying to protect Emily's identity.

"I'll go when I know Mavis is agreeable to this," Jamie stepped to the side to see the woman Mac was covering.

"Emily?" Then looked at Mac accusingly as Mac let Emily go. Jamie continued to stare at the two of them and Emily held her clothes tighter to her breasts and scurried toward the staircase unsure of what to say, how to explain away something she had not instigated.

As she left, she heard Jamie hiss, "What the hell are you doing? Starting your own harem?" By then she was too far away to hear Mac's answer.

Going directly to her room, Emily sat on the pretty pink and yellow quilt worrying about the argument she was sure was occurring downstairs. She wanted to go to Mavis and apologize or explain or assure her but Emily didn't know what she would say. She had to be honest. She enjoyed kissing Mac or rather Mac kissing her. Had enjoyed being pressed against the wall and treated like…the right term escaped her. But she felt desired.

She had never felt that way before. No man, no one had ever shown that sort of desire for her. Why Mac had done so wasn't anything she understood. Was it merely lust on his part? Had something she said or done triggered that action from him? This would be another night without sleep, she could tell. Having to explain to Mavis before Jamie said anything was the least of her problems. How was she to face either of the men after her display of weakness?

And it had to have been a weakness. What other woman responds to a man, a man engaged to another, with such abandon? She had responded. She had liked Mac's lips on her skin, sucking and licking. She wondered how far it would have gotten before one of them came to their senses? She was sure Mac never meant for it to happen and had tried to protect her from Jamie's curiosity. Now the three of them were aware of tonight's activities how was Emily to remain in the same house? She certainly didn't want to come between Mac and Mavis. Not after it seemed as if Mavis was beginning to warm to Mac.

But what was that supposed to mean for Mac and for her own relationship with Mavis? Mavis was her friend and she was possibly at this very moment deciding to marry Mac. What could she say to anyone? Mac? Jamie? Mavis? There were only questions and no answers. That is, except she was not so innocent she didn't understand the firm length of manhood pressed to her pelvis or the fact Mac was attracted to her - but to what end.

Neither Mac nor Jamie appeared for breakfast, which was just as well as far as Emily was concerned. She was losing too much sleep over the dramas occurring in this one house. She had decided she was either leaving or being Mavis's matron of honor. She felt Mavis had had enough time to decide if Mac was acceptable as a husband. If not, it was time to cut line as her father used to say and return to a bigger city and place another advertisement. This had already taken longer than either of them thought it would to decide. Emily, having no breakfast to clean up after, went outside to work in the herb garden trying not to think about the things she had no control over.

"We have to tell him. It isn't fair that both of us have to be unhappy so that Mac can be happy. And I'm not that sure he would be happy knowing how you feel about me," Jamie said as he sat on the edge of the bed pulling the standing Mavis into his arms. He rested his head against her soft womanly form.

Mavis stroked the top of his wavy hair. "I feel like I made a promise. Mac is depending on me to be the start of a family for him. I can't break that promise."

Jamie had started nuzzling into the space between Mavis's breasts and stroking down her leg to her ankle then up. Up under her skirt until he found the warm womanly skin at the top of her stocking. He moaned in appreciation and then started to roll the stocking down to give himself more expanse of skin to feel, to love.

Nudging her foot, she lifted it enough for him to slip off the shoe and the offending stocking. That encouraged him into more demanding stroking of the other stocking covered leg and soon she was straddling his knees and pushing into him as he took more liberties, stroking not only her legs but up to her derriere with both hands.

Mavis had never felt like this before. Wanted, desired and almost worshipped by the man holding and stroking her in such a way. She bent her head to place a kiss upon his lips when a conflagration started at the touch of their mouths.

Mavis covered Jamie's lips with a hunger that

almost undid him. One of his hands slid around between them while the other held her as close as he could get her with her skirts bunched up. Jamie found the most feminine part of her that his hand had been seeking, sliding between the folds to find and fondle the swelling nub. He imitated the motions he wanted to share with her.

She responded by pushing herself down unto the work-roughened hand that soon had an intense sensation building up inside her, something yearned to get out. Arching her back to push forward with more force, Mavis rode Jamie's hand, rocking with passion, trying to reach, she didn't know what nor could she imagine.

Jamie looked at her face, intense with the strain of trying to reach the unknown pinnacle and thought he had never seen such a beautiful sight. Instinctively knowing this was the first time Mavis had ever felt this intense pleasure. And he, Jamie, was giving her this.

He turned his hand so that it cupped her full orifice and Mavis began to keen first softly and then louder as she built to something that had to end before she exploded into a million little splinters.

Jamie realized immediately the implications of the sounds Mavis was emitting and tried to still her.

By this time, though, Mavis had taken over control of the physical coupling and had Jamie's hand pinched between her thighs, his fingers clenched between strong birthing muscles. She continued her keening, getting louder as she approached the finale of her efforts.

Mavis slumped forward in exulted exhaustion, leaning her head unto Jamie's shoulder. He felt like a genie having bestowed a gift no one else had ever given her. Then they heard it together. The calling of Mavis's name and light feet running up the stairs. Emily! They stared at each other with shocked expressions.

At the sound of Emily getting closer, Jamie dove under the bed. Mavis slipped on her shoes then turned toward the door just as a frightened Emily pushed it open and stopped abruptly upon seeing her friend standing there apparently unharmed. Mavis quickly turned back to the bed, afraid Emily would see some kind of glow or look in her eyes or something to give away the fact she had just experienced something so profound she didn't have a name for it.

"Just finishing up here. I'll be down to help with the dusting in a minute," Mavis said as she snatched up her still rolled stockings and brushed the wrinkles caused by their lovemaking out of the otherwise pristine cover.

"Oh, I thought I heard you crying out for help. I was in the kitchen garden so I ran as fast as I could," explained Emily still holding the doorknob as she caught her breath.

"Sorry, I was merely singing," Mavis said creating the lie as she went and then had to cough to cover a guffaw from under the bed.

Emily asked concerned, "You're sure you're all right?"

"Yes, I'm fine. You can get started and I'll be right down," Mavis again assured her, praying her friend wouldn't stay to help or offer to walk down with her. Mavis needed time to come to grips with what she had just done – with her intended's brother.

"All right, then." Emily left but worried about her friend. Mavis had never sung while she worked before and why wasn't she wearing stockings? Emily had noticed the bare legs when Mavis bent to smooth the bed.

Emily would have to watch for any other odd actions to make sure her friend had not found a liquor bottle Emily wasn't aware of.

Mavis reached down and pulled the cover up as Jamie slid out from under the bed still smiling. "I'm sorry, love." He stood and took her hand in his. "But I thought it would be worse if she came in here to find me with my hand up your skirt."

"Don't be crude, Jamie. What am I to do now?" she asked as she slumped on the bed.

Jamie was a little hurt and a little angry that Mavis refused to see the truth. "Tell Mac you don't love him. Tell Mac you love me. He's a big boy, he can take it."

"It's not that easy, Jamie. Those newspapers are full of women seeking husbands in the west. Mac turned down other women who would have been more than happy to come here, marry him, be a good wife to him and bear his children. I led him on. I raised his hopes for the family he feels he's missing out on. And what do I do about Emily? We had a plan," she tried to explain her conflicted thoughts.

"And what about me? Us? Don't I get a say in this? Don't you deserve to be with the man you love? Who loves you? I know, Mac, way better than you do. He wouldn't want a woman who's in love with someone else. And while you're thinking about poor Mac's delicate sensibilities, think how you'll tell him about what happened between you and me just now." Then he left the room - angry.

Mavis went to bed early again, giving Emily no chance to discuss what had happened between Mac and Emily in the kitchen before Jamie said something to her. Emily was sitting, rocking on the side porch worrying what to do. What was she supposed to do? This was a completely foreign territory for her. No man had ever shown such outright desire for her. She should not feel pleasure at Mac's attraction when it would mean disappointment for her friend and possibly the end to Mavis having a family of her own. If this attempt to find a husband didn't work out, Emily wasn't sure Mavis would take the chance again.

As Emily quietly walked through the house to the stairs, Mac called to her from the office door. "Can I talk with you a moment, Emily? I'll leave the door open if you want."

Emily was unable to discern his mood by the tone of his voice. When she entered the office, she looked around at the neat shelves lined with account books and brochures on livestock and farming. A large wood desk, with highly carved sides and piecrust edge dominated the room's floorboards, which were bare of rugs. Mac stood beside a chair that faced the window overlooking the yard to the barns and stable.

He watched Emily with worried eyes, then said, "I want to apologize for my conduct the other evening. There is absolutely no defense for a man to take advantage of a woman and I can't really explain what happened. I never meant to frighten you. I certainly don't want you to leave because of it." He rubbed the back of his neck and tried to continue.

"I'm not afraid of you, Mac. I didn't feel in danger but I think we need to be careful and make sure there are others around to keep anything that might be considered improper from occurring between us again," she told him, her voice firm with conviction.

"I, I guess that would be best. I just wanted to let

you know I still plan to honor the agreement I have with Mavis. And I want you to know you are welcome to stay here as long as you want after the wedding."

"Thank you, but I was planning on getting on with my own affairs once Mavis is settled. I appreciate the offer, though. So, we are agreed?" she asked and smiled letting him know there was no hard feelings on her part. That what happened would remain in the past and no one need explain it to one another. That didn't mean she was off the hook as far as explaining it to Mavis but between her and Mac, it was done.

"We're agreed." But Emily noticed Mac hadn't held out his hand to shake on the agreement. Maybe that was just as well. Emily liked remembering his hands on her in passion rather than friendship. It might help her keep warm in the long lonely years ahead.

The next couple of days fell back into the usual pattern except that Emily found herself on the side porch enjoying the mild evenings by herself. Mavis pleaded headaches, her menses, or tiredness and went to bed early. Jamie had business things that kept him from his bed till after Emily went up for the night when she would notice Jamie's room's door open and the room empty.

On the third evening, Emily told Mavis that she would accompany her upstairs since she needed to talk but didn't say that at the time. It was past time she confessed to her best friend that Mac had kissed her although she wasn't sure if she would explain how much she had enjoyed the kissing. How much she had thought about it since it happened and not with regret.

Since that night, Emily had had erotic dreams of her and Mac doing other things together. Things Emily had only heard about but had no actual knowledge of. Even without experience, she seemed to know what lovemaking would feel like. How it would make her feel warm and desired and want to climb into his skin. It was always Mac with her when she dreamed. Always Mac she shared that closeness with.

Then she would wake with such guilt she could barely look her friend in the eye each day. Felt she should say something that would perhaps help her forget those few minutes in Mac's arms. Forget what her body refused to forget.

When Emily followed Mavis into her room, Mavis turned and said, "I know what you want. You want to know if I've made up my mind to marry Mac. I don't know. I'm really worried we do not suit, that we are too different but I also feel that I owe Mac. I mean when we set off on this adventure it was just a matter of setting the date. Now I am worried if I should marry him. I know it isn't fair to anyone. I'm sorry Emily, I'm messing up all our plans and I feel so guilty."

Forgetting what she had planned on saying due to this confession, Emily's thoughts were to help her friend. It would be too selfish to add this new problem into Mavis's mix of worries. "Don't be silly, Mavis. This is a big decision. It decides what you will be doing for the rest of your life. You must trust in your husband and it isn't easy to be sure. But I might have to leave you to make that decision alone. I'm beginning to worry about what I'm to do. I gave up everything, too, and I feel I may need to go to a bigger town to find work." Her mind flew from one thing to another. Perhaps her leaving would be the answer to everything. Without her there, Mac would focus on Emily and any feelings growing between them would fade. Perhaps had already faded for

Mac since he hadn't appeared to have any urges to get her alone after that night. "We spent money on the new travelling outfits and then food on the trip here. I need to think what my choices are now that you're almost settled."

"Mac would give you money to get a start somewhere. He won't mind," Mavis offered.

"But Mac doesn't have any obligations to me. I am not the one he intends to marry and I certainly won't be taking any money from you or him for coming with you. But I do need to get on with my life. I'll come back for the wedding, to see you a married woman." She hugged Mavis before leaving the room.

It was too early for Emily to go to sleep and she had a lot to think about. How to leave Sweetwater and where to go when she did. Her life would be completely different than it had been the last three years but she was a much stronger person now and able to take better care of herself. She could go back to Chicago, possibly back to the hotel to see if there was a position available and if not, then she would keep applying until she found something. Jobs for women were opening up all the time, look at Abby and Callie. They both were working women. Emily felt she would be fine when she left Mac's house. She could take care of herself now.

What she wasn't as sure about was if she could forget about a steamy night when a man she had come to admire too much and desire as she should not, made her dreams come true. She woke from sweat soaked dreams panting as if she had been climbing a steep hill. Only remembering how it felt to be in his arms, feeling him want her, knowing she had a power over him if she wanted to exert it.

She knew she couldn't ever do anything like that again. It was wrong for both of them and she felt guilt over the dreams she had no control over. How would she ever face her friend, Mavis, if she and Mac lost themselves again? It was too big a chance to take and one she was afraid she would lose.

Three years disappeared as she thought about that night, she met Mavis. They were both out walking around in the middle of the night with nowhere to be and no one worrying about them. Mavis was standing next to a bridge railing contemplating the rushing river beneath her and Emily hadn't had any luck finding food thrown out by the nearby restaurants. She had learned to get there early before the cats and vermin picked it all over but that night there hadn't been anything worth scavenging.

She knew she looked what she was and probably smelled worse although her nose found nothing disturbing about herself. Since taking her home and giving her a bath was the first thing Mavis did, Emily could see now how she was living in a fantasy if she thought she didn't smell like the dustbins she had wallowed in.

It took days before Emily could even lift her head but after hearing Mavis's story, Emily felt a weakling. She had only lost a father. A man she had lived with her entire eighteen years of life and had all those memories of. Mavis had lost a husband of only four years and a son of three. How much worse it must have been for her. How many years had she lost that, if only her husband and young son hadn't fallen ill, she would have had with them? Emily had lost her father but Mavis had lost her whole world.

Acknowledging that truth made Emily stronger because if Mavis could live through that horrible time then Emily surly could as well and with less feeling sorry for herself. Yes, Mavis had turned to drink and it had tried to take over her life but it hadn't. It hadn't won and even though Emily knew why Mavis was on that bridge that night, her friend had stopped. Instead, she had taken Emily home with her to the boardinghouse and cleaned her up, fed her, then talked the landlady into allowing her to stay and share Mavis's room for an extra fee.

From then on, it was easier. For both of them but it took a while before they trusted one another enough to tell their stories and receive the counsel they needed. Emily found she could dare to feel something for someone again, find work and make a life for herself. Mavis found helping Emily allowed her to see past her tragic loss to a future that might include a husband and child, possibly more than one. They were both young woman and strong with their belief in one another. Both seeing the possibility of a future now that the grief had lessened.

Not that it was easy because it wasn't. Melancholy was a close friend, as well, but both women looked to one another to pull them out when it came insidiously calling to them. Both women knew the other wouldn't fail them. This was true at this time, also. Emily wouldn't get in the way of Mavis's happiness. She would help her friend achieve her goal of marriage to a fine man who could keep her well cared for and hopefully, provide her children, as well. Then Emily would move on and make a life for herself knowing she had repaid a long overdue debt.

On the porch, more content now that a plan was

forming, she heard the sound of boots coming from the front of the house. Emily stiffened, waiting for Mac to come into view. Instead, Jamie came up taking his usual chair. He didn't say anything at first and then stopped rocking and stared directly at Emily.

"If Mavis marries Mac, will you consider staying and marrying me?" Jamie asked seriously.

Emily responded, regretfully, "You don't love me, Jamie. It's just cupboard love. You will forget me a few days after I leave." Then something fell into place and Emily began remembering little incidences and whispered conversations. "Besides, I think you love someone else."

"But I'll be good to you, Em. I swear. I just know that Mavis will become sad once you've gone and then even Mac will see the truth between us."

"So you both know," Emily nodded sagely. "Why haven't you said something sooner. We...I could have done something to stop things from getting this far along. I take it Mavis knows how you feel?" At his pained look, she continued, "And, of course, she feels the same way about you but is willing to sacrifice both your happiness, your lives, simply to keep from disappointing Mac. He wouldn't want either of you to do that. He may be disappointed but he doesn't have as much invested in this relationship as you and Mavis do."

"You sound pretty sure of your facts. Is there something more? Something more than what I saw in the kitchen that night?" he asked his eyes dark with controlled emotion.

"I don't know much about men. But, yes, I think Mac is attracted to me and that has been holding him back from pushing Mavis to set a wedding date. He doesn't want to marry one woman while being just as attracted to another. Let me talk with him. Promise you two won't do anything foolish while I straighten this out?" She waited for the tenseness to leave Jamie's body as he nodded in agreement with her.

CHAPTER 6

After breakfast the next morning Mac headed to his office to do paperwork before going out to the stables. He closed the door before he had seen Emily sitting in the office chair, shoulders back and straight. Mac took a second to acknowledge she was really there before asking, "Did you need me?"

"We need to talk," Emily said quietly.

"All right, go ahead," he agreed leaning back against the door.

"When Mavis and I came out here to meet you and to see if the two of you would suit, Mavis did so in completely good faith. I was planning on paying you back for the cost of my ticket and I still am as soon as I get back to a larger city like St Louis and find employment. I have experience and letters of recommendation."

She looked at the inscrutable man before continuing, "I have to tell you that Mavis does not feel the two of you will suit. She is turning down your offer of marriage. That was the agreement between the two of you and I hope you understand that it isn't personal."

His brows drew down in contemplation but kept his gaze locked on her. "What does she plan on doing?"

"It's not my place to say," Emily answered evasively.

"Try."

"Mavis and Jamie are in love. I, I think they plan on getting married," she said in a rush.

"And you knew?" He stood up straight as if her answer meant something to him.

257

"No, I found out last night." Deciding to follow his lead and give as short an answer as possible.

"Does Mavis know about the other night in the kitchen?" Mac asked wondering if that pushed Mavis into Jamie's arms.

"I never told her. I don't think Jamie did either or she would have said something to me. She really is torn about letting you down but I told Jamie you wouldn't want them to ruin their lives merely to keep from disappointing you. That you wouldn't want either of them to do that. That you may be disappointed but you do not have as much invested in this relationship as Jamie and Mavis do in theirs."

"That's a lot of talk of what I do and don't want," Mac growled.

"Do you want a wife who is in love with your brother?" she asked bluntly.

"You know I don't. And don't look so smug. Somebody owes me a wife," he stated as bluntly.

"What do you suggest? Mavis is in love with Jamie. I am going to St Louis," Emily explained as if to a small child.

"Stay and marry me. We'd be as good a match, maybe better." He looked intensely at Emily for a reaction or answers to unasked questions.

"I'm not sure that would be a good thing for us. If only one of us is committed to the marriage, I don't think it would work. That it would last," she said seriously.

"I'm not much for quitting. Anything I enter into will last," Mac said firmly.

"I feel the same but I feel strongly about certain things and that makes my loss, any loss, more difficult," confessed Emily opening herself to be more susceptible to hurt.

Mac moved so swiftly, Emily didn't realize when he enclosed her in his strong arms and brought her up to his chest, bent his head and covered her mouth. Well, thought Emily, Mac was ever a surprise as she enjoyed his mouth lightly sucking her lips, lightly asking permission for entrance where his tongue dueled with hers, easing in and out again, imitating the mating ritual she was practically ignorant of.

Emily kissed Mac back, desire making her innocent virgin mouth eager for more of him. Mac sat in the chair taking Emily with him as he held her to his chest stroking her back to cup her butt as he satiated himself with her mouth. Emily lost conscious thinking and fell into a well of physical tingling with a buzzing in her ears, pliant in Mac's hands to do with as he wished.

"A cridhe," Mac whispered into her ear, over and over as he kissed her neck. "My heart, I should have known you from the start. Recognized who you were to me. I should have paid more attention."

Mac was the one to call a halt to the lovemaking. With a final quick kiss, he said, "That has to be the last. I won't be able to control myself if we keep going like this." He put his face into the curve of her neck and breathed in deeply. "I love the way you smell, the way you fit in my arms. I don't care if we don't have children, let Jamie fill the darn quilts with girls." Mac continued kissing the soft skin under her ear and made little suction noises enjoying himself with her body.

"Why can't we have children?" asked Emily not really thinking coherently with all the sensations he was causing to erupt from deep inside her.

"If you're barren, I don't care. Jamie will have to

have the daughters," Mac told her.

"Why does Jamie have to have daughters now?" She knew she was missing something but was too busy enjoying those tickles of joy he caused within her.

"My mother made a quilt for each baby she had. Mine was blue and pink because she didn't care whether she had a boy or girl. For the second baby she made a pink and green quilt because she thought pink was right for a baby girl but got Jamie instead. By the third, she was a little disappointed, not with Jeremy himself, but the pink and yellow quilt had been for her first girl, or so she thought. Then came Jessie, and the pink and white quilt was the last she ever made. She never had a girl and she made us promise that when we married, we would wrap our wives in these quilts to ensure we had daughters. To soften the hardness of the line she would say, especially when we got to rough housing and broke something. I guess I felt it was my duty being the oldest and I thought Mavis was a sure thing since she had already given birth once."

"I have no reason to think I can't have children. Why do you think that?" puzzled Emily.

"You were married before for several years but didn't have children. I just assumed you may be barren." He asked hopefully, "Or was it your husband?"

Emily wasn't sure how Mac was going to take this news. Telling a white-lie to a stranger was one thing but she had been living in this man's home and had evaded his direct questions concerning her marital state. Now she had to face the music. "I have never been married, Mac. I had to make that up years ago simply to get a job." She could see he didn't understand or didn't believe her. "When my father died, I had to give up our rented house.

I found most of the boarding houses didn't accept single women, especially young ones, because it causes too many problems with men hanging around. When I met Mavis, she introduced me to the landlady as Mrs and said she had known me before when our husbands were alive. Then she wrote letters of introduction and references using the Mrs so I appeared to be more mature and stable to prospective employers. Then it simply snowballed. No one knew me as a single woman and it was too dangerous to deny being a widow, so I became Mrs Emily Johnston."

"So you've never been married. Have you been with a man?" At Emily's shake of her head, Mac continued, "So that makes you a virgin."

"I guess," she admitted, shrugging.

"That's that, then," Mac said not making any sense to Emily but he placed her onto her feet. "You better get out of here. You have a wedding to plan and I have to talk with the minister. I'm going to town in the morning. I want you and Mavis to go to Abby and select a wedding dress and whatever else you want or need to become my wife and be happy living here."

Unseeing, Mac continued staring out the window. This time looking over the well-run ranch with the horse filled paddock and well-maintained buildings didn't fill him with pride. His mind was too busy thinking about other emotions, other feelings he had been ignoring. At the very least, pretending they weren't there.

Damn it, it didn't want to love his wife. He never wanted to feel such deep emotion toward another person so that if anything happened to them, he would become a shell of himself. Didn't want to become his father – but he had. He may as well acknowledge the fact. No matter how he tried to fight his feelings for Emily, how hard he tried to make things work between him and Mavis...it wasn't going to succeed.

Years ago, he watched as his father became half the man he was after the death of his wife. And Mac acknowledged that his parents were close being one of the few homesteaders out here and took contentment in being with one another. With four young sons where else would they be but at home. Even Mac could see the bond between them and he also saw how his father mourned when his wife passed.

The boys all missed her terribly, as well, but it seemed only Mac understood the hollowness of his father's heart. Maybe being the oldest, the one his father depended on the most with the ranch, made Mac more empathetic to his father's moods. Maybe because he and his father were the closest in temperament was the reason. Either way, he knew the pain of loss his father felt and the way his father looked forward to the day he would join her in the burial plot on the ranch.

Now, here he was over thirty years old and so in love it hurt to even contemplate her dying and leaving him. How had he let it happen? Or is that the whole point of love? Like with Mavis and Jamie. He knew his brother never set out to steal Mac's bride but it happened. Just as Mac's falling in love with Emily happened. He certainly didn't want to love his wife. Thought doing it this way, through the mail would have guaranteed it didn't happen at all. He hoped for a pleasant woman to spend the rest of his life with and to give him children that would complete his plan.

Now, he couldn't think of anything besides Emily. How she filled his arms and his heart. How precious she became the moment he allowed himself to think of her as someone other than his fiancée's best friend. How he would grieve if she ever left him – and he barely knew her.

He had thought them both widows. Women who knew the pain of loss and knew what to expect from a marriage. Especially a marriage of convenience. No long gazes into one another's eyes, no holding hands or being in one another's pockets. Instead, going their separate ways except for the intimate moments needed to produce a child. None of that appealed to him any longer. Perhaps it never had. Perhaps that was why he hadn't pushed Mavis for an answer in the first place. They had been here almost a month and he never got antsy about setting the wedding date. Never got anxious to seal their engagement with more than a peck on the cheek.

While at the same time, any thought of Emily had to come with an admonishment to himself. That she wasn't here for him. That she wasn't cooking those meals to impress him. That she wasn't a woman to be trifled with no matter how often his mind went there. And it went there often – too often recently. And he couldn't blame her for any of those thoughts. Never had she shown him in word or deed that she would accept his advances.

The other night in the kitchen merely wetted his appetite and he had worried whether or not he could keep his hands to himself afterwards. Had given himself 'the talk' more than once of how he could not lust over Emily. It was too dangerous – to his plans, to his heart. Now he needn't worry any longer. He could allow his hands, his mouth, his everything to partake of Emily any time he wanted. And he now could admit to himself, at least, he wanted her often. Perhaps his body would become bored with taking her but right now he didn't think so. Right now, he was mentally kicking himself for not keeping her on his lap longer.

He wasn't a highly sexual man or, at least, he never thought of himself as one. He never visited the ladies available in town, never had a convenient widow or even courted anyone. Abby was the closest he came to stepping out with a woman and that had been short lived. Now, his mind went to holding and kissing and doing as he wanted with Emily. All day, every day and he had been in a state of half arousal whenever they were together for too long. Whatever too long meant. Sometimes that wasn't a very long time at all.

And now he would have his chance to try out all those things going through his mind. But was he right? Did he know how to be a proper husband to a woman like Emily? A virgin who would look to him for guidance with their lovemaking. He had more worries than he thought. Emily was an unknown commodity, so to speak, and she would need him to help her through their wedding night. Hell, what did he know about virgins? Other than he felt like he wasn't too far from his own virginity, either.

Jamie entered the office but was distinctly on guard as he looked at his brother rocking back in the office chair with a scowl on his face. This didn't bode well for the talk Jamie thought they needed to have but he sure as hell wasn't giving up Mavis. If that meant leaving the ranch and starting over somewhere else, then so be it.

Jamie started the much-dreaded conversation, "We need to talk."

"Yep," replied Mac.

This was going to be harder than Jamie thought as

he began again, "We need to talk about Mavis and Emily." And he leaned against the big wooden desk.

"Yep." Another single syllable answer.

"I love Mavis and she loves me but we didn't mean to fall in love. It just happened and we're sorry if you got caught in the middle but we're getting married. If you can't live with that then I'll move out." There. Jamie felt he had laid it all out and now Mac would have to say more than one syllable.

"I know that, Emily told me. I'm glad for you. She's a great girl." Mac acted as if he had just woken up. "Why do you want to move out?"

"If it was too painful for us to be here, if you were angry that I'm marrying Mavis, if you were mad at me for stealing your fiancée? You pick which one. I can't read your mind and you don't tell me anything." Jamie ended in frustration. He never had trouble understanding his taciturn brother before but there was never anything remotely as important hanging on a conversation before.

"I never loved Mavis. I tried but I was attracted to Emily from the very first only was too dumb and single-minded to see it," Mac confessed to his younger brother.

"Why didn't you just say so and court Emily?" Jamie asked exasperated with his brother's lack of communication. All these nights of guilt and worry could have been prevented. Mavis's indecision and her worry would have ended without anyone being hurt. Some days he wondered about his brother's intelligence.

"Mavis was a proven commodity. She had conceived and borne a child while Emily had been married for what I thought was several years without conceiving. I pushed her out of my mind. I tried to ignore everything else my gut was telling me," Mac admitted.

"Mavis isn't a brood mare, for God's sake. Don't you have any sensitivity at all?" Jamie responded taking offence at Mac's thinking process.

Peering at his brother, Mac apologized, "I know. I'm sorry I didn't realize that I was so attracted to Emily. That it wasn't simply being close to a woman. If that was the case, I would have wanted to seek Mavis out instead of it always being Emily."

"Well, if we agree that I love Mavis and you want Emily, I guess we're okay. I'll live here until we find it doesn't work." Jamie stood to leave the room.

"Wait." Another one syllable. "I need your help."

"Can it wait till after the wedding?" Jamie asked wanting to go and tell Mavis everything was going to be all right. He knew she was upstairs worrying about what Mac was going to do and say once he learned about his and Mavis's relationship.

"No." Again, one syllable.

"All right, what is it?" asked Jamie willing to be more helpful since Mac was allowing Mavis her freedom without any complaints.

"I need help with…with Emily," Mac said as a rush of air escaped.

"What, didn't she agree to marry you? What did you say to scare her off?" asked Jamie worriedly.

"Not that. It's the afterwards. I'm not very experienced. I'm not sure what to do," the older brother confessed.

A grown man's confessions, especially coming from a man like Mac, had Jamie flummoxed. "But you've been with women?" he questioned cautiously.

Mac gave his brother an even deeper scowl and barked, "Of course, I've been with a woman. Just not a lot or often. I, ah, I have the doorman at the hotels I stayed at in Kansas City set me up." He looked embarrassed at having to confess even this much to his younger brother.

"And you've never visited Miss Lily's?" At Mac's shake of his head, Jamie continued, "I didn't think so but I had to make sure."

The two men sat in silence, neither meeting the other's gaze.

Finally grabbing the bull by the horns, Jamie began counseling his older brother on making love. "The main thing is to make sure your partner, ah, Emily, has, ah, enjoyed herself." At the silence from Mac, Jamie continued, "That she achieves as much pleasure as you do." Again, silence from Mac.

Jamie took a big breath and asked, "Do you have any idea of what I'm telling you?"

"I'm not sure," Mac admitted hating to feel so ignorant in front of his younger brother. It wasn't as if he hadn't taught the younger boys anything at all about women. He had trained them to treat women with respect, to be considerate and to always make sure the woman is comfortable. Tips on courting - not on having sex. His knowledge of sex was limited to farm animals and coming into season and covering mares and all sorts of what he now considered useless facts and figures. It didn't help that he could estimate to the day when a mare would foal and what sex that foal would be before it was born. Any horse breeder knew a colt would take longer than a filly. But how did that help him on his wedding night? On a night when his virgin wife will look to him for guidance.

Jamie dropped his head and whispered, "Jesus," into

his chest then tried again. "When you were with these women…" He began again. "When you were reaching the end, ah, finishing, ah, there was a climax…"

And here is where Mac barked out, "I know what a climax is, for Christ's sake!"

Jamie, getting angry at being yelled at when all he was doing was trying to help his brother, asked in a firm tone, "Yes, damn it, but did the women you were with? Did they enjoy you? Did they reach a climax?"

Dumbfounded Mac looked at Jamie and asked, "That's supposed to be part of it? They feel what I feel? Every time?"

"Yes, preferably every time. What do you think they're there for? Just to give you pleasure?" A silence lay heavily between them. "So, the answer to my question would be a, 'no', I take it?" Then Jamie said frustratedly, "I wish to hell I knew we were going to have this conversation. I would have brought drawings."

Staring Jamie directly in the eye, Mac asked, "You think I'm going to need them?"

"I hope not. This isn't easy. I've never really dissected my, er, technique. I mean a lot of it deals with what feels good to you and if your partner likes it, too, then you keep doing it. Or if your partner wants something and you don't mind either way, you do that anyway to make her happy," explained Jamie getting into the exchange of knowledge now.

"Like what?" asked Mac confused at what a woman could possibly ask for.

Jamie dropped his head to his chest again and said, "You're killing me here. What did you do with these women in Kansas City, for God's sake?"

Mac looked a little sheepish but answered honestly.

"Well, they showed up at my room and then undressed me, ah, and then if I wasn't, ah, ready, they touched me." Here he waited for any feedback from Jamie but there was none so continued, "And then we did it and I paid them. Oh, one time the girl pushed me down on the bed and got on top of me." He looked hopefully at his brother to see if that difference qualified him in some way.

"Mac, I'm glad that Emily has been married because she's going to have to be lead on this one."

"She hasn't." At Jamie's questioning look, Mac repeated a little louder, "She hasn't been married." Mac said almost sadly, "It's complicated but Emily is a virgin."

"So basically, you're both going into this blind," Jamie said just as sadly. "You may as well be a virgin for all the experience you've had."

"What makes you so much of an expert? Miss Lily's isn't all that fancy of a place. It's still a lot of one-hour visits to my thinking," Mac grouched.

"When I was in San Francisco for college, I lived with a very modern thinking woman a few years older than me. She had a wild imagination and broadened my tastes in food and drink and everything else. There wasn't a surface in that house we didn't make love on, there wasn't a position that two people could get into that we didn't try, and then the sex toys and lubricants …."

"Stop," yelled Mac. "I don't think I can take hearing about all of that let alone remember to do all of it."

"I'm not saying you should. You just have to do what you and Emily feel comfortable doing. I will add that since you're both virgins…." At Mac's look of denial, said, "Both practically virgins, you may want to ensure that she 'enjoy' herself by using your mouth. It's very enlightening, I've found."

"You mean," pointing downward, "down there?" Mac was making sure he understood before he made a terrible blunder.

"Exactly. Well, here goes the anatomy class and once I say this, we will never speak of it again, right?" At Mac's nod, Jamie disclosed some very personal secrets of a woman's body. Knowledge he had taken years to learn and techniques he practiced to perfection.

Mac was somewhat stunned when Jamie finally asked, "Do you understand? Did I go too fast for you?"

His eyes glassed over from too much information; Mac sat staring out the window. He felt foolish in his ignorance of what actually occurred or could occur between a man and a woman. How he understood his body more as well. Why he sought to be close to Emily, why he wanted to take her to his body and never let her go, why he felt alive whenever she was near him. Everything that Jamie had told him, Mac could see himself and Emily doing. Doing all those wonderous things to and with one another.

Jamie stood and on the way past his big brother patted him on the shoulder saying, "It'll be all right. The human race has continued for thousands of years so there must be some instinctive mating rituals that will come out once you've started."

For a morale booster it wasn't very strong but Mac hoped Jamie was right.

CHAPTER 7

Emily went back upstairs, still slightly unsettled by the conversation she had with Mac in the office and then the kissing that had occurred between Mac and her. She sat on the bed and thought about a future life with Mac, the man she had coveted for several weeks now. If she had read Mac's letter first then she could have been the one to come out to Sweetwater with plans of marrying him. She would have probably already been a married woman by now. She wouldn't have hesitated as Mavis had, she wouldn't have fallen in love with Jamie, and she wouldn't be second choice - but she was.

Emily thought about her future with Mac and although being his wife, enjoying his kisses, knowing his body was exciting, she still felt as if she was coming in second. And she feared that feeling would grow with the uncertainties of marriage to Mac, living here with Jamie and Mavis.

Spying her bag across the room, she decided she would follow her original plan. Leave Mac and return to a life she could control, one where she felt a part of, not merely accepted on sufferance. Married as if winning the second-place prize was sufficient since she had no other option anyway wasn't how she pictured her future. She couldn't live that way. Not after having the feelings for Mac that she had. She may never find a man who would move her in the same way but she wouldn't have the pain of wishing Mac felt for her what Jamie felt for Mavis.

Not that she begrudged her friend the happiness. She didn't and wanted the best for Mavis even if that had been Mac – but he had never been the right man for

Mavis. He was too big and brash and uncouth. Words she had heard Mavis use when trying to come to a decision. It should have been plain to both of them that the two, Mac and Mavis, would never suit. They had all been fooling themselves. Her most of all.

Emily left quietly by the back door and quickly made her way to the road. It would take her a couple of hours to get to town and she began the long trek down the dusty road. Hearing a wagon coming up behind her, she moved to the side of the road as the buckboard pulled to a stop.

"Howdy, ma'am, you one of the young ladies staying at the Macgregor's place? I'm Sully, foreman of the Harrison ranch," said an older man with a scruffy white beard and friendly smile.

"I'm Emily Johnston, the friend that accompanied the bride-to-be. I've been called away to return home." She fabricated the lie as she went, realizing how easily she fell into doing so. Covering her tracks and providing others with a viable story. The why and how of things that would sound plausible even if not the whole truth.

"I'm going in to town, can I give you a ride? Can't believe Mac didn't send a man to drive you up there himself," Sully said.

"To be honest, I didn't ask. They are so busy getting things ready for the wedding, I didn't want to disturb them. It isn't far but I would appreciate the ride," she told him as she climbed onto the seat next to the friendly man.

The two talked along the half-hour wagon trip, and when Sully pulled the team to a stop and tied them to the post in front of the mercantile, Emily got down and gave him her thanks. "I appreciate the ride and I'll remember Sweetwater for all its kind people."

"Well, you have a good trip. I hope whatever's having you headin' back home isn't too serious," he said taking the step up to the boardwalk.

Emily walked down to the train station at the end of the street and purchased a ticket with the money sent to them by Mac to ensure they felt safe. He had sent enough to pay for their way home and she had originally thought to return it to the man when he married Mavis. Now, she would make sure to repay it once she got a job and some money saved up.

She sat waiting for the next eastern running train to come in. She had almost everything she owned in the carpetbag by her feet. She knew Mavis would send on her few other things as soon as she knew where she would be living. Emily's heart beats sped up as the sound of the train first announced its presence. What she was doing was dangerous and she knew she should have probably talked things over with Mavis. One of her problems was that she was too emotional and made rash decisions when frightened. Perhaps there was a better way to end things but this is the only one she could think of where she wouldn't be talked out of doing what she felt was best for her. She didn't want Mavis to join her out of guilt. Jamie and Mavis belonged together and Mavis could help Mac find the right wife for him later. Someone who could live with a man knowing he didn't actually want her, that she was second choice.

Mac, dressed in his best suit and tie was waiting to help Emily sit at the supper table when Mavis came in carrying a pot roast surrounded by potatoes and carrots and placed it in front of him for carving.

Mac waited a moment, then asked, "Where's Emily?"

"I thought she might come down for dinner but she's been in her room all day. Told me this morning not to disturb her. That she wasn't feeling well and had a lot of things to think about so I've left her alone," Mavis said as she sat down and Jamie pushed her chair in.

Mac was gone from the table taking the stairs two at a time, worried their conversation of the morning was weighing too heavily on Emily. After all, it hadn't been much of a marriage proposal. Mac realized that right after Emily left his office but he couldn't chase after her in his physical condition, which didn't return to normal for at least half an hour. He kept focusing on how well she felt sitting in his lap, against his chest, beneath his lips.

Mac stopped at the closed door and tapped, not meaning to disturb her if she were sleeping but wanting to hear her voice, offer her solace if she needed it. He tapped again and after no response opened the door and peeked in. The bed was made and there didn't seem to be any signs of Emily, no brushes, no shoes, no dresses hanging on the clothing hooks.

"Jamie," Mac bellowed. "What do you know about Emily leaving?" He clomped heavily down the stairs.

"What do you mean? When did Emily leave?" He seemed as confused as Mac was. "Maybe she went for a walk or is rocking on the back porch," Jamie said as he stood and turned toward the kitchen and rear door.

"All her things are gone. She's gone. I think she went because you and Mavis are together and then I might have put pressure on her to fill Mavis shoes, so to speak," Mac confessed. "She might think I expected her to replace Mavis."

"You did what?" demanded Jamie. "That isn't how

you explained it to me. You said she was in agreement to marry you. That you preferred her."

"I might not have exactly asked her to marry me," replied a worried Mac.

Jamie looked at Mavis and with a big sigh asked, "What exactly did you say to her, then?"

"I, I, that I wanted children and she and I should get married and that she could go to Abby's and buy whatever she wanted, her and Mavis," Mac recalled.

"Did you tell her that she was special to you? That you had been attracted to her from the beginning?" Jamie asked trying to ignore Mavis's exclamation of surprise.

"Hell, no, I didn't realize that myself until just this morning as she and I were talking," bellowed Mac, now adding anger to his worry about Emily. "I can't tell her something I didn't rightly know beforehand, can I?"

At the quiet that fell over the room, Mac said going toward the back door, "I'm heading into town. Maybe she's still there depending on when she left the ranch."

"Do you want me to go with you?" Jamie asked as Mavis urged him to follow his brother to make sure he wouldn't hurt Emily.

"No, I'll bring her back with me. I guess I didn't make myself clear enough to her," Mac added, admitting for the first time aloud that he didn't communicate very well, especially with the finer sex.

Once in town, Mac headed directly to the train station and asked Gene, the ticket seller, if a woman fitting Emily's description had been around.

"Yep, bought a ticket on the first train heading east. Boarded the three-thirty. Right pretty. Isn't that the lady that came with your fiancée, Mac?" commented Gene in his usual friendly manner.

"She came with Jamie's fiancée. I'm still looking," explained Mac to Gene's raised eyebrows. "Give me a ticket on the next train east. I'm going to leave my horse at the livery for Jamie to come get. Is there time for that?" he asked the ticket seller.

"Sure, I'm afraid you got about two hours and twenty minutes before it gets here and another ten to twenty minutes for unloading the freight," Gene said thinking out-loud.

"Be back then. I'll grab dinner, left the ranch without eating." Then Mac rode his horse back to the livery that wasn't too far from the hotel restaurant.

Emily entered the front doors of the Kansas City hotel and went to the desk, signing in under her supposed married name to seem more respectable in the desk clerk's eyes, eyes that she had felt run over her hat and dress, leaving a price tag on each item in his mind. But Emily stood straight and met his gaze, knowing her ensemble was above reproach and appeared much like any other female's in the hotel's grand foyer except her skirts might have had a little travel dust on them.

Evidently passing muster, the clerk hit the bell for a porter to take her bag to her assigned room. The young porter was much friendlier and Emily passed him a coin as he opened her door and set her bag inside.

Looking around the neat room, she noted the dresser with matching mirror, a wash-sink and small table by the side of the bed, a desk and chair as well as a wide bed covered by a very nicely embroidered coverlet and pillowslips. Removing her hat, she took a deep breath finally able to calm her nerves which had been at frayed ends. She was hungry but decided to ignore the hunger pangs to stretch the money she had until she found work.

That she would do after a sound night's sleep.

Although she knew she was tired, Emily had difficulty falling asleep in the noisy city. She had gotten so used to the quiet of the ranch, the howl of a coyote calling to its mate or sometimes the bellowing of cattle if they had been brought in closer to the ranch in case of a storm. And she couldn't stop thinking about that last morning with Mac. Perhaps she had been a fool to run, to leave the ranch and Jamie and Mavis. Pretty much the only people she had cared about since her father died.

Emily let the tears drip off her cheeks unto the pretty pillowslip but was unable to stop them when she tried. Feeling sorry for herself wasn't a trait Emily allowed so she soon had her emotions under control and plans in place of where to go to look for her next job.

This wasn't a town she was familiar with but all big cities seemed alike. She wished she had those letters of recommendation Mavis had written years ago. At least when she went to apply this time, she had real experience and any prospective employer could contact her previous one to get a proper review of her work. She knew the hotel where she last worked had been very pleased with her performance and accepted her resignation reluctantly knowing she was traveling west with Mavis. They also knew she had plans of finding a husband, as well. Would they mention that fact if contacted by a potential employer? Could she find a position without divulging more personal information about herself? Would a future employer worry she was merely biding her time until she married and left their post as well?

If she had thought her funds would stretch, she would have travelled all the way to St Louis but instead stopped in Kansas City giving her more funds while looking for work. She would ask around for a safe, less expensive boardinghouse tomorrow. But probably not the desk clerk who signed her in just now. She would approach someone she could trust. Possibly someone in charge of hiring staff for the hotel. He would know where his employees stayed.

Mac made his way through the crowds at the train station or rather the crowds parted for him. Several tracks ended at the city, people coming and going at all hours of the day and night making the station a hub of humanity twenty-four hours a day. The trains never slept so that meant people had to change their lives to meet the train's needs. Men to replenish the coal or wood or water that fed the noisy engines. Men to sell the tickets, clean the train cars, wash the windows and bring the gleam back to the glass up and down the sides of the train so the passengers could see out. Someone to sell the newspapers that were de rigueur at each stop, and men who created the magic that occurred in the dining car. Now that had to be an act of God to turn raw product into the fine dining that accompanied the rocking and jerking of the trains.

Once out in front of the station, Mac realized he had no idea where to go. The parts of the city he knew centered around the auctions and cattle yards. There were so many people, all going in different directions. Mac kicked himself mentally for not paying more attention when Emily and Mavis talked about their lives while living together, if they ever did so. How was he to find one little women in all this chaos?

Hailing a cab and on an off chance asked if the driver had seen a woman like Emily to which the helpful driver told Mac, no, but he could take him to a house that probably could find one that would suit his needs.

Mac declined. Evidently, he hadn't needed to ask the doorman for aid in finding women. The cab drivers were just as helpful with such things. "Take me to the Winston, would you? They know me there." Mac reminded himself he would need to drop in to his bank and get funds. At least he was known to them and there was no telling how long it would take him to find one small woman in a city this size. He knew she had been a cook in a hotel restaurant so he would check in those places first.

Emily woke early. The street noise so long forgotten intruding on the sleep she had finally succumbed to. She got up and washed, missing the large tub at the ranch already. Taking a damp towel, she wiped it against the dust at the bottom of her travelling gown. Finally satisfied it looked presentable for job searching, she set the fashionable hat onto her head and tied the ribbons under her chin.

Bypassing the hotel's dining room knowing it would have the most expensive food in the city, she continued a few more blocks off the main thoroughfare. She headed to a little restaurant seemingly used by locals. It was similar to the one where Mavis and she would sometimes eat when they felt flush with cash, which wasn't very often. Or when their jobs caused the two women to miss the meals furnished with their room.

She would need to purchase some paper and writing supplies so she could put in resumes and apply to an employment agency. Emily felt she was qualified to sew now with all the experience she had making clothes with Mavis but her strongest skills were her cooking and baking. Perhaps she would get a job like Callie had as a ranch hands' cook. That would have her living away from big cities and their noise and commotion, a place where she could sleep at night listening to the crickets. How did one apply for a position like that?

Once seated, Emily ordered a breakfast knowing it would be the least expensive on the bill of fare but skipped the tea or coffee because of their added cost. She left a small gratuity and then went in search of a newspaper, finding one discarded in the foyer of the hotel, which she quickly put under her arm with her other purchases.

Returning to her hotel room Emily found the maid had been in and cleaned. The room smelled of polish and lemons as Emily sat at the desk to write out letters in response to the adverts she hoped to find in that section of the newspaper. Since she had a limited number of sheets of paper, she would only send inquiries to those positions that had the most potential. Anything remotely possible for her to qualify as a candidate would receive a request for a personal interview.

Using her neat script, she sent an inquiry to two employment agencies explaining her experience and reason for leaving her last position. She could only hope they understood her need to help her closest friend travel to meet her future husband. She wished she had written recommendations but hoped the employment agency would ask her previous employer for one themselves. Now, she would wait to hear about those and read through once more for anything she could possibly get by showing up. Some jobs were by the day and she had lived off those her first few weeks once Mavis had explained how they worked.

The jobs weren't glamorous and paid little but it was

something and the chance to be hired in full time. Most of the work was by the piece like sewing certain parts of a shirt or adding monograms onto handkerchiefs that then sold three to a package. She could do those sorts of things now that Mavis had shown her how. Right after her father died, she had very little talent for the type of things people were paid to do. She had run her father's rented home with a charlady but had no saleable ability. She was glad she had never run into those men who procured for the brothels that Mavis warned her about. Just one more way Mavis had saved Emily's life.

Trudging home, or rather back to the hotel, she admitted she needed to find a less expensive place to stay. It was a good address to leave with prospective employers but not so easy on the pocketbook. She should ask when next she stood in line for a day job. The other women will know where the safe rooms were.

Mac was grumpy and almost frantic. He had taken time out of his search to purchase a couple of shirts that had to be made to order and another tie, all arriving at his hotel yesterday morning. He ordered a union suit to fit and now felt he had enough clothes to keep him presentable for a few days by using the hotel's laundry service. He stopped into the barbershop each morning just off the hotel's lobby and the newsstand, looking at help wanted advertisements that may appeal to Emily. He wanted to catch her applying for one of the positions but most of the adverts for women, Mac hoped, wouldn't appeal to her. They seemed demeaning and beneath Emily's skills and intellect.

The boot-boy had just finished as the barber whipped the cape off Mac, causing the hair clippings to dance in the morning sunlight. Mac paid them both and took the paper with him as he went to have breakfast and search for any new jobs, he hadn't tracked down already. He was to meet with a Pinkerton, too, now that he had more information from Mavis as to where she thought Emily might go or positions, she would apply for.

Mac was still angry at himself for not making his feelings clear to Emily. She might not have run if he hadn't kissed her that morning or if he hadn't told her he cared for her. Emily might not have run off if she hadn't been afraid of him, his big body, his plain stupidity.

The Pinkerton was professional, taking down notes in a little book he kept in his suit jacket pocket. Mac felt a little relief thinking that now there would be two people looking for Emily but was a little disturbed the investigator never questioned Mac's reason for searching for the young woman. What if Mac was a mental case and wanted to harm Emily, would this man help Mac get Emily anyway? Then Mac thought it didn't matter. Mac was in over his head in this and it was going to take too long with only himself looking, especially in the city where Mac was totally out of his element.

Mr Andrews, the Pinkerton, snapped his book shut and returned it to the inside coat pocket, saying as he grabbed his derby, "I make a daily report, Mr Macgregor. Don't worry. I've chased down quite a few runaway wives in my time." Mac looked skeptically at the peach fuzz still on the young man's cheeks. "They can run but they can't hide. They begin to stick out like a sore thumb after a while. At least, someone used to the city can spot them."

"I don't want her hurt or anything, just let me know where she is and I'll talk to her. If she wants to come back with me fine, if she doesn't then I have my answer," he told the man opposite him, letting his own feelings show more than he wanted but it was a true statement. He wasn't there to force Emily into doing anything. He simply wanted, no needed, to know she was safe. If she would accept money to get started again, he would gladly leave her some, or at least, a loan if she refused to accept a gift. He didn't want her staying somewhere she wasn't safe. Somewhere where unscrupulous men could take advantage of her innocence. Men unlike him.

Emily felt herself being watched and glanced up quickly from the map she was studying to catch the young man staring directly at her. She turned her back on him and studied the map again, letting him know that she wasn't interested in him coming over and speaking with her. His type she could deal with, the drunk she ran into last night while coming home from an interview was a different story. She had to stomp on his foot with her heel and then do an un-lady-like sprint to the hotel and the doorman's startled expression.

When she looked up to check the street sign, the young man was gone so he must have gotten Emily's un-worded message. Looking at the height of the sun, Emily turned toward the address in the paper only to run into a long line of women in all forms of dress and all ages, which were also applying for the same position. Her hopes were dashed as she saw the line slowly, one by one, enter the building door, and one by one come out without much optimism. Then a man came out and waved all the prospective job seekers away, saying they had their quota and didn't need to see anyone else.

The dejected women turned in various directions, their shoulders a little more bent, their smiles all but gone, unable to meet the gazes of their sisters in need.

Emily felt a little desperate herself but not as desperate as some of these women looked. She wished she could help them because that was where she was when she had met Mavis.

Emily had given up hope when she found Mavis on that bridge, the small gin bottle as empty as Mavis's eyes. But together each found someone to help, to be needed by, and together they found a way through the pain and loss and made new lives for themselves. Well, at least, Mavis had. Emily wondered if Mavis was married yet. Had Jamie finally stood up to his brother and let him know Mavis belonged to Jamie? Then those thoughts brought the image of Mac into her mind. Would Mac go back to letting his hair grow out and hiding behind that bushy beard, hiding his emotions deep inside again?

Emily thought that thinking about Mac while walking back to the hotel might have made her think she was seeing the big bear of a man standing in front of her hotel talking with the doorman. At the doorman's nod towards her, even in the dusk, she knew the man was none other than Mac.

Instinctively turning, Emily tried to flee but it was difficult in long skirts and a bustle to outrun a man who took such long steps. Mac didn't grab her but touched her arm gently and in what sounded like a plea asked, "Let me talk with you, please, Emily. You said I had to learn to talk to people but then people have to listen, too, don't they?"

Emily stopped and gazed up into those beautiful green eyes, at the face that had become so dear to her, the one she had missed so much the last two weeks. She was emotional and felt the tears burn at the back of her eyes, which Mac must have realized. "If you trust me, I'll take you back to my room and we can talk in private."

Emily, not trusting her voice, nodded and followed his lead as he walked with her several blocks to the more central business section of the city where he led her past the doorman as the uniformed man opened the door and welcomed Mac back.

"Mr Macgregor," a supercilious voice rang out across the foyer from the front desk. "We are not that kind of hotel!"

Mac turned on his way with Emily to the main stairs and with a look that would wilt any man less than six-foot-four said firmly, "I am taking my wife to my room after her long journey. Please have tea and sandwiches sent up."

The man who had called out lowered his gaze, unable to meet Mac's hard glare and said, "Certainly Mr Macgregor, right away, sir. And welcome, Mrs Macgregor."

Emily remained quietly on his arm but dropped her hand as soon as the door to his room was closed behind them. "I'm-m-m not s-s-sleeping with you," she stuttered.

Mac looked at her in surprise. "I didn't expect you would. I just said that to the little twerp to shut him up. It was either that or punch him. Should I go back down?"

"No, no, of course not. It's just that you make me nervous and I say the wrong things," she explained.

"I thought that was my job," he replied teasingly. "To say the wrong things, do the wrong things? Expect people to know what I want and need without telling them. Like not asking you to marry me properly. I simply took for granted you knew how I felt about you. How

I've always felt about you."

He steered Emily toward the wingback chair where he pulled her onto his lap, the lap that felt so much like home to Emily she curled her knees up and laid her cheek against his chest making all his words sound like thunder under her ear.

"I am sorry. I must not have been listening very well if I missed all that, too," she said, offering him an olive branch that she may have been at fault, as well.

"I know I'm not a good communicator. You taught me that much about myself but I never meant to scare you into running away." Here he pulled her closer saying, "I was so worried for you, here alone in this city, with no one to help you if you needed it. But I'm here to let you know if you can't find it in your heart to stay and be my wife at the ranch then I'll help you set up a business in town, in Sweetwater, I mean. It's safe for a woman on her own and there's Abby and other women around and other men, so maybe you can find a man you could care for. Have a family with."

That was one of the longest statements Emily had ever heard from Mac, at least one of the most informative. "I could see myself coming back to Sweetwater - with you - if you really want me. Not just to please Mavis or make it easier on yourself."

"I don't think you'll ever make it easy on me, a coure. You about killed me when I saw you tonight and then you turned around in fear and practically ran from me." He kissed the top of her head, missing the little hat she was so proud of.

"I wasn't afraid of you as much as I was of running into your arms just to find out Mavis sent you to check up on me while you were in town for business or something," she confessed, loving his scent, the strength she could feel beneath his shirt.

"I got in the city right after you did and I've spent the whole time trying to figure out where you were. Even hired a Pinkerton and today was the first time he brought me anything useful. The name of the hotel you are staying at. I thought you'd be at a boardinghouse and one of those places that accepts ladies only," he explained, letting his thumb rub her wrist where the sleeve pulled away from her glove.

Emily stretched so her face was up, just under his. "I didn't have a job yet so I didn't want to commit to a part of town and then find I had a long walk or expensive trolley ride to work each day."

Mac took her invitation for what it was and bent his head to take her lips into his like he had in the office that last morning.

"You're a very good kisser," she complimented him when he finally let her mouth free.

"Tell Jamie. He thinks I'm inept at everything to do with women." And he took his time kissing her the second time, too.

"I'll tell everyone if you want me to," she teased the large man that others were afraid to tease.

Mac laughed saying, "Now that I don't need the ladies of Sweetwater to pay me any attention, I have an advocate of my abilities."

"Don't get too carried away there, lover boy. I'm not going to brag you up simply so some other woman can wedge herself between us." Emily wasn't teasing any longer. She had made a decision and now that meant she would fight to keep what she thought of as hers.

"I kind of like that you're possessive. Makes me feel

wanted," he told her truthfully, a man still unsure of his place in her heart, even in her life.

"Mac, I love you and I should have stayed and fought for you if I had doubts about your feelings for me. But it was just that Mavis had found her true love and I couldn't face being second place, even if it was to Mavis," she confessed.

"And I love you. You have always been the one in my dreams, in my bed when I thought about being married. I was dumb to think that one woman could replace another. That was at first, before I learned what my feelings toward you meant, ones that never surfaced when I was near Mavis. Nice woman but didn't make me want to grab her and press her up against the kitchen wall." He brought Emily's body up so he could bury his face in her neck.

"That's good because I kind of liked that myself. Maybe we can try it again without an audience. See what happens," she said enjoying the man holding her.

"We better stop talking about that night or we'll end up in that bed and although I would be fine with it, I don't want to scandalize the hotel staff any more than we have. Mavis and Jamie are waiting for us to come back before they will marry and since they are sharing a bed already, the wedding shouldn't be too long in the future."

"Oh, dear, I expected as much - the bedding I mean. There's a lot of passion in you Macgregor men." Then an irrelevant thought crossed her mind. "What if you couldn't find me or I wouldn't go back with you? They really waited?" Emily asked amazed at her friend's loyalty.

"Mavis said she wants a double wedding or something like that. Jamie's happy, he's already bedding her and I'm under pressure to get you back home, back to Sweetwater before a niece or nephew makes an appearance."

"Then tomorrow it is. I know Mavis would want it all to be legal as soon as possible," Emily said as she snuggled deeper into Mac's lap.

An almost silent knock at the door had Mac putting Emily in the chair in his place and opening the door, accepting the tea trolley after slipping the gratuity to the porter. He pushed it over to Emily who smiled and said, "I haven't enjoyed tea since leaving the ranch." She poured herself some fragrant brew, letting the scent sooth her, although she felt relaxed in Mac's presence. How quickly life can take an unexpected change. How quickly she felt everything would be right now Mac and she were together.

Emily offered Mac a sandwich quarter and said, "I can't eat all they sent up and these macaroons look good, have some of those, too."

Sitting in the chair at the desk, he watched as Emily ate. When she was finished, he got up and taking her hand raised her so she was standing in front of him.

"Miss Emily Johnston, will you do me the honor of becoming my wife and making me the happiest man on earth?"

Emily looked up at the man she loved and said, "Yes, I will."

Mac bent and kissed her and took out a ring box. "I've had this for days. Bought it just for you, hoping I'd get a chance to put it on your hand. I wasn't going to leave until I found you, made sure you were safe and secure, but hoping you'd accept this ring and agree to come home with me. I don't think I would have gone back without you."

"Well, that isn't an issue now." She answered as he kissed her again. "I'm returning with you,"

"We have to stop this or we'll end up like Jamie and Mavis." He stepped back from Emily to put space between them.

"There's a water closet at the end of the hall and a tub room if you want to take a bath," Mac explained.

"No bath, I'm not prepared but I'll take advantage of the other." And she left him for a few moments.

When Emily returned, Mac said, his voice rough with desire, "Take off your dress and things so they don't get wrinkled then get into bed. I'm sleeping on top of the sheets so I think you'll be safe enough."

Emily thought about offering him more, for him to get into bed with her but then realized she wasn't ready for that and this wasn't the right place. She smiled as she removed her dress and underskirts finally slipping into bed in her camisole and bloomers.

Mac had kept his head turned busying himself with removing his own clothes. Then he turned out the light and said to the dark, "We'll pick up your belongings in the morning and head straight back to Sweetwater. I want to have the right to sleep with you as a husband."

Mac slept the soundest that night since leaving Sweetwater to find Emily. She slept the soundest since that very same day. The morning came too soon for them both.

CHAPTER 8

"Abby, these materials are lovely. Your taste is superb," enthused Mavis. "I'm impressed and now I am in a real dilemma as to which ones I should choose."

Smiling widely, Abby said, "That's high praise from someone with your experience in the design business. I do get to choose from a lot of good distributors because I go in with a friend who has a fashion house in St Louis. It saves me money, which I pass on to my customers but better than that, I have access to great fabrics and trims I would never see brought to Sweetwater.

"But you are both lucky brides-to-be since both of you have an open account. Your men told me to let you have anything you want and that was not limited to your wedding assembles. Mac in particular thought you would like the hat second from the edge in the window. Said he would like to see you in it when you got home."

Those words started a bevy of activity trying on hats and matching fabric to trim and ribbons. Emily, smiling and continuing to admire the new hat now posing on her head, took a moment to bless whatever angel that led her to make the decision to stay with Mavis when she first found her so lost to life that she had all but given up. And again, coming with Mavis to Sweetwater bringing her to her destiny.

After several hours of looking at materials and selecting the right trim and accessories, the ladies stopped for a cup of tea and cookies. Still talking about fabrics, hats and shoes, Abby changed topics.

"Mavis, you've been married before and Jamie is a great man but Mac isn't, um, as well travelled as Jamie."

Both of the other ladies turned toward Abby, their interest peaked by her opening statement. Abby cleared her throat and continued, "I just learned, of course, that Emily is single and I can assume that means, not that I'm judging if you're not, but I assume you have not been with a man, in that way, as husbands and wives are." The usually blunt Abby actually blushed with the effort of making herself understood.

She looked expectantly at the two other ladies just as brightly colored as she was. Both tried to speak at once, and then Emily began, "I am aware of what goes on between a husband and wife. Well, in concept, that is. I think we will be fine. Mac is really a very kind and considerate man. He's not rough or course like some people might think considering what he used to look like." She defended her future husband.

Abby rushed to explain, "I'm not saying anything against Mac. I never would. He has done too many kindnesses for me in the past and I am proud to call him a friend but he is really very shy as you may know, and I guess I'm asking that you give him a little time. You know, to be a husband, if he needs it." She looked expectantly at the two women again.

Mavis took her turn to try to decipher the hidden message in Abby's coded words. "I think you're referring to the pleasure that can be part of the marital bed? That Mac may not be experienced in giving such pleasure?"

Beaming, Abby said, "Exactly." Nodding her head in agreement.

"Well, I've been married and I had not experienced the pleasure which you speak of but I know I will enjoy it with my next husband. On the other hand, I know

Emily is not aware of what we speak and I think it best she and Mac start at the same point. Don't you agree? I assure you Emily is very sensitive to her future husband's needs and will be able to help him through with the love and empathy that is an integral part of her make-up."

An un-said message passed between the two other women and Emily wanted to ask what they were discussing but felt that if Mavis felt she and Mac could over-come any problems together, she would trust Mavis's judgment. Mavis knew Emily better than anyone else at this time in her life and her friend would help her with anything Emily needed to know.

The ladies finished for the day when Jamie came in to the shop to say he would wait for them outside. A smile was sent to Abby as he tipped his Stetson and left. The ladies picked up their packages to start on their dresses and left Abby to put together the main sections. Another day of sewing them together would be all that was needed.

A few days later, again in the room of the dress shop, Miss Lily stood back and admired her handy-work. She had been helping the brides get ready for the ceremony that was scheduled in less than two hours.

"Oh, that's beautiful, Miss Lily. I knew you were the right one to get for this. They both look lovely, the pearls wrapped in Emily's hair is pure brilliance," Abby said coming up behind Miss Lily and admiring Emily.

Emily was staring at herself in the mirror, not believing that the elegant woman appearing there was her. It was astonishing what this friendly woman could do with Emily's usually unmanageably fine hair. She noted she would need to pay a visit to Miss Lily's to dress her hair often from now on.

Mavis entered and did a slow turn as the other ladies complimented everything from her hairstyle, another treasure done by Miss Lily, to the light blue dress skimming her slender form that she had designed and did much of the smocking and beadwork on. She had a cute little straw hat that sat in the center of her head tilting a little forward. The snow-white dove, its wings outspread as if in flight held the Swiss dotted veil in place.

"Oh, Mavis, you are stunning. I so wish I could draw well enough to keep this day forever. Jamie will be so proud to have you on his arm," Emily enthused.

"And you've finally found someone to tame that beautiful hair of yours. I would have never thought it could be made to keep such a style. It really makes your eyes appear larger. You look so doe-like. Mac is going to fall in love all over again," Mavis said with tears in her eyes.

"Don't cry. Please don't cry or we'll all be watering pots by the time we get to the church. I don't want red eyes when I get married," said Emily, her eyes already shiny with unshed tears.

Miss Lily stopped the melancholy mood by saying, "Come now, ladies. We must get Emily dressed. I, for one, am anxious to see how she looks all put together." She ushered Emily behind the curtain doorway to change into her wedding finery. When Emily reemerged both Abby and Mavis couldn't withhold their awe.

"I never dreamt my design would look so beautiful but I think it is the wearer more than the garment. It was definitely a good choice to go with that fabric. The cream silk with just a hint to the pink tones brings out the gold in your hair and makes your skin glow. I would be a bit jealous if I weren't so sure of Jamie's love," said Mavis.

Miss Lily came bustling up to them saying, "The hired buggy is standing outside whenever you're ready. I wish you the best and also to your husbands. They were always two of my favorite boys." The kind lady dabbed at the tears now forming in her eyes.

The brides stared at each other and a look passed between the two of them but they held back the grins they both wanted so much to let escape. They thanked Miss Lily for her help and asked her to please attend them at the wedding as Abby was doing, which she accepted with gracious sincerity.

The hired buggy driver helped the brides dismount and side by side, the two women who had begun this journey to new lives together, walked up the church steps and into the little white church of Sweetwater. They had already met the Reverend Walters so wasn't surprised to be welcomed by that good man. Abby and Miss Lily arrived and walked down the aisle first, followed by Emily and Mavis.

The brides were focused on their future husbands and both brides knew when their prospective husbands realized who the attendants were walking down the aisle. Both men blushed from their shirt collars up but met the gaze of their respective brides without guilt.

Once the husbands-to-be saw their future wives, they both took a deep breath. Jamie flashed that wide, devastating grin and Mac's eyes gleamed with promised passion. Both brides, holding the elaborate bouquets their husbands had gotten for them, stepped forward and stood next to their chosen life-mates.

After the quiet ceremony, Mac and Jamie kissed their brides and then kissed, less passionately, of course, their brother's bride. The two couples went back down the aisle and as they reached the outside door, they heard a squeal of delight from Abby who was immediately behind them.

She burst past the newly married couples and practically threw herself into a stranger's arms who welcomed her warmly with a kiss that would have rivaled in passion the ones the brides had just received from their husbands.

Both husbands were smiling and hugging their wives next to them. Mac bent down explaining, "That's Callie Harrison's, brother. He evidently knows Abby very well but I hired him to take photographs of our wedding day. These beautiful dresses will be forever saved to show our grandchildren."

"That is such a thoughtful plan. I'm deeply touched you would think of it," said Mavis very pleased with her new brother-in-law.

"Well, it seems it might take a little longer since Matthew seems a bit preoccupied." They all looked at the man, Matthew St Michaels, clearly besotted with a starry-eyed Abby.

CHAPTER 9

The newlyweds looked around their borrowed lodgings. Abby had told the couple days ago that they could use her apartment over her shop so that Mac and Emily could be alone, too. There was a bottle of Champaign on the table with two glasses and a note from Abby telling them to enjoy it.

"Where do you think Abby got the wine?" marveled Mavis.

"Probably from Matthew. I'll have to get him a thank you gift in return," Jamie said paying more attention to his new wife than he did the wine.

Jamie smiled at his bride asking, "Did you ever think we would be here? Together? Married and allowed to do any of those delicious things you promised me?" he teased kissing Mavis with more passion than he thought he could restrain. Mavis opened her lips so Jamie could once again take his fill of her sweet warmth.

"I don't know about you but I have been dreaming about a certain morning and haven't been able to get it out of my mind," she said between kisses.

"I think I have been having the same dream. Does it include a bed? And you pulled close to me, like this?" Mavis was pulled closer to the bed where Jamie sat, his cravat already laying on the comforter beside him.

Putting both hands under her dress, he made quick work of removing her stockings and stylish wedding shoes. She allowed him this liberty and even helped when he wasn't moving fast enough for her. Unbuttoning the front of her dress, she soon had it pulled off over her head, eliminating one of the main obstacles in Jamie's way. Mavis untied the corset and let it hang at her waist so Jamie took this opportunity to help lift her camisole over her head, too.

Mavis smiled a satisfied feline smile as she unbuttoned Jamie's shirt. The expanse of tanned torso had Mavis purring in pleasure as she pressed her palms to his chest and massaged the strong muscles through the soft blond curls found there.

Jamie was ignoring her ministrations, mesmerized by the sight of Mavis's breast like small perfect pendulums swinging with her movements in front of his watering mouth. He nuzzled between the enticing pink tipped orbs, covered one and suckled. Mavis's breath caught as she wrapped her arms around his head holding him in place. Pleasuring her as he went from one breast to the other trying to assuage his own hunger.

Mavis pulled away and bent forward, unbuttoning Jamie's trousers and freeing his engorged erection that was soon encased in a warm, silky haven as she straddled his hips. Both participants welcomed the joining of their bodies and stayed, enjoying their first union as man and wife.

That quiet moment didn't last long as Mavis raised herself slightly on her knees, which were on either side of Jamie's hips. She let herself down slowly, drawing out the sensation she had remembered in her dreams and now in reality. She rose again and Jamie placed his hands on each side of her waist to help guide her and they were soon in synch with Mavis beginning to keen her pleasure.

When Mavis became quiet, Jamie said, "Go ahead, love. No one will hear you. Enjoy yourself, please, enjoy me." With his permission, Mavis let herself relax and the keening began and went into a crescendo as she reached her peak. Jamie stiffened and followed in a much quieter release. The two stayed joined as long as they could and then pulled back the covers and slept.

A few hours later, Mavis was awoken by Jamie as he nestled his hips against her in spoon fashion. His arm wrapped her closer to him and he played with the nipple of one breast making his claim on her plain. His erection nudged her for permission to enter and Mavis moved to accommodate the eager member. Nuzzling the back of her neck, he hummed his pleasure as he entered and then eased from her body in ever-pleasing strokes. His hand moved down to envelop her curl-covered mound and slid fingers to the nub seeking attention.

Mavis had been rocking with Jamie and as the speed increased so did the keening to again end in a high-pitched "ah-h-h-h" as Mavis met her release. Jamie reached his final possessive ecstasy then held tightly to Mavis until sleep claimed them again.

Chapter 10

Emily sat on the edge of the bed. She had crawled into it once already and then decided perhaps that wasn't where she should be, like presuming he wanted her there. But then if he didn't want her there, he wouldn't have married her and then sent her up to his room to get ready. But if he wanted her to know where he wanted her, shouldn't he have come up with her to help her get ready? Her mind began churning as she wondered, get ready for what?

Tapping on the door, Mac entered the bedroom he had had for the past thirty-three years. He hadn't had time or inclination to move into the room his parents shared after his father died so it has remained unused. Maybe they should turn it into a nursery. He smiled at that thought and then that smile widened even more when he saw his wife sitting on his bed in his room. Could life be more perfect?

He could see Emily was nervous. He was hoping she wasn't frightened. He didn't want her to be frightened of him, of what they were about to do. He didn't have much experience when it came to having sex but this was making love so he was hoping some unknown instinct kicked in to help things along as Jamie had hinted.

Emily - his wife - was looking at him timidly. She was plucking at the pink and light blue quilt on his bed. Well-worn and washed many times, it had always been there. Sitting on the bed next to her, he held her hand. It trembled in his big paw. He looked down at the sheer fragility of it saying, "Please don't worry. I can wait until you're used to being married. I just came in to tell you I love you and you don't have to love me back but I know you'll love our children and that's what's most important to me."

"What do you mean? You think I don't love you? Why do you think that? I told you that I loved you," said a puzzled Emily.

"I know that was mostly to get me to feel better about letting Mavis go, to let Mavis be with Jamie. I would have done that anyway. All they had to do was explain they had feelings for each other. I'm not insensitive."

"No, you are not and that is why I love you. I trust you with my life, which is what becoming a wife means. It has to be total trust and I have that with you. I have from the beginning." Emily tried to convince her new husband of her sincerity.

"I almost wish you had been married before. There feels like a lot of pressure to make sure you enjoy being married. You know, enjoy the marriage bed. Jamie tried to give me some pointers but you know there are some things that are just too personal even between brothers." He forced a smile, trying to hide how difficult this was for him being open about his worries.

"I know. Abby was trying to explain things to me but everything seemed to be going over my head. I simply kept nodding and finally I think she realized that and merely said to be patient. That everything would probably work out eventually. If it didn't, the two of us would have another little talk in a couple of weeks," she said helpfully.

"Good God, protect me from women." Shaking his head, he continued, "I'm afraid I'm no Romeo. I know the basics and I have good instincts. Now you ready for me to tuck you in?" he said going to rise from the bed.

"Not yet." She pulled him down to her so her mouth reached his and laid back on the bed taking him with her. He rolled up and brought both arms around her body, holding her to him without putting his weight on her. He took over the kissing. Evidently, he had practice at that or was simply a quick study.

Either way, he kissed and took little sucks on the soft inviting skin of her neck, along her jawline and her eyelids and finally back to her lips, waiting to be caressed with his, opening under his entreaty for entrance. His tongue delved into the warmth, imitating the lovemaking motions.

His hand came over Emily's breast and the nipple hardened into his palm. He made a little moan and placed one of his legs over her body to hold her in place as if there was a chance, she would try to leave him. The front of the nightgown had little buttons Mac tried to undo, but soon small hands were there helping him reach his goal.

Her perfectly shaped breasts were soon free for his foraging hand and he suckled the pink gift till it was pebble hard before administering the same to the other.

She had been lying there, eagerly accepting every pleasure Mac was giving her when she could no longer hold back. She had no idea if she was supposed to participate but she wanted to touch Mac so much she finally dared to.

Pushing him away from her so she could unbutton his shirt, she pulled it out from his trousers. Then she ran her hands up his torso and back down trying to memorize every muscled hump and rock-hard surface. She let her fingers comb through the nest of masculine fur and she found herself humming with pleasure. Mac must have liked it since he returned to her with heated passion.

Emily reached the top of Mac's trousers in her mapping of his charms. The top button was already undone and she tried to reach the others but Mac was pressed against her hip and she couldn't budge him.

"Just a minute, love." He stood up reluctantly and pulled the bedding back to help her unto the sheets. Unbuttoning his trousers, he slid them to the floor. He had already removed his shoes and socks somewhere else in the house. Emily kept her eyes on the ceiling but wanted to look at him, at all of him but was afraid.

"Emily, if you want to stop, I can do that. I understand this is all new to you," he said quietly.

Turning toward the man she married, she looked fully at him, from foot to head and then back to his erection jutting proudly from a nest of fur the same color as that on his chest. She was a little intimidated when she remembered Callie saying something to Mavis about IT fitting. Even if it seems too large, it fit.

Emily raised both arms out to welcome her husband as he kneeled onto the bed and leaned over her saying, 'Let's get rid of this, too." He pulled her nightgown over her head and tossed it to the floor next to his things.

Mac kissed Emily thoroughly and then descended to administer his attentions to both of those delighted peaks. He stroked down Emily's body enjoying the soft curves and planes, memorizing her shape and noting what she seemed to respond to. He found the mound covered in golden curls and was rewarded by a small gasp followed by a soft sigh as he let his middle finger slide into her silken woman's heat.

Mac was almost taken back by the overwhelming feeling of possession as he searched for and found the protruding nub. He kept kissing his way to her narrow waist and the tiny indent there and went still lower.

Emily grabbed his head to prevent further descent when he whispered against her stomach, "Please, don't deny me." Loosening her hold, she held her breath unsure as to what he planned on doing. Curiosity superseding embarrassment.

Mac's mouth replaced his hand. He thought he was going to be involved in a perfunctory activity. Something to give Emily pleasure or to get her ready for his possession but instead found himself completely engulfed in this new sensation. He felt as if he was fully in control of her pleasure, of making this a night for her to remember, a night when he made love with her for the first time.

He toured his captured haven and found delight in every sign or movement it caused. By this time, Emily was petting his head and inadvertently sending him signals as to what she liked. When she held his head in place, Mac concentrated on that one area, that one spot, which seemed to bring Emily to that euphoric ending Mac had wanted for her.

After the quivering of Emily's thighs stopped, Mac raised himself and held her to him and kissed her to calmness. "Are you, all right? Did you enjoy that?" Making sure he had done things correctly. He had gotten so involved in the love making, everything Jamie had told him went out of his mind and he acted instinctively, doing what he liked and responding to Emily's silent signals of enjoyment.

"I didn't know. I mean, I didn't understand what all the fuss was about. This was indescribable but I'm really happy you knew what you were doing." She shyly hid her face into Mac's neck.

"Me, too." He kissed her laying full length against her, his erection protruding between them like a third leg. Emily wiggled against him, encouraging contact with the movements of her hips and opening her legs so he fit between them.

"Are you sure, mo cridhe?" Mac whispered through his kisses.

"I am very sure. I love you, Mac," she whispered back.

Mac raised himself up and over Emily sliding her to lay flat against the mattress. He was hesitant because he was unsure of how painful this was going to be for his wife but she wrapped her arms around him and encouraged him to proceed with entering her.

He lost all sense of time once he felt the welcoming warmth of the soft satiny passage feeling as if he'd come home. "Mo cridhe, my heart, my love," Mac whispered in her ear.

Settling himself fully into Emily, he held his weight off her with his forearms. His hips instinctively began to raise and lower, Mac enjoying the sensation the slight friction was having on the rest of his body.

Taking up the rhythm, she followed his lead, and soon, too soon, Mac was convulsed in a climax stronger than he had ever imagined possible. He collapsed, breathing hard and holding his weight up so he didn't mash the small woman beneath him.

Emily held her husband, now truly her husband, close to her listening to his heart beats as rapid as she had ever heard. She felt as if she had presented him with a gift as pleasurable as he had given her. And she was amazed that when he found his release, she could feel his seed enter her, possibly giving life to the child they both wanted so much.

When Mac tried to lay to the side of his wife, now truly his wife, she prevented him and said, "Can you stay on me a while? I loved having you in me, filling me with your body. I feel so safe and secure. I feel cherished. I've never been happier."

Mac complied with her request kissing her on her head and keeping her tightly under him. He never thought he was going to enjoy being married so much. Why had he waited so long?

Then he looked down at the beautiful woman asleep beneath him and he knew why. He had been waiting for Emily. He slid off of his now sleeping wife and spent the next half hour watching her and making plans for their future.

Emily woke up snuggled against her husband's hard chest but as soon as her lashes flickered, Mac began kissing her awake. He massaged her breast making the pink peaks button into hard pebbles that invited Mac's mouth to take his fill of them. Emily was soon writhing beneath his questing hands and mouth, but when he tried to descend and pleasure as he had earlier, she prevented his descent.

She begged, "No, please fill me like you did before. I really want your weight on me, claiming me as your wife."

Mac couldn't deny her plea and entered the slick passage as he had before. Emily began the rhythmic movements before Mac and he smiled a little at his wife's anxious lovemaking. This time Mac could control his release, especially when he realized that Emily's little sighs and moans was signaling her mounting pleasure with his actions. He concentrated on her breathing patterns and soon Emily was meeting Mac's increased pace and stiffening with the ecstasy he followed her into.

"Oh, Mac, I don't know how married people ever get out of bed. This is so wonderful, I'm not sure I want to ever get up," she told him after finding her breath.

"Well, we have to get up at some point to eat, mo cridhe." He kissed the top of her head smiling

Petting the hair on his chest she asked, finding the words strange on her lips, "Mo cridhe. What does that mean?"

"My heart, you are my heart and I couldn't live without you," he admitted openly.

"I am glad you think of me like that but there is more to life. Are you hungry? I can make you something," she offered.

Mac tucked her back under his arm and murmured sleepily, "Maybe later after I've loved you one more time, maybe with you on top of me this time."

Emily snuggled down and thought about what her husband had said. She realized he was a lot more inventive than she thought he would be. She was really going to enjoy being married even if they didn't actually stay in bed the whole time.

A word about the author...

Author Susan Payne has always loved to read which meant she often found herself reading books she was too young to fully understand. That didn't stop her. She found a dictionary and looked up anything that she questioned. She still thinks reading a thesaurus is a fun way to spend an afternoon.

Raising a family of five children kept her busy but also allowed her time to read. Often more than fifty books a month with her children playing at her feet. That's where her love of history met her love of words and she read the new historical romance genre.

In her forties, she decided to try her hand at writing but became discouraged when she never reached the conclusion to the many stories she began. She 'retired' even after joining the local chapter of Romance Writers of America and saw how many of them seemed to write with ease.

Later, Susan found her mind filled with characters all clamoring to tell her their stories. All wanting to be heard. All wanting her to tell the world how happy they were with their chosen partners. How they had gotten through loss and survived as well as thrived.

At over eighty manuscripts, Susan is still hurrying to get the words down so that she can write the next. All stories of men and women who made their mark on life and then moved on.

Highland lairds, Berserkers from northern Europe, Georgian and Regency then on to the western US up to

1890.

THarrisonRanchandMacgregorsMailOrderBride_978150923 0280_covhe stories keep coming and the couples keep finding their happy-ever-after.

This author has published the Sweetwater series of a fictitious town in 1873 Kansas by The Wild Rose Press beginning 2019 and Montana Lineman to be released in 2020 by Literary Wanderlust.

www.ingramcontent.com/pod-product-compliance
Lightning Source LLC
Chambersburg PA
CBHW070047030726
47506CB00002B/384